"BACK YOUR PLAY."

A stark silence settled over the gaming room. Earl saw Monte turn from the twenty-one layout, her eyes round with fear. He stared at the miner with a straight hard look. When he spoke, there was a soft, menacing lilt to his voice.

"I'll only ask you once. Tell everybody you were mistaken and we'll let it drop here."

"Or else?"

"Or else," Earl said quietly, "back your play."

The miner glowered across the table a moment. Then his features twisted in a murderous expression. He kicked the chair aside and clawed at the pistol stuck in his waistband. Earl's hand dipped inside his jacket and reappeared with the derringer. He cocked and fired in a single blurred motion. . . .

THE
BRANNOCKS

MATT
BRAUN

St. Martin's Paperbacks

This is a work of fiction. All of the characters, organizations, and events portrayed in this novel are either products of the author's imagination or are used fictitiously.

THE BRANNOCKS

Copyright © 1986 by Matt Braun.

For information address St. Martin's Press, 175 Fifth Avenue, New York, NY 10010.

ISBN: 978-0-312-96490-0

Printed in the United States of America

Signet edition / May 1986
St. Martin's Paperbacks edition / November 1996

10 9 8 7 6 5 4 3

TO BETTIANE

More than yesterday,
less than tomorrow

I

EARL BRANNOCK EMERGED FROM the Denver House. He paused a moment in front of the hotel, lighting a slim black cheroot. Then he turned and walked off along Larimer Street.

Springtime lay across the land with fiery brilliance. The earth shimmered under a late-morning sun, and the streets, knee-deep in mud only a week before, were now baked hard as stone. Far in the distance the snowcapped Rockies pulsed and vibrated as the sun neared its zenith.

Sauntering along the boardwalk, Earl proceeded downtown. His pace was unhurried and he puffed the cheroot with an air of easygoing good spirits. The Civil War was scarcely a month ended, and the close of hostilities had acted as a restorative on the people of Denver. A sense of celebration still lingered throughout the town.

A native Missourian, Earl had come to Denver in 1861. The menfolk of his family, including his two brothers, had rushed to serve under the Confederate flag. But he'd thought the war a senseless waste, the work of politicians and hot-tempered fools. He had traveled far enough west to outdistance the conflict, and the zealotry of both sides. Denver, while not neutral ground, had been largely untouched by the slaughter.

Four years later, in early May of 1865, the town was in the midst of a boom. Apart from mountain men, Anglos in large numbers first appeared in Colorado during the summer of 1858. A band of prospectors had discovered gold in the foothills of the Rockies, near the juncture of the South Platte River and Cherry Creek. The following year some fifty thousand men trekked westward at the height of the Pikes Peak gold rush.

By 1860, richer lodes of ore were discovered deeper in the mountains. There, scattered at random across the landscape, a dozen or more mining camps were established. The original discovery site, where gold quickly petered out, was transformed into a settlement of tents and crude log structures. The townspeople named it Denver, and a year later Colorado was granted territorial status.

On a level plain, situated beside Cherry Creek, Denver shortly became the principal supply point for outlying mining camps. Commerce and trade, as well as land speculation, created a thriving and relatively stable economy. By the end of the war, Denver's population was approaching five thousand, and upper Larimer Street was the heart of the business district. The town had a bank, several dozen stores and shops, a brick kiln, and one newspaper.

Still, for all its growth, Denver was very much a mountain settlement. While log cabins had given way to frame houses and brick buildings, there were no paved streets and the only trees were cottonwoods scattered along the creek bank. Boardwalks had been constructed in the business district, and more recently in the downtown sporting district; but spring and winter the side streets were a morass of mud, often impassable except on foot. The town was prosperous, bustling with trade, though far from elegant.

Earl Brannock considered it home. By profession a gambler, he made Denver his headquarters. He kept a permanent room in the hotel and occasionally he played poker in some of the town's gambling dens. Yet, for the most part, he was an itinerant, traveling the mountain circuit. Three weeks out of four were spent in the outlying camps, where miners and their gold dust were easily separated. He lived very well on his winnings, and he answered to no man. He came and went as it suited him.

A dapper man, Earl wore a black broadcloth coat, with matching vest, gray-striped trousers, and kidskin boots. One pocket of his vest held a gold watchpiece and the other concealed a blunt-snouted .50-caliber derringer. Beneath a low-crowned hat, his hair was wiry and red, and his eyebrows were a pale ginger. His manners were impeccable and his normal expression was one of amiable bonhomie. He gave other men a sense of false security, and they often misjudged his cold resolve. He had killed three of them over card-table disputes.

Crossing over to Blake Street, Earl entered the downtown sporting district. By local ordinance, all saloons, gaming dives, and hurdy-gurdy dance halls were restricted to a three-block section on the south side. One block east, on Holladay Street, another section was devoted to dollar cathouses and a handful of high-class parlor houses. As a whole, it was lusty and depraved, a carnival of vice. The revenue it generated from license fees was the town's major source of taxes.

Halfway down Blake Street, Earl entered the Criterion Hall. Unlike most gambling dens, the interior was paneled in dark wood, with ornate carvings and the floor waxed to a high polish. A gleaming mahogany bar occupied one entire wall, backed by a French mirror and rows of sparkling glasses. The gaming tables, including roulette and dice layouts, were situated along the opposite wall. To the rear four poker tables afforded a degree of privacy by their location. A piano provided the sole musical diversion.

A tall, rather dignified man stood alone at the bar. His gray hair and neatly trimmed mustache were in marked contrast to the somber elegance of his black cutaway coat. From a bone-white china cup, he sipped coffee laced with cognac while he watched three bartenders prepare for the noon-hour rush. His debonair bearing in no way detracted from his look of iron authority. The bartenders hustled about busily under his quiet scrutiny.

"Good morning, Henry," Earl greeted him. "I see you're still drinking up the profits."

Count Henry Murat turned from the bar. His sharp features creased in a congenial smile. "A proprietor," he said, lifting his cup, "needs constant fortification. The trials and tribulations of a gaming impresario are many."

"In other words, the hair of the dog that bit you. I take it you had a rough night."

"Long and tedious," Murat acknowledged. "A succession of pinch-penny players devoid of sporting blood. I drink to keep myself from crying."

Earl shook his head, grinning. "My heart goes out to you. It's a wonder you're able to keep the doors open."

"Well . . ." Murat chuckled, eyes twinkling. "I'm hardly a candidate for the poorhouse. With luck, the good nights even out the bad."

"Luck, hell! It's the house odds that line your pockets."

Count Henry Murat was one of Denver's premier gaming operators. He claimed kinship to a noble of Napoleon's court, blithely sidestepping questions about his lack of foreign accent. He and his wife, Countess Katerine, were among the earliest settlers in Denver. The town's first American flag flew on the roof of their log cabin, sewn by the countess from red flannel underwear and a blue cloak. With a stake from a gold-mining venture, Murat had opened a classy saloon and gambling parlor some years past. The Criterion, so he said, was operated along the lines of a European casino. No one in town begrudged him the illusion.

"You're envious," Murat said now with heavy good humor. "Tell the truth, my friend. Wouldn't you prefer the house odds on your side?"

"I do pretty well on my own."

"Indeed you do! But the life of a vagabond cardsharp takes its toll. Don't you agree?"

Earl feigned a wounded look. "You do me an injustice, Henry. Educated hands aren't necessary to trim the suckers. Poker is a game of skill."

The point was well taken. Earl Brannock's reputation was that of a square gambler. He never resorted to cold decks or other cheating devices common to the profession. A keen mind and an intuitive grasp of human nature gave him all the edge needed. He seldom lost.

"I was jesting," Murat said lightly. "You're not a cardsharp in the literal sense. But admit it or not, you're very much the nomad."

Earl took a draw on his cheroot. Head tilted back, he blew a perfect smoke ring toward the ceiling. Then, waiting for it to widen, he puffed a smaller oval straight through the center. When he spoke, there was a sober tone to his voice.

"There are times," he confessed, "when it gets old. I'm headed for Central City tomorrow, and halfway wish I weren't. Lately, it's come to seem like a job."

"No challenge," Murat said. "All the spice gone from the game."

"Yeah, something like that."

"So, I was right! You do tire of the gypsy's life."

"One day . . ." Earl paused, exhaled smoke through a wide smile. "When I put together a stake, I'll open a place that'll knock your socks off. The Criterion won't hold a candle to it."

"I wish you well," Murat said philosophically. "For most men in our profession, it's a pipe dream and nothing more. Perhaps you'll prove the exception."

"Bank on it," Earl said with a raffish smile. "All I need is the right time and the right pigeon—the big game."

"Speaking of which," Murat observed, "I've arranged a private game tonight. A Texas drover brought in a herd of cows yesterday. He's flush and eager to buck the tiger."

"Who's sitting in?"

"Jim Gaylord, Sam Boyle, and Jack Tracy. And, of course, myself."

"Impressive company," Earl noted. "How much to get a chair?"

"Table stakes . . . twenty thousand minimum."

Earl slowly wagged his head. "Too rich for my blood."

Murat pursed his lips, nodded. "Perhaps another time."

"And a few more trips to Central City."

"You'll find your mark, my friend. No pun intended—it's in the cards."

Earl joined him in a coffee and cognac. He rarely drank before sunset, and never before breakfast. Today seemed like a good day to start.

2

CENTRAL CITY WAS SOME thirty miles west of Denver. Earl stepped off the stagecoach late the following afternoon. He swatted dust from his suit jacket and walked toward the center of town. As was his customary practice, he'd brought along no baggage.

Among local boosters Central City was called "the richest square mile on earth." It was no idle boast, for upward of a hundred thousand dollars a week was gouged from the mountainous terrain. Placer miners, who worked the streambeds, still accounted for much of the gold. But hard-rock mining, with shafts bored into the mountainsides, was now the major producer. Such wealth was a lodestone for hundreds of newcomers who arrived daily.

The town itself was scattered along a gulch almost two miles long. Surrounded by mountains, the frame buildings and log cabins were wedged side by side throughout the camp. Main Street was designed to provide places of business with a look of permanence. The illusion of a second story was created with false fronts, framework structures attached to roofs, often topped by cornices and complete with sham windows. The business district looked substantial and built to last.

Earl traded greetings with several merchants along the street. He was a familiar figure in Central City, generally staying over a week on each trip. Unlike Denver, where the town fathers had pretensions of respectability, there was no stigma attached to a gambling man in the mining camps. Cardsharps and bunco men operated at their own peril, exposure often resulting in sudden death. But an honest gambler was looked upon as just another businessman. His stock-in-trade was luck and chance, the odds of the game.

Nowhere was this tolerant attitude more evident than with the sporting crowd. Saloons and dance halls and gaming dens were liberally scattered among more legitimate businesses. Even whores were viewed with grudging acceptance, one of the mainstays of any mining camp. Girls employed by a saloon or a hurdy-gurdy also worked the backroom cribs where love for sale was priced by the minute. The respectable people of Central City viewed all this with broad-minded amusement. Miners, by nature, were a randy breed. And women for hire were simply a part of everyday life.

Crossing an intersection, Earl mounted the boardwalk on the other side of the street. He went through the batwing doors of the Metropole, one of the few two-story buildings in Central City. A combination saloon, dance hall, and gaming dive, it was his regular haunt while in town. With something to suit every taste, the Metropole drew large crowds. Liquor was four bits a shot, the girls were a dollar a dance, and the gaming tables offered a variety of ways to go broke in a hurry. Whatever a man's preference, he got his money's worth at the Metropole.

The interior was brightly lighted by coal-oil lamps. Opposite the bar were crude tables and chairs, with a cleared area for dancing. The customers' casual indifference to spittoons was marked by a floor stained dark with tobacco juice. Toward the rear, gaming layouts were ranked closely along one wall. On the other wall were several tables set aside for poker, and a twenty-one layout was positioned in the center of the gaming area. The woman behind the twenty-one spread was the Metropole's star attraction.

Her name was Monte Verde. She was compellingly attractive, with raven hair, bold dark eyes, and a sumptuous figure. She wore a green velvet gown, her shoulders bared and an emerald pendant suspended over the vee of her breasts. Her expression was at once sensuous and humorous, and her eyes danced with a certain bawdy wisdom. She gave Earl a dazzling smile.

"Hello there, stranger."

The evening rush hour had not yet begun. There were no players at the table, and Earl stopped directly in front of her. He smiled, looking her over with undisguised relish.

"Hello yourself," he said pleasantly. "How's tricks?"

"Another day, another dollar."

"Sounds downright boring."

She laughed. "Not the way I deal."

The statement was more truth than jest. The game of twenty-one originated in France, and *vingt-et-un* was reputed to have been Napoleon's favorite. Imported to New Orleans, the game became popular on riverboats and eventually made its way to the mining camps. It was fast, decided on the turn of a few cards, the closest hand to a count of twenty-one being the winner. Whether there was one bettor or more, every player was on his own and went directly against the house. Monte Verde was the only woman dealer in the camps, and men waited in line to try their luck. Her looks, and her joking manner, made losing almost a pleasure.

Earl was perhaps the only man in Colorado who knew Monte Verde's real name. Like him, she was a native Missourian, and as two wayfarers in a remote mining camp, they'd been drawn together. For the past three years he had shared her room upstairs, and her bed. He kept a spare change of clothes in her closet, and everyone in town considered her his woman. He was her confidant as well, and late one night she'd told him her darkest secret. Monte Verde was a woman with a past.

At the outbreak of the Civil War, Missouri was divided in its sympathies between the North and South. But the state legislature, in the spring of 1861, voted to side with the Union. Shortly afterward the federal army established its headquarters at St. Louis. The city teemed with Confederate sympathizers, one of whom was the young kinswoman of a prominent Missouri politician. Her name was Belle Siddons.

Her social position was above reproach, and she soon developed many admirers among the officers assigned to Union headquarters. Her escorts squired her to military balls and various loyalist functions, and their wartime secrets were never secret for very long. In 1862, after arousing suspicion, she was arrested as a spy. Following interrogation, she confessed her guilt, proudly boasting that she had kept Confederate forces informed of Union troop movements. She was tried and convicted before an army tribunal.

Only the intervention of President Lincoln spared her the gallows. Sentenced to prison, she was released after four months, and much political dickering, on condition that she exile herself somewhere beyond the Missouri River. Traveling westward, she sought a new life in Colorado Territory and the gold fields. She changed her name, and with time and experience she became a skilled twenty-one dealer.

Among her clientele were outlaws, gunmen, prospectors, and the legion of adventurers who populated the mountain settlements. Yet, in those first few months, she kept her admirers at a distance, aware that personal entanglements and the business of gambling were a dangerous mix. No one questioned her past, for westerners considered any breach of privacy as the cardinal sin. She remained, instead, the lady with the strange name. And one of the great mysteries of the Colorado gold camps.

Earl Brannock was the exception. She sensed in him a kindred spirit, another exile, and allowed their lives to become entwined. Yet their union was one without bonds, or promises. She was his woman while he was in Central City; neither questioned the other about the times they were apart. Still, their arrangement had lasted three years, and there was an unspoken understanding between them. She was always waiting when he returned to Central City.

"Good to be back," he said now with a suggestive smile. "After a few days, Denver gets to be a lonesome place."

She touched his hand, laughed a low gloating laugh. "I missed you, too, lover."

"Guess I'll get cleaned up. Haven't seen any high rollers around, have you?"

"Why, are you looking to make a killing in one night?"

"I take 'em where I find 'em—for all they're worth."

Her lips curved in a teasing smile. "You are a scoundrel, Mr. Brannock."

"Would you have me any other way?"

"Any way at all suits me . . . tonight."

"By God, I have been away too long!" Earl laughed and walked toward the staircase at the end of the bar.

She followed him with her eyes, tingling inwardly with anticipation. When he glanced back on the stairs, she gave him a slow, naughty wink.

The overhead lamp bathed the players in an amber glow. Seated around the table were three miners and another man Earl took to be a drummer. The game was five-card stud, with a ten-dollar limit. By mutual agreement, it was a cutthroat game, check and raise allowed.

Earl was ahead almost five hundred dollars. He'd been the steady winner, drawing unbeatable cards for the past four hours. The drummer was dealing now, and Earl considered the board as the fifth card was dealt. He calculated that the best hand on the table was two pair, jacks and hidden treys.

He had two queens showing, and a third in the hole. He checked the bet.

Across the table, the miner holding jacks grunted sharply. He was a barrel-gutted man with muddy eyes and a face pebbled with deep pockmarks. All night he'd held second-best hands, losing consistently to Earl. When the other two miners also checked, he bet the limit. The drummer, seated beside him, folded his cards. Earl tossed a twenty-dollar gold piece into the pot.

"Raise you ten."

The next two men dropped out. The miner opposite him sullenly matched the raise. "You're called."

Earl turned his hole card. "Three little ladies."

"Sonovabitch!" the miner snarled. "You done it to me again."

"Guess it's my lucky night."

"In a pig's ass!" the miner said, jerking a thumb at the drummer. "You and this slicker are in it together. He's been dealin' you winners all night."

"Who, me?" the drummer bleated.

"Harsh words," Earl said with a clenched smile. "I suggest you apologize to our friend."

The miner gave him a querulous squint. "Your friend, not mine! You think I can't spot a couple of sharpies when I see 'em?"

A stark silence settled over the gaming room. Earl saw Monte turn from the twenty-one layout, her eyes round with fear. He stared at the miner with a straight hard look. When he spoke, there was a soft, menacing lilt to his voice.

"I'll only ask you once. Tell everybody you were mistaken and we'll let it drop here."

"Or else?"

"Or else," Earl said quietly, "back your play."

The miner glowered across the table a moment. Then, his features twisted in a murderous expression, he kicked the chair aside and clawed at the pistol stuck in his waistband.

Earl's hand dipped inside his jacket and reappeared with the derringer. He cocked and fired in a single blurred motion.

A burlesque leer of disbelief spread over the miner's face. He stared down at the puffy hole on his shirtfront and saw a growing crimson stain. The pistol dropped from his hand and he slowly corkscrewed to his knees. He toppled over backward on the floor.

Earl regarded the other players with great calmness. When none of them moved, he put the derringer away and slowly pocketed his winnings. Standing, he walked from the gaming room, nodding to Monte as he went up the stairs.

Monte Verde took her hand from a small pistol secreted beneath the twenty-one table. As a couple of housemen carted the body out, she deftly shuffled the cards.

She smiled engagingly at the huddle of miners gathered before the layout.

"Place your bets, gents. Twenty-one wins every time!"

3

A WEEK LATER EARL returned to Denver. As he stepped down from the stagecoach, he looked like a man in need of a stiff drink. His features were set in a troubled expression.

Following the shooting, his luck had turned sour. There was no problem with the law, for he'd killed to protect himself. The miner had drawn first, and the Central City marshal wrote it off as justifiable homicide. But Earl's fortunes at the poker table were another matter entirely. He began drawing second-best cards, so bad that even a decent bluffing hand rarely worked. He contained his losses by playing conservatively and folding often. For the week, he was down almost three hundred dollars.

Earl was not a superstitious man. Most gamblers religiously stuck to certain quirks or idiosyncrasies. Some believed that it was bad luck to count their winnings during a game. Others thought the way to change a losing streak was to walk three times around one's chair. An even hoarier notion was that it inevitably brought bad luck to sit in a game with a one-eyed gambler. Earl subscribed to none of the bugaboos commonly associated with misfortune. Yet, despite himself, he felt somewhat snakebit by the shooting. Killing the miner had done nothing to improve his bankroll.

The only high point of the trip was Monte. A week spent in her company was like an elixir, often intoxicating and always pleasurable. While she'd been unable to change his luck, she had done much to restore his spirits. Her lovemaking had, if anything, been more ardent and uninhibited than usual. She had assuaged his losses with kittenish sensuality and long nights of physical pleasure. But her revitalizing effect had worn off long before the stage reached Denver. He now felt down at the mouth and just a little frazzled. For the first time in a long time, he'd returned a loser.

Entering the hotel, he proceeded across the lobby. Several acquaintances, fellow members of the gambling fraternity, were seated on the horsehair sofa and a collection of easy chairs. He nodded to them, rushing on, reluctant to be drawn into a conversation about his trip. As he approached the stairs, the desk clerk called out. "Mr. Brannock!"

Earl paused, turning. "Yes."

"I wanted to let you know, Mr. Brannock. Your brother is upstairs."

"Brother!" Earl repeated, stunned.

"Yes, sir," the clerk replied. "He arrived yesterday and I . . . Well, I hope you don't mind, Mr. Brannock. I put him in your room."

"Which one?" Earl demanded.

"Pardon me?"

"Which brother—Virgil or Clint?"

"I'm not exactly sure. I don't recall asking, just offhand."

Earl spun away, bounding up the stairs. On the second floor he hurried down the hall and burst through the door of his room. A large man, tall and wide through the shoulders, rose from a chair beside the window. Framed in a shaft of sunlight, his chestnut hair and full mustaches gave him a ruddy look. Earl moved forward, hand outstretched.

"Virge! By God, it's really you."

Virgil Brannock clasped his hand, then pulled him into a tight bear hug. At thirty, Virgil was the eldest of the three brothers, a year older than Earl. Since they'd last met, he appeared to have aged, flecks of gray streaking his sideburns. He released Earl, stepping back with a warm smile.

"Well, you're looking fit and then some. The mountains must agree with you."

"No complaints," Earl said, tossing his hat on the bed.

"How about yourself? Where the hell did you spring from? How'd you get here?"

"One question at a time," Virgil said genially. "I got here by stage, pulled in yesterday. As to the where, my last stop was Missouri."

"You've been home, then?"

Virgil nodded. "Went there when I was mustered out. Took close to three weeks' travel from Appomattox."

Earl stared at him. "You were with Lee . . . at the end?"

"Gordon's Second Corps," Virgil acknowledged. "Got myself a souvenir the last day of fighting."

He extended his left hand. The ring finger and the little finger were scarred and bent, drawn inward like talons. To all appearances, the crippled fingers were locked rigid in place.

"Jesus," Earl muttered. "Can you move them?"

"A wiggle here and there. But the truth is, I got off luckier than most. Lots of men were killed right up to the cease-fire."

"Sounds like it was pretty rough."

"I doubt I'll ever see worse."

Virgil went on to explain that Union forces had trapped Lee and the Army of Northern Virginia. Heavy fighting raged during the early days of April, with the ring drawing ever tighter around the Confederates. On April 9, when General John Gordon sought to halt the advance of Phil Sheridan's corps, Virgil had been wôunded in an artillery exchange. An hour later Lee formally surrendered to Grant at Appomattox.

At the field hospital, an army doctor had ordered Virgil's fingers amputated. Having seen too many amputations, Virgil refused and went away with his hand swathed in bandages. Under the terms of the surrender, officers were allowed to keep their horses and personal belongings. Virgil, who was then a captain, rode out three days after the cease-fire. He'd arrived at the family farm outside Harrisonville, Missouri, on April 27.

When he finished, Earl nodded stolidly. "How are Uncle Ezra and Aunt Angeline?"

"All things considered, they came through it fairly good."

"Any word of Clint?"

"Last we heard, he'd been shipped to a Yankee prison. Somewheres in Ohio."

Their younger brother was two years Earl's junior. At the outbreak of the war, both Virgil and Clint had volunteered. Earl, who had denounced the war as madness, refused to join them. While Virgil accepted his decision, Clint angrily branded him a traitor to the cause. The division alienated Earl and the youngest brother, and Clint had departed for the war without attempting to heal the split. Not quite two years later the family had been notified of Clint's capture during the battle of Vicksburg.

"I wonder—" Earl mused aloud. "You think he's been released . . . or what?"

Virgil shook his head. "Hard to say. I figured we would've heard something before I left. The Yankees are pretty good about that sort of thing."

"What do you mean?"

"Well, you know, notifying the next of kin."

"Are you saying you think he's dead?"

"I don't know, Earl. I wish I did."

Virgil grew silent, staring at a spot of sunlight on the floor. His expression was abstracted, a long pause of inner deliberation. Finally he glanced up, his face stern as a deacon's. "Guess you heard about the folks?"

"Yeah," Earl answered, his eyes grave. "Uncle Ezra wrote me when it happened."

"I visited the cemetery while I was there. The family chipped in and gave them real nice headstones."

Their parents had been among the first civilian casualties of the war. The Missouri-Kansas border region was bitterly divided between Confederate and Union sympathizers. Savage guerrilla warfare was a natural outgrowth, and hot-blooded men of both states rallied around self-appointed leaders.

William Quantrill, who was active in the proslavery movement, organized a band of Missouri guerrillas. With such recruits as Jesse and Frank James, he spent the balance of the war terrorizing abolitionist strongholds in Kansas.

Quantrill's counterpart in Kansas was Charles "Doc" Jennison. A sinister and unusually gifted leader, Jennison rose to prominence on the eve of the Civil War. Under a banner of antislavery, he formed a guerrilla outfit known as the Jayhawkers. Operating as the Seventh Kansas Regiment, they began a campaign of murder and looting throughout western Missouri. Their first major blow was struck during the summer of 1861, when they pillaged Harrisonville and the surrounding countryside. James and Sarah Brannock, their farm burned to the ground, were killed in the course of the raid.

However unrealistic, Earl blamed himself in large part for his parents' death. He had departed Missouri for the Colorado gold fields in early May, only two months before the Jayhawker raid. He'd often thought that had he stayed, he might have somehow prevented the tragedy. It relieved his conscience none at all to realize that he, too, would have been killed by the guerrillas. He was still ridden with guilt.

"I never went back," he said after a prolonged silence. "Maybe I should've, just to visit their graves. It's hard to know what's right."

"What's past is past," Virgil said gently. "You made a life for yourself here and it does no good to look back. Besides, it wouldn't have changed anything anyhow."

Earl sat down on the edge of the bed. He scrubbed his face with his palms, seemed to collect himself. "Well, like you say, it's water under the bridge now. So tell me, Brother Virge. What brings you to Denver?"

"A fresh start," Virgil said, suddenly smiling. "By all accounts, you seem to have prospered out here. I thought I'd give it a try."

"You"—Earl looked amazed—"a gambler?"

"God A'mighty, no! I'm not cut out for the sporting life. Figured I'd try my hand at business."

"What kind of business?"

"Good question," Virgil said, chuckling softly. "To be honest about it, I haven't got the least idea. Guess I'll have to scout around and see what strikes me."

"How about money?" Earl inquired. "Have you got the wherewithal to get started?"

"Yes and no," Virgil said. "I sold the farmland back home, even though it didn't bring much. And of course, that's to be split three ways—including Clint."

Earl brushed the offer aside. "Keep my share and welcome to it. Matter of fact, I'd be willing to stake you to anything reasonable. I'm pretty well fixed."

"Well, we'll see how it goes. They say Colorado's the land of opportunity, and plenty to go around. I'll have a look for myself."

"I could show you the ropes. There's not much I don't know about Denver and the gold camps."

Virgil turned. "Wouldn't it be something if Clint popped up all of a sudden? The three of us back together again!"

Earl's voice lowered, his eyes downcast. "I'd give a heap for that, Virge. All I own."

"So would I."

Virgil turned to the window. His gaze went past the streamer of sunlight and he seemed to stare off into the middle distance. His features set in a look of somber introspection. "So would I."

4

THE NEXT COUPLE OF days were spent looking around town. Virgil was quickly convinced that Denver was the major trade center for the Colorado settlements. Yet he sensed that all business and trade was tied directly to the gold camps. He decided that the camps were the place to start.

Earl suggested a week's trip to Black Hawk. Located a few miles east of Central City, Black Hawk was the second-richest camp in the mountains. Upon arriving there, Virgil discovered that the town was in the midst of a transformation. Once Earl found a poker game, his time was his own, and he set about investigating the process of mining gold. He found there was more to it than a greenhorn might suspect.

Any gold rush began with traces of the yellow metal being located in streambeds. Gold derived originally from veins deeply encased in mountainous rock formations. Over long periods of time, erosion due to weather broke the rock apart and loosened subsurface pockets of ore. The runoff from seasonal rains then carried the gold from the vein and eventually deposited it somewhere downstream. The churning action of water and stone abraded the ore until finally it was reduced to nuggets and thin flakes, or even fine dust.

These streambed deposits were the discoveries located by prospectors. The task of separating gold from solid rock had been done by nature, and by panning the streams, which was known as placer mining, the prospector was able to work the deposits. Within a short period of time, however, these surface deposits quickly played out. The prospector then resorted to ever more elaborate methods of dredging the streams for pockets buried beneath tons of mud and silt. Ultimately, the labor required to uncover an ounce of gold amounted to little more than day wages.

When the placers played out, the next step was to undertake quartz mining. After tracing the vein to its origin, mine shafts were excavated, and the backbreaking job of transporting the ore to the surface was begun. Quartz mining, which was sometimes called hard-rock mining, was essentially a problem of freeing the gold from lodes buried deep within the earth. Yet extracting the gold from a quartz vein was a complex operation that required elaborate machinery.

The mined ore was first crushed in a stamp mill, which was a mechanized version of the ancient pestle and mortar. Ore was then passed over shelves of quicksilver, which adhered to the gold and separated it from the crushed rock. The final step was to free the gold in pure form by distilling it from the quicksilver. The process was laborious, time-consuming, and far more costly than panning a streambed. It required both a knowledge of mining techniques and a heavy investment of capital. For all intents and purposes, quartz mining was big business.

Virgil soon scratched mining off his list. He had neither the experience nor the necessary funds to undertake a venture of such magnitude. Instead, he spent the remainder of the week poking around the business district of Black Hawk. He quickly became aware that a mining camp was dependent on the outside world for virtually every item of daily life. Food and clothing, hardware and utensils, even the grain for work animals, were imported from elsewhere. One staple, which seemed indispensable to the rigors of a mountainous climate, was imported in vast quantities. Miners, so he observed, consumed prodigious amounts of alcohol.

By rough count, Virgil estimated that there was one saloon for every hundred people in Black Hawk. Casual conversation with saloonkeepers confirmed that the ratio was approximately the same in Central City and other mining camps. One of the favorite libations among miners was an explosive concoction known as Taos Lightning. A product of New Mexico Territory, it was made in Don Fernando de Taos and transported by ox wagon over 350 miles of mountain passes. Aged only a week or so, it was a potent strain of *aguardiente*, distilled from corn or wheat. According to local legend, a sudden jolt of Ol' Towse had been known to stop the drinker's watch and snap his suspenders.

Yet miners were nothing if not connoisseurs of alcohol in all its hybrid forms. They consumed rye and bourbon, brandy and champagne, and even beer in almost equal doses. Water was all but a foreign substance, used principally to pan gold and wash dirty socks. Upon returning to Denver, Virgil's initial assessment was borne out by a testimonial to the celebrity of John Barleycorn. As he stepped off the stage, he saw an eighty-wagon caravan, loaded entirely with liquor, pull into town. The wagons were jammed with 2,700 barrels of popskull whiskey and 1,600 cases of imported champagne.

Further investigation revealed that alcoholic spirits had been a staple of trade since the days of the mountain men. Western fur traders discovered that firewater was the most profitable of all freight items. It could be packed and carried with relative ease, and not a drop of spoilage. Further, and all the more significant, the price it commanded was sky-high in relation to its weight. A hundredweight of flour went for thirty dollars in the mining camps. An equal measure of whiskey, when sold by the drink, fetched upward of three hundred dollars. Clearly, there was a fortune to be made in quenching the thirst of miners.

Because of harsh winters, wagon traffic from eastern shipping terminals began in April and ended in early November. Throughout the summer and fall, teamsters offloaded tons of alcohol in the mining camps. Yet, with the onset of bad weather, the distribution system ground to a halt. Either saloonkeepers overstocked during the summer—thereby laying out a king's ransom in cash—or it proved to be a long, dry winter in the mountains. With profits figured at 1000 percent per drink, there was no choice but to overstock.

After scouting around, Virgil determined that there was only one wholesale liquor house in Denver. It seemed that no one was willing to commit the necessary investment capital to supply the mining camps both winter and summer. Barkeeps, as a result, contracted with middlemen who sold their consignments of liquor to the highest bidder. As Virgil assessed the situation, there was a ready market for a wholesaler who would sell at established prices on a year-round basis. Insofar as he could judge, the one local wholesaler was barely able to meet the demand of Denver's sporting district. He saw the mining camps as an opportunity literally dusted with gold.

Virgil estimated that he needed twenty thousand dollars to stock a warehouse and carry the business through the initial turnover of inventory. Twenty thousand would allow him to stock various types of bottled liquors, as well as barrel whiskey and a limited selection of champagnes. From the sale of the family farm he had two thousand, and Earl, after listening to his proposal, agreed to loan him another three thousand. That left him fifteen thousand dollars short, and no hope of raising it from private sources. He decided to try Denver's only bank.

Virgil had his one suit sponged and pressed. He put on a clean shirt, with a four-in-hand tie, and spruced up his boots with bootblack. Finally, after dusting off his hat, he inspected himself in the mirror. He thought it would have to do.

Some minutes later he walked through the door of the First

National Bank. A teller informed him that Mr. Walter Tisdale was president of the bank, and pointed him in the right direction. He crossed the room, halting before the open door of an office. Behind the desk sat a rotund man, with a moonlike face and bushy muttonchop whiskers. Virgil rapped on the door.

"Mr. Tisdale?"

Tisdale looked up from an accounting ledger. "Yes."

"I'd like to see you a minute."

"Of course." Tisdale motioned him forward. "Please step inside."

Virgil introduced himself and they exchanged handshakes. Tisdale offered him a chair, casually examining his shiny store-bought suit and worn boots. He waited until Virgil had seated himself.

"Well, now, what can I do for you, Mr. Brannock?"

"I need a loan," Virgil said without preliminaries. "I figure to open a business here in Denver."

"Indeed?" Tisdale said blandly. "Are you new to the city, Mr. Brannock?"

"Yessir, I am. Arrived here a week ago Friday."

"May I inquire where from?"

"Missouri. A little town called Harrisonville."

"And what prompted your move west?"

"Couple of things," Virgil said. "I aim to better myself, and I heard Denver's growing by leaps and bounds. As to the second reason, my brother has been living out here four years now. You might know him. His name's Earl Brannock."

"I know of him," Tisdale said without inflection. "People say he's one of the few honest gamblers in town."

"That's Earl," Virgil affirmed. "Square as they come."

Tisdale steepled his fingers, peered across the desk. "Were you in business, back in Missouri?"

"No, sir, I wasn't. I've been a farmer most of my life."

"I see," Tisdale said in a carefully measured voice. "And what sort of business do you plan on opening here?"

"Wholesale liquor," Virgil told him. "Way I calculate it, the mining camps are a wide-open market."

"How did you arrive at that conclusion?"

Virgil related his investigation of the past week. He went into some detail with respect to the seasonal nature of the liquor trade. Then he explained that the saloonkeepers, to avoid overstocking for the winter, would gladly switch their trade to a responsible wholesaler. He ended on a note of confidence.

"The market's already there," he observed. "And it's waiting for somebody to meet the demand at reasonable terms. I intend to be the man."

Tisdale appraised him with a thoughtful look. The banker prided himself on being a shrewd judge of character. Virgil's practical manner and his logical assessment of the liquor trade indicated an astute and orderly mind. Moreover, his determination and assured attitude outweighed his lack of business experience. Tisdale found himself favorably impressed.

"Denver needs men with your spirit, Mr. Brannock. The bedrock of a solid economy is commerce, not gold. Few men have the foresight to look beyond a bird in the hand."

"I'm here to stay," Virgil announced, "and I figure I'm on to a good thing. I aim to make my mark."

Tisdale nodded wisely. "What size loan are we talking about?"

"I've got five thousand," Virgil said. "I'll need another fifteen to do the job right."

Tisdale studied him a moment. "I'll grant the loan on three conditions, Mr. Brannock. First, instead of renting a building, I suggest you buy property and erect your own warehouse. Second, the bank will hold a lien on the warehouse and land, as well as all equipment."

Virgil looked at him questioningly. "What's the third condition?"

"I believe it's a mistake to undertake any enterprise with limited funds. Fifteen thousand would allow you no cushion, nothing to offset unforeseen contingencies. So I would insist that we make the loan for twenty-five thousand.''

Virgil appeared dumbstruck. "Well, I'll be . . ." He stopped, shook his head. "That's damned generous of you, Mr. Tisdale."

"Not at all," Tisdale said with a sly grin. "I'm simply protecting my investment. Incidentally, the interest rate is twenty percent per annum on a three-year note. I'll expect quarterly payments, promptly and on time."

"Whatever seems fair," Virgil said buoyantly. "Way I see it, I'll be rolling in money before the summer's out."

"No doubt," Tisdale agreed. "When things are properly under way, perhaps I'll introduce you to some of our more civic-minded businessmen. It pays to develop the right contacts."

"I'd be obliged, Mr. Tisdale. Mighty obliged."

After the loan agreement was signed and Virgil had departed, Tisdale suddenly remembered something. The lapse was unlike him, particularly upon meeting an ambitious and halfway presentable younger man. He'd forgotten to inquire if Virgil Brannock was a bachelor.

5

THE TRAIN CHUFFED TO a halt outside the Harrisonville depot. Up front, the conductor swung down from the lead passenger coach as the stationmaster crossed the platform. Only one passenger stepped off the train.

Clint Brannock paused a moment on the platform. He scanned the depot as though it were an unexpected curiosity. Four years ago, when he rode off to war, the railroad had not yet extended to Harrisonville. The trip from Ohio, where he'd been confined in a Union prison camp, was in fact his first ride aboard a civilian train. He thought it a big improvement over horseback.

A strapping six-footer, Clint still wore the tattered remnants of a Confederate uniform. Normally robust and muscular, he was now painfully thin from more than two years' imprisonment. Yet his features were ruggedly forceful under a thatch of sandy hair. With a square jaw and a wide brow, his smoky-blue eyes gave him a determined look. His mouth seemed fixed in an implacable line.

The stationmaster gave him a puzzled once-over, then hurried forward. "Well, bless my britches! Everybody about give you up for dead, Clint."

"Hello, Amos." Clint accepted his handshake, nodded at the depot. "You're with the railroad now?"

"Have been the last year or so. We ain't heard hide nor hair of you since you was took prisoner. Where you been?"

"Ohio," Clint said flatly. "Yankee prison."

The conversation was cut short as the train got under way. Clint nodded and moved across the platform. On the other side of the depot the town appeared unchanged. There were a couple of new buildings, but Main Street looked much the same as when he'd gone off to war. Like most farm communities in Missouri, little varied from season to season. Somehow, even though it stirred memories, Clint experienced no sense of homecoming. He turned and walked off along a dusty road leading south.

The vestiges of war were with him still. On July 3, 1863, he'd been captured in Mississippi. At the time, he was acting as a courier from besieged Vicksburg to Port Hudson, another Confederate stronghold two hundred miles downriver. After being jumped by a Union patrol, he had tried to outrun them and complete his mission. A slug through the shoulder knocked him off his horse, and he ended up in a Yankee field hospital.

Later, he would learn that the dispatch he carried, intended for the Port Hudson commander, was of far-reaching consequence. General John Pemberton, commander of the Vicksburg garrison, had decided to surrender his beleaguered troops. To that end, he had requested a conference with the Union leader, Ulysses S. Grant. The surrender had been effected the next day, July 4. Following his recovery, Clint had been transported to a Union prison camp.

Life in prison had been far worse than the battlefield. Conditions were primitive, and food rations, at best, were meager. After six months, Clint had been offered a pardon, on condition that he become a "galvanized" Yankee. The term applied to Southerners who swore an oath of allegiance to the Union and were transferred west to fight Indians. Clint spent his time instead trying to escape prison camp and rejoin the Confederacy. His last breakout attempt had occurred only three weeks before the war ended. He'd drawn solitary confinement, and regulations required that he serve out the two-month sentence. On May 12, fully a month after the cease-fire, he had finally been released.

Four miles outside Harrisonville, Clint turned into a farmyard. His uncle, Ezra Brannock, was chopping wood near the back door. But it was his Aunt Angeline who spotted him first and came running from the kitchen. She threw her arms around him in a maternal hug, tears streaming down her face. She was a large woman, in her early forties, her skin prematurely lined. He remembered her as gentle and infinitely wise, and he allowed himself to be fussed over like a fuzzy-cheeked boy. For the first time, he felt as though he'd come home.

Ezra, who was his father's brother, greeted him like a son. Ezra's only boy had been killed in the war, and his daughter had married a man in town. While Clint bathed and changed into leftover clothes of his dead cousin, Angeline went to work in the kitchen. She laid out all the fixings: fried chicken and corn bread, mashed potatoes and greens, and a savory mincemeat pie. Clucking and scolding, she forced him to eat until he felt ready to burst. Home cooking, she declared, would put a little meat on his bones.

After supper, Ezra and Clint retired to the front porch. There, settled back in rockers, they watched the sun sink westward. While they had spoken of Virgil and Earl, there had been no mention of Clint's parents. Finally, wondering whether he should broach the subject, Ezra fired up his corncob pipe.

"Maybe tomorrow," he said, puffing smoke, "we can ride out to the graveyard. I reckon you'd like to see where your folks was laid to rest."

Clint merely nodded. His eyes were faraway and clouded, as though wrestling with something that resisted words. When at last he spoke, his mouth was clamped in a bloodless slash and ugly lines strained his face. His voice was toneless.

"Tell me about it," he said. "How it happened."

Ezra took a deep breath, blew it out heavily. "Jennison's raiders split up into two parties. One ransacked the town, cleaned out the bank, and killed five men. The other bunch hit the farms nearest to town. They was mainly lookin' for saddle horses."

"Go on," Clint said dully.

"Your pa put up a fight. Him and your ma forted up in the house, and he let loose with a shotgun. Killed three of the bastards before they set fire to the house. Just for spite, they burned down the barn, too."

"So the folks never had a chance?"

"They might've," Ezra said darkly. "But your pa probably figured he could hold 'em off. He never was one to back away from a fight."

Ezra thought the youngest son was much like the father. Hot-tempered and handy with his fists, Clint had been the wild one of the three brothers. Since childhood, he'd had an affinity for guns and hunting; always off in the woods, he'd been what men called a natural shot. To himself, Ezra wondered now how those skills had been honed by the war.

Clint looked at him with a disquieting stare. "You say Jennison was the leader. Was it him that raided the house?"

"No," Ezra said, remembering. "Jennison stayed in town. His second-in-command was a no-account by the name of Jack Quintin. He's the one that killed your folks."

"You sound like you know him."

"Just his name. Toward the end of the war, he got to be a regular visitor around these parts."

"How so?"

Ezra briefly explained. In the aftermath of the raid, the Union army had disowned Doc Jennison. Thereafter, Jennison and his chief lieutenant, Jack Quintin, had operated the Jayhawkers as irregular guerrillas. Their plundering raids into western Missouri continued through 1864, when Jennison had been killed in a skirmish with proslavery forces. Quintin had then assumed command and led the Jayhawkers until the end of the war. With the return of peace, he had quickly dropped from sight. Everyone assumed he had taken sanctuary in abolitionist Kansas.

Clint was silent for a time. "Any idea what this Quintin looks like?"

"Nothin' to hang your hat on," Ezra said slowly. "Why do you ask?"

"Only seems fair," Clint said with an odd smile. "I wouldn't want to kill the wrong man."

Ezra squinted at him with an owlish frown. "That's a damn-fool notion if ever I heard one. Seems like you would've had your fill of killin'."

Clint's eyes were suddenly fierce. "Let's just call it a blood debt. I aim to collect."

Ezra Brannock was a simple man. His hands were large and gnarled, calloused from the hardships of a lifetime spent tilling the soil. He abhorred violence, and he thought revenge was the poorest of excuses for killing another human. Yet, since the younger man had walked into the yard, he'd sensed a strangeness about Clint. He was colder and harder, somehow brutalized by the killing ground of war and his years in prison. Then, too, his eyes were pale and very direct, mirroring a personal insensitivity that was curiously detached. He looked like he'd forgotten the meaning of compassion and mercy.

"Vengeance won't get you anywhere," Ezra said at length. "All it does is eat away at your soul. God knows, it won't bring you no peace."

Clint rocked his hand, fingers splayed. "The Yankees burned my soul out of me, Uncle Ezra. I reckon I lived through it for a reason, though. Today, I learned his name."

"Thunderation!" Ezra said gruffly. "Nothin' good'll come of it, boy. You'll wind up destroying yourself."

"Not before ı square accounts with Quintin."

"And how the devil you figger to do that? You haven't got a glimmer of where to start lookin'."

Clint heaved himself to his feet. "Think I'll have another piece of that mincemeat pie. Aunt Angeline sure knows her way around the kitchen."

Left alone on the porch, Ezra struck a sulfurhead and rekindled his pipe. He knew now that argument would avail him nothing. He could talk himself blue in the face and it wouldn't change a thing. The boy, like his father before him, would never turn the other cheek. And like his father, it would probably get him killed.

Ezra stared morosely off into the gathering twilight.

Four days later Clint walked back into town. He was ten pounds heavier and ruddy good health showed in his features. He hadn't eaten so well, or so much, since before the war.

Stuffed deep in his pocket were five twenty-dollar gold pieces. Though Ezra and Angeline Brannock were themselves hard-pressed, they had dipped into their hoard and provided him with a stake. His Aunt Angeline, trying to choke back the tears, had entreated him to join his brothers in Denver. He'd promised nothing, and his uncle hadn't reopened the argument. They watched from the porch until he was out of sight.

In town, Clint's first stop was at the local livestock dealer's horse pens. There, after suitable haggling, he bought a dun gelding and a used saddle. His bankroll reduced by half, he then rode the gelding uptown. Several stops and twenty dollars later, he had himself provisioned with camp gear and a week's supply of vittles. He next walked across the street to the hardware store.

With the war scarcely ended, firearms were in short supply. Yet luck, or perhaps fate, was with him today. Confederate officers, upon being paroled, were allowed to retain their sidearms. A local man, after being mustered out of the army, had traded his pistol for farm tools. It was a Colt Navy .36 cap-and-ball revolver, somewhat worse for wear but still serviceable. Beside it in the display case was the companion military holster.

For sixteen dollars, Clint bought the pistol and holster. Another three dollars went for gunpowder and a bag of .36-caliber lead balls. He strapped on the flap-top holster, which was inverted according to military custom, carrying the pistol butt forward. Then, while the store owner watched silently, he loaded and charged five chambers. Holstering the Colt, he walked back across the street.

A warm noonday sun beat down as he rode out of town. Behind him were unexpired emotions and some memories best forgotten. There was nothing to look back for, no reason for staying.

He turned the dun gelding toward Kansas.

6

THE THIRD WEEK IN May brought crisp sunshine to the mountains. Aspens budded emerald leaves and brilliant patches of wildflowers dotted the slopes. Above the timberline snow-capped spires still towered against the sky.

The mines were once more operating at full capacity. After the winter slowdown, fair weather brought increased activity throughout the mountains. The quartz mines went back on double shifts, and the camps were again jammed with thousands of workers. Placer miners also began working their claims with renewed vigor. While the yield from streams was lower than last year, there was still gold to be found. Springtime was a season of optimism for men determined to strike it rich.

Earl returned to Central City on a sun-drenched Monday. As he stepped off the stage, he was greeted by still another aspect of springtime. Sanitation in the mining camps was of a rudimentary nature. Outhouses were crude affairs and never constructed in adequate numbers to accommodate thousands of men. Drainage ditches were frequently clogged, and sewage inevitably spilled over into the streams. Winter stifled the odor, but warm weather brought on the breathtaking stench of human waste. Old-timers in the mining camps learned to breathe through their mouths.

The week began on an auspicious note. With optimism running high in the camps, Earl had brought his entire bankroll. He had five thousand in greenbacks and coin, which he deposited with the Metropole cashier. Then, biding his time, he waited until a modest table-stakes game developed. The limit was twenty-five dollars, and luck was with him throughout that first night. He won slightly more than a thousand dollars.

The following night he put together an even larger game. With a limit of fifty dollars and a continued run of good cards, he cleared almost three thousand dollars. Fortune smiled on him Wednesday night and Thursday night as well. The faces of the players changed, but there seemed no scarcity of men willing to risk high stakes. Friday night was no exception, and the game lasted until daylight. When he deposited the night's take with the cashier, he was somewhat taken aback by the total count. He'd won eighteen thousand dollars for the week.

Monte was no less stunned by his good fortune. For years she had watched him work the camps, winning consistently, but never pulling down the big strike. Now, all in the space of five nights, he'd more than tripled his bankroll. Yet she was perhaps more cautious than Earl. She had seen big winners, professionals as well as amateurs, push their luck one step too far. A man on a streak too often developed a sense of invincibility, believed himself unbeatable. Then, suddenly, the caprice of fate dealt him a lesson in reality. The cards turned sour and luck went by the boards. The victor became the vanquished, and lost it all.

Upstairs, following the Friday-night game, Monte urged him to take a breather. She feared his run would end as abruptly as it had begun. Moreover, she was concerned that five grueling nights at the tables had worn him down, both physically and mentally. A player's stamina and the mental agility essential to high-stakes poker were an exhaustible resource. Even the most vigorous of men needed a break, time to relax and revitalize themselves. She pleaded with him not to press his luck further. Not until he'd taken a few days off.

Earl blithely ignored the warning. His nerves were strung tight and he seemed galvanized by nervous energy. He paced their room like a caged panther, replaying hands he'd drawn and reveling again in the size of the pots he'd won. He agreed that it was unwise to discount the odds, press luck beyond certain limits. But some visceral instinct told him that he'd not yet reached the end of his string. Whether gambler's intuition or ordinary gut hunch, he believed it was no time to quit. When she persisted, he finally promised that he would stop after one more night. A final grab at the brass ring.

Word of Earl's remarkable run had quickly spread through the camp. As so often happens, men who considered themselves gamblers began lining up to take a crack at the big winner. Some perversity of the mind, long recognized by professionals, goads certain men to test their luck against another man's hot streak. On Saturday night, four such men appeared at the Metropole. Three were owners of large quartz mines, and the fourth was Tom Spainyard, a gambling man of some repute. All of them were high rollers of considerable note, addicted to table-stakes poker. They each thought themselves the one to put the quietus on Earl Brannock.

The game was five-card draw, Western rules prevailing. In some Eastern casinos, the traditional rules of poker had been revised to create even more enticing odds for inveterate gamblers and wealthy high rollers. Introduced into the game were straights, flushes, and the most elusive of all combinations, the straight flush. The highest hand back East was now a royal flush, ten through ace in the same suit. By all reports, the revised rules had infused the game with an almost mystical element.

Poker in the West, however, was still played by the original rules. There were no straights, no flushes, and no straight flushes, royal or otherwise. The game was governed by tenets faithfully observed in earlier times on riverboats and the Creole gaming salons of New Orleans. Whether draw poker or stud poker, there were two unbeatable hands west of the Mississippi. The first was four aces, drawn by most players only once or twice in a lifetime. The other cinch hand was four kings with an ace, which precluded anyone holding four aces. Seasoned players looked upon it as a minor miracle or the work of a skilled cardsharp. Four kings, in combination with one of the aces, surmounted almost incalculable odds.

Shortly before five in the morning, Earl drew an unbeatable hand. The all-night game had weeded out two of the mine owners, both departing ten thousand dollars poorer. The third mining man was dealing, and down to his last thousand dollars. By mutual agreement, the game was table stakes with no limit, check and raise. Earl and the other gambling man, Tom Spainyard, were each roughly fifteen thousand dollars ahead. Until now, they had butted heads infrequently during the course of the night.

On the first go-round, Earl was dealt three kings. He was under the gun, seated next to the dealer, and he opened the betting for a thousand dollars. Spainyard studied his cards a moment, then called and raised two thousand. The mine owner, unable to match the three thousand, dropped out. Earl called the raise and, with only a slight hesitation, bumped it another two thousand. Spainyard gave him a peculiar look and just called.

When the dealer announced ''cards to the payers,'' Earl drew two cards. He collected them as they were dealt and slipped them beneath the three kings. Without looking at them, he began riffling the cards one over the other, awaiting Spainyard's call. Spainyard tossed two cards into the deadwood, silently extending two fingers. The mine owner slid two cards across the table, and Spainyard folded them into his hand. He also began riffling his cards, staring now at Earl.

There was something impenetrable about Earl in a poker

game. His composure was monumental and his expression betrayed nothing of what he was thinking. He held his cards slightly above table level and slowly spread the three kings. Then he inched the fourth card into view, saw the ace of diamonds. Finally, with a flick of his thumb, he spread the fifth card. He sat there a moment, his face unreadable, staring at the case king. He'd drawn an unbeatable hand.

Folding his cards, Earl pushed three stacks of chips into the pot, "Opener bets three thousand."

Spainyard squeezed his fifth card into view. He grunted and looked up with a wide peg-toothed grin. "See your three and raise . . . five thousand!"

"Your five," Earl said impassively, "and another five."

A muscle twitched in Spainyard's cheek. He scrutinized Earl a moment, then shook his head. "I think you're bluffing, Brannock. How much you got in front of you?"

Earl carefully counted his chips. He glanced up, his features wooden. "Six thousand and change."

"Close enough," Spainyard said with a terse nod. "I tap you out."

Spainyard shoved all his remaining chips into the pot. By now, a crowd had gathered in the gaming room. They watched intently as Earl moved stacks of chips to the center of the table.

"You're called," he said in a neutral voice.

Spainyard laughed, fanning his cards faceup. "Read 'em and weep, sport. Four jacks!"

"Other way 'round," Earl said, spreading his hand on the table. "I caught the fourth king."

A hush settled over the room. Spainyard stared down at the cards with shocked disbelief. His face was white and pinched around the mouth.

"Some people—" Spainyard faltered, slowly sank back in his chair. "Pure shithouse luck, that's all it was!"

"I couldn't agree more, Tom. Tonight was my night."

"Goddamn if it wasn't."

Spainyard rose and pushed through the crowd. As Earl sat staring at the mound of chips, a buzz of excitement swept through the onlookers. He wagged his head, finally allowed himself a smile.

Some while later Monte joined him in the room upstairs. He was seated on the edge of the bed, staring at the wall with a slightly dazed expression. She closed the door, leaned back against it.

"How much did you win?"

"Including tonight," he said in a low voice, "it tallies out to sixty-seven thousand."

"Will you stop now?"

"You'll never guess what I plan to do."

"Oh?" she said softly. "What's that?"

Earl looked at her. "Altogether I've got seventy-two thousand dollars. I'm going to open the damnedest gaming parlor anybody ever saw. I want you along as my partner."

Her eyes danced merrily. "Are you talking about a business arrangement?"

"Nobody draws a crowd like you do. Together, we'll make a couple of fortunes and more. Hell, we can't miss!"

"When you say partners"—her chin tilted—"does that mean personal ties . . . or just business?"

"You tell me," Earl said. "How do you want it?"

"No strings," she replied. "And no promises. Why spoil what we've got?"

"Fair enough," Earl agreed. "Anytime you get tired of my company, you're free to walk. And vice versa."

"Where do you plan to open this gaming emporium?"

"Where all the high rollers are—Denver."

"And how do we split the ill-gotten gains?"

"Well, of course, I'm putting up the money. So I figure we'll divvy it seventy-thirty, my favor. Sound fair to you?"

Monte's eyes suddenly shone, and she laughed. "Hello, partner."

She crossed the room and halted in front of him. The light scent of her perfume and the warmth of her body seemed to envelop him. She cupped his face in her hands and leaned forward with a minxish smile. Her lips were moist and inviting.

He pulled her down on the bed.

7

WALTER TISDALE'S HOUSE WAS in the uptown residential district. There, in an exclusive area around Fourteenth Street, the wealthier families of Denver had built imposing brick homes. Men of position and status wouldn't live anywhere else.

Virgil turned into the walkway shortly before eight o'clock. The house blazed with lights, and he wondered how many dinner guests were attending the party. Tisdale had invited him earlier in the week, mentioning that several prominent men would be there. He'd promptly splurged on a blue serge suit, new boots, and a narrow-brimmed hat. He felt tricked out like a sporting house dandy.

The dinner invitation was clearly a stamp of approval. Over the past three weeks Virgil had worked night and day organizing his business. After purchasing a lot in the downtown area, he had contracted to have the warehouse built. To acquire an initial inventory, he had outbid everyone else on a ten-wagon caravan of liquors and champagne. His next move was to purchase four delivery wagons and teams, and hire drivers.

By stagecoach, he'd then made a three-day swing through

Central City and Black Hawk. His proposition made sense to saloon owners, and he met with little sales resistance. All of them were in favor of reducing their own inventories and thereby reducing their overhead. Some were skeptical, but most agreed to let him stock their shelves on a weekly basis. When he returned to Denver, he had more than twenty new accounts on the books. He forwarded an order to St. Louis for a thirty-wagon caravan of liquor.

Flushed with success, Virgil was anticipating the dinner party. He thought it could only improve his prospects to be on a chummy basis with the town's movers and shakers. Walter Tisdale admitted him at the door, noting his new suit with a glance of approval, and took his hat. The banker seemed genuinely pleased to see him.

The parlor was large and ornate. A vast Persian carpet covered the floor, and a number of sofas and settees were scattered around the room. The wallpaper was a lush red damask, and velvet drapes bordered the front windows. Several armchairs and a divan were arranged before a black marble fireplace. Virgil was surprised by the lavish furnishings, and suitably impressed. The banking business, from all appearances, was a highly profitable venture.

Tisdale's wife and daughter were waiting in the parlor. Mrs. Tisdale was short and plump, with shy eyes and a tittering manner. Her daughter, who was in her early twenties, looked nothing like the mother. Elizabeth Tisdale was rather tall, with enormous hazel eyes and exquisite features. She was vivacious, with a sumptuous figure, her dark hair upswept and fluffs of curls spilling over her forehead. She wore a demure gown that did nothing to hide her tiny waist and magnificent hips.

When they were introduced, she gave Virgil a glance full of curiosity. Her hand was firm, and her appraisal of him was deliberate, almost searching.

"Father has told us a great deal about you, Mr. Brannock."

Virgil returned her gaze with open admiration. "Not a whole lot to tell, Miss Tisdale."

"Oh, quite the contrary!" She looked at him with impudent eyes. "To hear Father talk, you're very much a man on the move."

There was an awkward pause. Virgil saw something merry lurking in her eyes, and he wasn't quite sure how to respond. The arrival of the other dinner guests provided a welcome diversion.

William Byers, owner and publisher of the *Rocky Mountain News*, entered with his wife. A moment later David Hughes, the town's leading attorney, led his wife in from the vestibule. The last to arrive was Luther Evans, whose business seemed related to real estate. Virgil assumed that he was a single man, since he was unaccompanied. He caught a look that passed between Evans and the Tisdale girl. Her smile was perhaps too quick, somehow uncomfortable.

Still new to town, Virgil was nonetheless aware that these men were members of an elite crowd. Denver was a relatively new community, one where social status was not determined by an old family name or inherited wealth. Whether a man sought fortune or political power, the Colorado frontier was a place where everyone started even and built from bedrock. Those who achieved eminence and success, however, soon monopolized many aspects of a town's growth. In time, they gravitated together and joined to form the core of the local power structure. Virgil sensed that he was among such a group here tonight.

Dinner was served promptly at eight. The dining room was darkly paneled, with a crystal chandelier suspended over the table. Bone china, fine silver, and stemware glasses were formally arranged on immaculate linen cloth. A black manservant, dressed in a starched white jacket, served the meal. From tableside conversation, it became apparent that his wife was the family cook. Virgil was now doubly impressed by the style in which the Tisdales lived. He thought a man could easily grow to like it.

Throughout dinner, the conversation centered around local affairs. The topic of most interest was a volunteer group, recently formed, to raise funds for a theater and opera hall. Virgil listened attentively, offering comments only when he was addressed directly. He was seated opposite Elizabeth and found it difficult not to stare. She was animated, laughing happily at witty remarks, and on occasion darted him another of her curious glances. He noted as well that she tended to ignore Luther Evans, who was seated at her side and tried to engage her attention. He idly wondered if Evans was a frustrated suitor.

After dinner, the ladies retired to the parlor. The manservant appeared with a decanter of brandy and a humidor of fine cigars. Drinks were poured and the five men lit up in a blue haze of smoke. Quickly it became apparent that the others deferred to David Hughes, allowing him to set the tone of conversation. He was a stocky bulldog of a man, with steady dark eyes and a deliberate manner. He seemed to dominate the table with an air of magnetism and enormous confidence.

Scrupulously polite, he looked at Virgil with a calm judicial gaze. "Well, now, Mr. Brannock, how's your new business doing? We're interested to hear of your progress."

"Going real well," Virgil said, clearing his throat. "So far, things have worked out pretty much the way I expected."

"Yes," Hughes said, puffing importantly on his cigar. "Walter told us how you surveyed the field and found an untapped market. Very impressive."

"No great credit due," Virgil remarked. "Somebody would've stumbled on it sooner or later."

Tisdale chuckled out loud. "You're being far too modest, Virgil. The market was there for the past four or five years. No one had an inkling of its existence until you came along."

"Indeed!" Hughes added expansively. "You deserve congratulations, Mr. Brannock. The winner jumps in where others dare not tread.''

"Well, I've barely got my feet wet. There's a lot of ground still to be covered.''

"Tell us about it.''

Virgil made an offhand gesture. "I've only covered Central City and Black Hawk so far. That leaves a whole slew of mining camps I haven't seen.''

"Expansion.'' Hughes nodded sagely. "You have the right idea, my boy. Sew it up fast and tight, discourage competition.''

"Tell you the truth,'' Virgil said, smiling, "I was thinking along those lines myself. I figure I found the lode, so it ought to be me that mines it.''

Hughes strummed his nose. "I like your style. Denver's growing, and we need men of vision to help it along. Don't hesitate to call on me if I can be of assistance.''

"Thank you, Mr. Hughes. I might just do that.''

"Anytime,'' Hughes said bluffly. "To quote the Lord, I believe in helping those who help themselves.''

The other men laughed dutifully at the jesting remark. Virgil became aware that they were looking from him to Hughes and back again. He had the fleeting impression that he'd just been subjected to some sort of test, and passed. Yet there had been no apparent drift to the discussion, no obvious purpose. He found it strange and somehow unsettling.

Elizabeth suddenly appeared in the doorway. "All right, gentlemen! Enough of your stinky cigars and brandy. We insist that you join us in the parlor.''

The men laughed and rose in unison from their chairs. As Virgil stood, Elizabeth whisked across the room and took his arm. She vamped him with a winsome smile and steered him toward the doorway.

"Come along,'' she said pertly. "I want to hear all about this marvelous enterprise you've undertaken. May I call you Virgil?''

"Well, sure thing," Virgil said, somewhat astounded. "I'm not much for formality."

"Good, neither am I. So I insist you call me what all my friends call me—Beth."

Virgil grinned and allowed himself to be waltzed into the parlor. She squeezed his arm as they went through the door, chattering gaily. He looked like a cat with a mouthful of feathers.

8

TOPEKA WAS SITUATED ON the banks of the Kansas River. It lay some fifty miles west of the Missouri border, and it was there that Clint began his search. He rode into town on the first day of June.

Laid out in 1854, Topeka was the original Free State settlement. Sentiment against slavery was strong, and the Free Staters soon turned the area into a hotbed of abolitionist supporters. The climate gave rise to such men as John Brown, who four years later led the first guerrilla raid into Missouri and liberated eleven slaves. A year later, in 1859, Brown sealed his own doom by leading the raid on Harpers Ferry, Virginia.

When Kansas entered the Union in 1861, Topeka became the state capital. By then a major trade route, it was the original site of the Oregon Trail ferry crossing. Thousands of westward-bound settlers poured through the town on their way to the Promised Land. A short distance outside town was the juncture with the Santa Fe Trail, which branched off southwesterly toward New Mexico Territory.

The bloodbath of the Civil War somewhat tempered abo-

litionist sentiment. Kansas was still antislavery in mood, but
defeat of the Confederacy had cooled the hatred of past years.
By 1865 Topeka was a thriving farm community, as well as
a railroad terminus. While animosity still lingered along the
Missouri border, most people felt it was time to heal old
wounds. Few men admitted to having ridden with the Jayhawkers on their infamous guerrilla raids.

Clint thought of Topeka as a starting point. He was a tyro
manhunter, with no experience in tracking cutthroats and
murderers. So he began where the abolitionist movement had
been centered during the war. A guerrilla leader such as Jack
Quintin would be known there, and remembered. Someone,
Clint told himself, might very well provide information as to
the former Jayhawker's whereabouts. Or, with luck, the hunt
could end in Topeka itself. Quintin could easily have taken
sanctuary among wartime comrades.

Unversed in the subtleties of detective work, Clint took the
direct approach. He toured the town's saloons, casually striking up conversations with patrons and bartenders. One way
or another, he managed to introduce the subject of the Jayhawkers and Jack Quintin. He was looking for a reaction,
some tipoff that Quintin was known to the speaker. It occurred to him that he might encounter hostility or run into
trouble with a former guerrilla. Yet the risk seemed unavoidable, one of the hazards of the hunt. He had to start somewhere.

Shortly, he discovered that the Jayhawkers were something
of a sore point. People in Topeka seemed hesitant to discuss
the subject, as though they wanted to forget the years of border strife. Guerrillas were no longer considered admirable,
and most men became evasive when the topic was raised.
Toward the end of the day, Clint began having second
thoughts about his approach. Even when he offered to buy a
round of drinks, no one seemed inclined to talk. It was as if
Jayhawkers had become a dirty word.

Then, not long after sundown, he stumbled across a loquacious drunk. The man was a barfly, apparently a permanent resident in one of the town's seedier dives. His brother had ridden with the Jayhawkers, only to be killed a few months before the war ended. A few drinks unlocked his tongue even further and put him in a bragging mood. He heard things, he informed Clint slyly, for there were men in Topeka who had served with his brother. None of them spoke openly about their guerrilla days, but they talked freely among themselves. Jack Quintin was one of the names most frequently mentioned.

At the close of the war, the drunk revealed, the Jayhawkers had scattered to the four winds. Some Kansans were already branding them robbers and murderers, common outlaws. There was talk of bringing them to justice, since they had operated independently of Union forces. With time, however, the authorities lost interest in pursuing the matter. Former guerrillas still laid low, but they were no longer hiding out. Only recently word had surfaced about their leader, Jack Quintin. His hangout these days was thought to be Fort Riley.

Several drinks elicited little more information. The barfly had told all he knew, and most of it secondhand hearsay. Still, it was the only lead Clint had uncovered, and it had the ring of truth. A man on the run would logically head for unsettled areas, the Western plains. Once there, he might very well stay until all threat of prosecution had passed. Or he might find reason to stay there forever. Men like Quintin were misfits in normal times and civilized places. The lawless frontier was more their natural element.

From Topeka, Clint followed the Santa Fe Trail westward. Two days later he sighted Fort Riley, where the river made a slow dogleg to the south. Established in 1853, the cavalry post provided protection from Indian attacks for settlers and trade caravans. Not far from the garrison, the small town of Junction City stood framed against the endless plains. A night spent in the local saloons uncovered still another lead. Quintin had been there and gone, departing almost a month ago. The grapevine had it that he'd drifted on down to Fort Larned.

Well over a hundred miles to the southwest, Fort Larned was an isolated frontier outpost. Built with a view to permanence, it was constructed of stone a short distance from the muddy waters of the Arkansas River. In recent years, it had served as a base for army campaigns against the Cheyenne, as well as the Kiowa and Comanche. Trade caravans, bound for New Mexico Territory, plied the Santa Fe Trail during good weather. But ordinary travelers were scarce, and few settlers had dared venture so far west. Hostile Plains tribes made life on the frontier a chancy proposition.

On June 8, Clint rode into Fort Larned. Dusk was settling as he approached the squalid collection of buildings outside the garrison. For the most part, the log structures appeared to be saloons and dance halls, catering to the gamier tastes of soldiers. There were no hotels, but Clint found a ramshackle livery stable on the outskirts of town. For four bits a night, he made arrangements to stall the dun gelding. The livery owner agreed to let him sleep in the loft at no extra charge.

By the time he emerged onto the street, night had fallen. Stars were scattered like flecks of ice through a sky of purest indigo, and a pale moon bathed the fort in a spectral glow. Walking downstreet, he entered a saloon that was lighted by lanterns hung from the rafters. There were two soldiers at the bar and a civilian seated alone at one of the tables. A slatternly-looking woman stood by a door at the rear, which apparently led to the backroom cribs. She gave him a bored once-over as he moved to the bar.

The barkeep was bald as a billiard ball and smelled rank as bear grease. He ambled forward, nodding indifferently.

"What'll it be?"

"Any chance of getting a meal?" Clint asked.

"Yeah, if you're not too particular. I could have the girl rustle you up a steak."

Clint smiled. "She cooks, too?"

"In between times," the barkeep said amiably. "When she's not workin' the back room."

"Maybe I ought to have a drink beforehand. How are you fixed for bourbon?"

"Friend, it all comes outta the same barrel."

After he was served, Clint sampled the snake-head whiskey and smacked his lips. "Got a bite, doesn't it?"

The bartender chortled softly. "Soldiers would drink horse piss if it was laced with alcohol."

Clint hooked an elbow over the rough plank counter. "Guess you know everybody around these parts."

"What makes you ask?"

"I'm looking for a friend. Last I heard, he was headed for Fort Larned. Figured to sign on as a scout."

"Your friend got a name?"

"Quintin." Clint paused, took another swig of whiskey. "Jack Quintin."

The barkeep gave him a fish-eyed look. "If I was you, I wouldn't say that name too loud. Not around the soldier boys, anyways."

"Yeah?" Clint lowered his voice. "Why's that?"

"Your friend's got a price on his head. The army wants him on a charge of horse stealin'."

"No joke!" Clint sounded surprised. "How'd he get mixed up in a thing like that?"

"Search me," the barkeep said. "But he's a goner if the army lays hands on him."

"Any idea where he headed?"

"Don't wanna know. I try to tend to my own knittin'."

"How about somebody else? I'd hate like hell to lose track of him altogether."

"You might talk with Hobart."

"Who?"

The barkeep nodded across the room. "Joe Hobart. He's a gamblin' man. Him and Quintin used to share a bottle pretty regular."

Clint turned and casually inspected the lone civilian. Hobart was a lean, rawboned man with a hooked nose and a downturned mouth. He sat with a bottle and glass, dealing solitaire. His hands worked the cards with effortless grace.

"Much obliged," Clint said to the barkeep. "Guess it never hurts to ask." He crossed the room, halting beside the table.

Hobart glanced up from the cards with a thin smile. " 'Evening, cousin. You look like a man who might enjoy a hand or two of poker."

"Another time, maybe," Clint said pleasantly. "I'm looking for a little information right now."

"What sort of information."

"A friend of mine, Jack Quintin. The barkeep said you might know where he's headed."

Hobart's eyes hooded and his face went cold. "Why would I know the whereabouts of a horse thief?"

"I understood you and him were drinking buddies."

"You understood wrong," Hobart said sullenly. "Suppose you just turn around and go on back to the bar."

Clint gave him a tight, mirthless smile. "Why get your nose out of joint? I'm just trying to locate a friend."

"Friend, hell!" Hobart grated. "You got the smell of a lawdog, mister. And I'm not especially fond of the breed."

"How about Jayhawkers?" Clint's voice was edged. "Way you talk, you might've rode with Quintin during the war."

Hobart fixed him with a corrosive glare. "Walk away and leave me be. I've done said all I'm gonna say."

Clint made a snap decision. To press the issue now would get him nowhere. Instead, he would wait until later, when the saloon closed. Then, outside in the dark, he would manage to take Hobart prisoner. Any man could be made to talk, and he felt certain the gambler was no exception. All it required was the proper form of persuasion.

"Have it your own way," he said bluntly. "Lots of people

are bound to remember Quintin. I'll just ask around somewhere else.''

With a curt nod, he turned and walked toward the bar. The bartender looked up, then suddenly stared past him. Something in the man's eyes alerted him, and from the direction of the table, he heard the scrape of chair legs. His response was instinctive and fast. He dived headlong to the floor.

A slug whistled overhead and thunked into the bar. Clint rolled sideways, clawing at the flap-top holster, as the report of a gunshot echoed through the saloon. He saw Hobart standing, arm extended, smoke curling from the barrel of a small revolver. As he fumbled with the holster, Hobart fired again, hurrying the shot. Splinters exploded from the floor directly at Clint's side.

Still on his back, he finally managed to pull the Colt. His arm came level and he sighted quickly over the top of the barrel. He fired even as Hobart was in the act of cocking his own pistol. The gambler's left eye winked in a spurt of blood. Then the back of his skull blew apart, splattering gore and brain matter across the wall. He dropped to the floor as though his legs had been chopped off.

Clint levered himself to his feet. The two soldiers and the woman were staring at him, watchful and silent. He holstered the Colt and collected his hat off the floor. Finally, he looked around at the bartender.

"You got any law out here?"

"Nothin' except the army. And they ain't gonna worry theirselves about a tinhorn gambler."

"Then I reckon I won't either."

The barkeep looked puzzled. "What the hell did you ask him?"

"One question too many."

Later, stretched out in the livery stable's hayloft, Clint realized he was at a dead end. All leads had disappeared when he pulled the trigger on the gambler. By now, Jack Quintin could be anywhere. New Mexico Territory was one possibil-

ity, and Colorado was another. Still, Quintin seemed to be
drifting westward, where there was no law and few lawmen.

From all Clint had heard, the gold fields in Colorado were
just such a place. The remote mountain camps were a haven
for outlaws of every stripe. No one asked questions or pried
into a man's past. And they cared even less about border raids
and Jayhawker guerrillas. It sounded made to order for a man
like Jack Quintin.

Early next morning Clint rode west, toward Colorado Territory.

9

BLAKE STREET WAS QUIET. The noonday rush was over and Denver's sporting district appeared somnolent. High overhead, a brassy sun stood fixed in a cloudless sky.

Later, with the first shadows of twilight, the sporting district would come alive. Banjos and rinky-dink pianos would flood the street with discordant music. Every joint, from the rawest saloon to the hurdy-gurdy dance halls, would vibrate with the laughter of ruby-lipped charmers. Decked out in spangles, their faces freshly painted, the girls would begin another night of sweet-talking the customers. So long as a man's pockets jangled, he was fair game once the sun went down.

Earl crossed the intersection of Blake and Fifth. The girls of the sporting district were very much on his mind. He already envisioned the type of gaming parlor he planned to open. Since girls were a distraction and tended to cheapen an establishment, he'd decided against them. The only woman on the premises would be Monte Verde, for she very definitely fitted in with his ideas. He intended to run a classy operation.

The Alcazar was one of the few establishments that suited his plan. Located on the corner of a busy intersection, it was a frame building with saloon and gaming facilities on the ground floor. The upper floor was now used for girls, but Earl had other plans for the space. He'd heard that the owner, Jack Tracy, was looking for a buyer. So the story went, the price was fifty thousand for the whole shebang. He thought Tracy might be persuaded to take considerably less.

The interior of the Alcazar was somewhat shoddy. There was sawdust on the floor, and prints of bare-knuckle prizefighters adorned the walls. Behind the bar, a couple of lascivious nude paintings framed a mirror that was cracked top to bottom. Walking through the main room, Earl decided that the bar itself, along with a roulette table, weren't too bad. Otherwise, he would have to gut the place and start all over. He found Jack Tracy in a backroom office.

" 'Afternoon, Jack.''

"Well, well,'' Tracy greeted him. "Long time no see. Where you been keeping yourself, Earl?''

"Here and there,'' Earl said, seating himself in a rickety chair beside the desk. "Got in last night from Central City.''

"Now you mention it . . .'' Tracy gave him a sly look. "Word's out you made yourself quite a score. How'd you do?''

"No complaints,'' Earl said evasively.

Tracy realized he'd overstepped himself. He chuckled, pressing the matter no further. "Well, anyway, what brings you around here?''

The Alcazar's owner was a slender man with innocent brown eyes and an affable manner. Earl knew him to be a former grifter, who looked upon gambling as a rather sophisticated bunco game. By all accounts, every table in Tracy's dive was rigged.

Earl lit a cheroot, exhaled smoke. "I hear you've been trying to sell out. Any takers?''

"Not yet,'' Tracy admitted. "Why, you interested?''

"I might be . . . if the price was right."

"Hell, it's a bargain," Tracy said jovially. "The place does better'n two thousand a week. I'm only asking fifty."

"Out of my league," Earl informed him. "I'm not anywhere near that well fixed."

Tracy cocked his head, one eye squinted. "What sort of offer did you have in mind?"

"I also hear"—Earl paused, blew a plume of smoke toward the ceiling—"you've got troubles with Ed Case."

The name made Tracy blink. Ed Case was the undisputed czar of the sporting district. By dint of political connections and a squad of strong-arm thugs, he controlled the world of vice in Denver. According to the rumor mill, he'd already put Tracy on warning. Payoffs from the Alcazar were too little too late, and growing worse.

An indirection came into Tracy's eyes. "What's Case got to do with anything?"

Earl spread his hands. "Nobody has made you an offer because they don't want to deal with Case. For the right price, I might be willing to risk it."

"So . . ." Tracy peered across at him. "Make me an offer."

"Thirty thousand."

"Jesus Christ!" Tracy yelped. "You're trying to steal it. I wouldn't take a nickel less than forty."

"Yeah, you would," Earl said equably, "and you've just heard my best offer . . . take it or leave it."

Tracy pondered it at length, eyes narrowed in concentration. Then, with a hangdog smile, he nodded. "You just bought yourself a dive."

Earl asked for a pen and a piece of paper. He drafted a sales agreement specifying a thousand dollars down and the balance within ten days. They were both aware that he would forfeit the down payment—and never pay the balance—unless he came to terms with Ed Case.

After the agreement was signed, Earl counted out a thousand dollars. He shook Tracy's hand, stuffing the paper in his pocket, and walked from the Alcazar. On the street, he turned left and proceeded along the block. Directly ahead was the Progressive Club, one of the town's better gaming parlors. On the opposite side of the street was the Palace, a combination saloon, gambling den, and variety theater. Both of the establishments were owned by Ed Case, and Earl knew that they were only the visible symbols of one man's power. What counted most went on behind closed doors.

Ed Case had arrived in Denver the spring of 1859. Unlike most men who joined the gold rush, he evidenced little interest in prospecting. For a time, he managed a prizefighter and promoted other sporting events. His first gambling dive, known as Denver Hall, was a log cabin with a canvas roof and dirt floor. As the town grew, he increased his holdings along Blake Street and slowly put together a gang of back-alley hooligans. By the time Denver's first elections were held, he was the vice lord of the sporting district. As such, he controlled the swing vote and thereby dictated the outcome of any election. While unproved, it was commonly accepted that he'd struck a deal with the uptown crowd and with city hall. So long as they gave him a free hand in the sporting district, he delivered the vote.

Earl was under no illusions about the risks. Case's strong-arm boys collected weekly payoffs from every dive, including Holladay Street whorehouses, throughout the sporting district. There were no exceptions, and anyone who rebelled got worked over with saps and brass knuckles. Those who resisted too strenuously met with strange accidents, or just disappeared. To take over the Alcazar, Earl would first have to settle the delinquent payoffs account. Only then could he broach the even riskier plan he'd concocted. And hope his luck was still running strong.

Case's office was on the second floor of the Progressive Club. A burly thug with a pug-nosed scowl guarded the door. After listening to Earl's request, he rapped lightly on the door and stepped inside. Several moments elapsed, then the guard returned and waved him into the office. Earl knew the underworld boss on sight, but they had never before met. He walked forward with breezy self-assurance.

"Appreciate your seeing me on such short notice, Mr. Case."

Case made no offer to shake hands. Nor did he indicate that Earl should take a chair. He was a tall man, with angular features and hair prematurely gray. Impeccably dressed, he wore a cutaway coat, dark trousers, and a somber tie. His eyes were like a matched set of ball bearings.

"What can I do for you, Brannock?"

Earl took a deep breath. "I've just made a deal for the Alcazar. I'd like to work out some sort of arrangement with you."

Case gave him a short look. "I'm listening."

"Word's out that Jack Tracy owes you money. Does the account have to be squared before I can buy the place?"

"Why ask a question when you already know the answer?"

"Then I think I can show you how to collect."

Case's eyes veiled with caution. "Go on."

"Give Tracy the word," Earl said with a guileless smile. "Tell him I have to settle with you and he gets anything left over. That way he can't skip town on you."

Case smiled humorlessly. "And you don't get stuck with his mistake. Isn't that the gist of it?"

Earl opened his hands, shrugged. "A man has to look after himself first."

"All right," Case said. "I'll break the bad news to Tracy."

"There's one other thing," Earl went on quickly. "Before I actually buy the place, I'd need your agreement on a certain matter."

"What's that?"

"I understand the weekly payoff is ten percent."

"So?" Case answered stiffly.

"I plan to run honest games."

"How does that concern me?"

"No whores, either," Earl replied indirectly. "Strictly a high-class gaming parlor."

"You still haven't made your point."

"Square games and no girls lowers the take. To make it on house odds, I'll need a cushion. Five percent ought to do it."

"Five percent!" Case repeated with a sudden glare. "You want me to cut the payoff in half?"

"I figure it's the only way."

"Why should I make an exception for you? Lots of people operate square games."

"Not altogether," Earl corrected him. "Some tables are square and others are rigged. The suckers never know which is which."

"That's their lookout. Let's get back to what I asked. What makes you the exception?"

Earl looked him directly in the eyes. "Nobody else has the guts to fight you. I do, if you force me to it."

"Wouldn't be much of a fight. You'd lose before you got started."

"Not if I hired myself a crew of headbusters. I could hold out long enough to cause you serious trouble."

"How long?" Case insisted. "A week, two weeks? Don't make me laugh."

"You wouldn't laugh if the idea spread. All it would take is a few dive owners following suit. You'd end up with a revolt on your hands."

Case watched him with a thin, fixed smile. "You could wind up dead. Or hadn't you thought about that?"

"I'll take my chances," Earl said evenly. "But if you ever try, make damn sure your boys don't miss. Otherwise it's open season."

"You'd risk your ass for a lousy five percent?"

"I guess I already have."

Case deliberated a moment. Earl Brannock was not the sort of man he wanted as an enemy. Nor could he run the chance of creating a martyr, one who might sow the seeds of rebellion. Then, too, there was the matter of Brannock's brother. According to his friends in city hall, Virgil Brannock was already in thick with the uptown crowd. All things considered, it seemed better to play along, appear to compromise. When the time was right . . .

"You're in business," he said at length. "Just don't get foolish and start talking out of school. Our arrangement is on the q.t., strictly private. Understood?"

"Whatever you say," Earl agreed. "So far as I'm concerned, it ends here."

"One last thing."

"Yeah?"

"Don't try pushing me into a corner again. You've used up all your credit."

Earl flipped him an offhand salute, turned away. When the door closed, Case tilted back in his chair. His eyes were cold and a muscle in his jaw knotted. He stared off into space.

Some men were as they appeared to be, and other men were deeper, hidden. He wondered about Earl Brannock.

10

Virgil stood by the loading dock. A wagon and team was backed up to the platform, and one of his drivers was man-handling crates of liquor out of the warehouse. He carefully checked each item against an invoice.

As he watched, it occurred to him that he needed more help. His workday began at sunrise and rarely ended before ten or eleven at night. He kept the warehouse organized, wrote out invoices and tallied the books, and took a weekly inventory. When time permitted, he squeezed in a trip to the camps and solicited new customers. His accounts ledger now had more than fifty entries.

Yet time was at a premium. There were only so many hours in a day, and he was one man. He knew his time would be more profitably spent in the camps, adding new accounts. The potential for a hundred customers or more was out there, wait-ing to be tapped. But he first had to free himself from the routine duties of operating a business. He decided to hire a bookkeeper and a warehouseman, no later than the end of the month. Next month, he might even add another wagon and driver.

When the loading was completed, he began totaling the invoice. He finished and quickly wrote out a duplicate by the time the driver had the crates lashed down tight. His policy was that all orders were to be paid for on delivery. The drivers collected the money after unloading and were responsible for the full amount on the invoice. The system neatly eliminated deadbeat saloonkeepers and past-due accounts. Since opening for business, Denver Wholesale Liquors had maintained an enviable cash position.

As the wagon pulled away, Virgil walked back through the warehouse. He had been operating slightly more than a month, and he was justifiably proud of what he had accomplished. Any day now, the forty wagons of liquor he'd ordered would arrive. Yet, from the way the business was growing, he already planned to double the order next time around. By the end of the summer, when he began looking ahead to a winter inventory, he might very well have to expand on the warehouse. He was thinking of ordering a hundred wagonloads of liquor and champagne.

Still, for all the progress, he was constantly on the alert to new opportunity. Beer, no less than whiskey, found a ready market in the mining camps. A couple of German immigrants had established a brewery and were producing beer of reasonably high quality. By importing the raw materials overland and constructing their own barrels, they were able to undercut the price of Eastern breweries. But miners, particularly in the summer, were not fond of warm beer. As a result, an offshoot of the brewery business had quickly developed.

Several independent operators were currently supplying the demand for ice. During the winter, rivers and lakes throughout the mountains froze solid. Tons of ice, free for the taking, was harvested with manpower and long saws. Then the blocks of ice were stored in specially constructed log buildings heavily insulated with sawdust. While there was some shrinkage, the low temperature generally ensured a supply of ice through the summer. Saloonkeepers paid dearly to keep their kegs cooled and the miners happy. Since the alternative was hot beer, no one complained too loudly.

A quiet inspection had convinced Virgil that ice could be developed into a profitable sideline. The independent suppliers were disorganized and small, strictly hand-to-mouth operations. He felt confident that the icehouses could be bought piecemeal, and for fairly reasonable sums. Then, once the business was consolidated under a single management, any newcomers would not be able to compete on price. The upshot would be a small monopoly, and one that complemented his liquor business. He planned to make his move toward the end of summer, when the suppliers' icehouses were all but empty. He thought they would be receptive to any fair offer.

Emerging from the warehouse into the office, he was reminded of the old saw about all work and no play. His last night out had been the evening he'd attended the dinner party at Tisdale's home. One thought triggered another, and an image of Elizabeth Tisdale sprang to mind. After dinner that night, seated beside her in the parlor, she had listened raptly to his plans for the future. Later, at her father's insistence, she had played several selections on the melodeon. He remembered thinking how beautiful she looked, warm and young and vibrant. The vision was with him still, enhanced perhaps by the passage of time. He wondered how he could arrange to see her again.

His office was sparsely furnished as a monk's cell. A battered rolltop desk, bought used, stood against one wall. Before it was a wooden armchair, and grouped around a potbellied stove were four straight-back chairs. The only other stick of furniture was a large table, used as a catchall for boxes of foolscap and assorted supplies. The top of the desk was littered with paperwork and accounting ledgers. He wearily lowered himself into the chair.

Some minutes later, the street door opened. He glanced up from making an entry in the ledger and all the color suddenly drained from his face. The pen dropped from his hand as Clint closed the door and stepped into the office. He rose from the chair with a shaken expression.

"Clint—"

Words failed him, and he strode forward, enfolding the younger man in a mighty embrace. Four years and more had passed since they'd ridden off to war. In all that time they hadn't corresponded, their only communication being messages passed along through relatives. Between them was the special bond of eldest and youngest, and now, their eyes misty, they struggled to collect themselves. Clint found his voice first.

"You better let go," he grumbled, "before you smother me to death."

Virgil released him with a low chuckle. "How'd you find me?"

"Asked at the hotel."

"No, not that! I mean, where'd you come from?"

"Missouri," Clint said easily. "By way of Kansas and points west."

Virgil's gaze turned somber. "You've been home, then? You know about the folks?"

"Yeah, I know. Uncle Ezra told me the whole story."

There was a moment of strained silence. At last, Virgil grinned and shook his head. "Well, by God, you don't look any the worse for wear. Yankee prison camp must have agreed with you."

"I got by," Clint said, nodding at Virgil's hand. "Looks like you weren't so lucky, though."

"Nothing much," Virgil said lightly. "A souvenir to remind me of Appomattox."

"Uncle Ezra told me you were with Lee. I reckon it's something you're not likely to forget."

Virgil briefly recounted his last days with the Army of Virginia. In turn, Clint spoke of his capture outside Vicksburg and the time he'd spent in prison camp. Then, with anger spilling over in his voice, he told of his futile search for Jack

Quintin. He went on to say that Denver had seemed the next logical stopping point. All the more so because Virgil now lived there.

"That's about it," he concluded. "I figure the mining camps are as good a place as any to look for Quintin. From what I've heard, the rougher it is, the better he likes it."

Virgil gave him a long, searching stare. "Hunting a man down and killing him is dirty business. Are you real certain that's what you want to do?"

"Goddamn right!" Clint swore. "I'm surprised you'd even ask. The sonovabitch killed our folks."

"What he did and what you've got in mind are two different things. I suspect we all did things in wartime we're not exactly proud of."

"What the hell's with you, Virge? Are you trying to excuse the bastard?"

"No, I'm not," Virgil said pointedly. "I'm just saying there's a difference between the battlefield and cold-blooded murder."

Clint gave him a lightning frown. "You've got it a little bass-ackwards. Quintin's the one that committed murder. Whatever he gets he damn sure deserves."

"So you've set yourself up as his executioner . . . is that it?"

"Why not?" Clint said hotly. "Nobody else seems keen on the job."

"How about the law?"

"We're a far piece west of Missouri. You think the law out here would be all that interested?"

"Probably not," Virgil conceded. "I just don't like the idea of . . ."

His voice trailed off and there was a beat of silence. Clint looked at him strangely. "Go ahead. You don't like the idea of what?"

Virgil shook his head ruefully. "Funny thing about revenge. Once a man gets it in his blood, it's like a poison that eats him alive. I'd hate to see that happen to you."

Clint's mouth hardened. "Don't trouble yourself about me. I'll dance on Jack Quintin's grave and enjoy every minute of it."

"Yeah," Virgil said heavily. "I reckon that's what has me worried."

Clint smiled. "You always were a worrywart, anyway. Appears things haven't changed."

The tension between them eased somewhat. Clint turned sportive, inquiring how a God-fearing farm boy got into the business of demon rum. Virgil took him on a tour of the warehouse, proudly relating all he'd achieved thus far. Clint was impressed and Virgil went into some detail about his future plans. As they returned to the office, Virgil gave the younger man a sideways glance.

"You haven't asked about Earl."

"Why ask?" Clint said tightly. "I don't give a damn one way or the other."

"Hold on now," Virgil protested. "Earl's your brother."

A stony look settled on Clint's face. "I got over the way he felt about the war. But he shouldn't have gone off and left the folks like he did. Except for him, they might still be alive."

"You're wrong," Virgil said heavily. "Earl couldn't have changed what happened."

"Guess we'll never know, will we?"

"Maybe it'll help if I tell you that Earl feels the same way. He blames himself for the folks' death."

"Too little too late. He should've thought about that before he took off."

Virgil was the peacemaker of the family. In earlier days, when Earl and Clint had gotten into fights, it was Virgil who pulled them apart. As the eldest, he'd always commanded their respect and their loyalty. He reverted now to a familiar role.

"What's done is done, and nothing's to be gained in looking back. I want you and Earl to patch things up."

"Virge, I suppose we just see things different, that's all. Earl and me are quits."

"No!" Virgil thundered. "I won't have it, by God. You're blood kin, family. You've got to at least make the effort."

"Give me a good reason why?"

"Because Ma and Pa would have wanted it that way. You know damn well I'm right, Clint."

Clint spread his hands in an empty gesture. "The folks were good Christian people, real forgiving. I'm not sure it rubbed off on me."

"You'll try, though," Virgil pressed him. "At least give it a chance."

"What the hell," Clint said with a tired smile. "If it means that much to you . . ."

"Let's go!"

"Where?"

"Don't ask so many questions."

Virgil laughed and led the way out the door. Clint followed along with a look of deep misgiving. They walked toward Blake Street.

II

THE BELLA UNION OPENED with considerable fanfare. Crowds were drawn at first by curiosity and no small degree of cynicism. A full-page ad in the *Rocky Mountain News* declared all games to be "square and aboveboard." The proprietor offered $10,000 to anyone who could prove otherwise.

Far from an idle boast, Earl made the offer in earnest. Dealers and croupiers were paid top wages, ten dollars a day. Before being hired, they were treated to a lecture on the virtues of fair-and-square. Any man caught cheating, Earl told them, would never deal again. To illustrate the point, he placed his hand on the bar and demonstrated how easily fingers could be squashed with a bungstarter. No one failed to get the message.

The saloon's interior had been gutted and revamped from scratch. Along one wall, the mahogany bar now stood waxed and polished to a high gloss. The back bar was a glittering array of glasses and mugs, all arranged before a magnificent diamond-dust mirror. The walls were decorated with paintings of voluptuous women, scantily clothed and leaving little to the imagination. Tables and chairs were positioned along the opposite wall, and the hardwood floor gleamed with beeswax. Set in a rear corner was a small stage where musicians and a ballad singer held forth nightly.

Toward the rear, a wall now separated the saloon from the gaming room. A wide entranceway opened onto the twenty-one table, where Monte Verde held court every evening. Immediately behind her were three roulette wheels, chuck-a-luck and dice layouts, four poker tables, and six faro banks. The odds at faro were the most favorable of any form of Western gambling, which accounted for its wide popularity. While other games gave the house a six-point edge, there was less than a 2 percent spread in faro. Betting was made on a layout, with each player attempting to guess the order in which a given card would show. By midevening, men were ganged around the faro banks three and four deep.

Earl was somewhat philosophical about faro. The small house percentage meant a low return, and there were nights when all six banks lost money. Still, apart from Monte Verde, faro was the Bella Union's biggest draw. Once the banks became crowded, the spillover was quickly diverted to other games. Gamblers, by their very nature, were compelled to wager; denied a spot in one game, they simply moved over to whatever was available. Thus far, the take on any given night ranged upward of a thousand dollars. The house, given the odds, was always a winner.

Afternoons were a time for mundane chores. Earl and Monte shared a suite upstairs, which had been redecorated and lavishly furnished. As their nights were long, they generally slept late and lounged about in the morning. Several housemen, who were quartered in individual rooms, were responsible for opening at noontime. By two o'clock, Earl was invariably seated at his desk in the downstairs office. Between then and the evening rush, he checked the books and attended to the myriad details of running a gaming parlor. He'd discovered, much to his surprise, that he had a knack for business.

Monte found him there shortly before three. Later, she would change into an evening gown with a peekaboo neckline. But for now she wore a tailored day dress that buttoned demurely to the throat. She put an arm around Earl's shoulders and gave him a soft peck on the cheek. He muttered something under his breath and went on running figures in an accounting ledger. She stepped back, hands on her hips.

"Aren't you the lover boy?" she said with a mock pout. "All I get for my trouble is a grunt."

"C'mon, Monte," Earl grumbled. "I'm trying to operate a business here. Save it for the boudoir."

"That's a joke! All you do lately is fall asleep and snore. I think I liked you better as a gambler."

Earl looked around, finally smiled. "You've got a sharp tongue for such a pretty lady."

"Humph!" she sniffed. "Flattery will get you nowhere, Buster. It's action that counts."

"Tell you what," Earl said with a slow grin. "Tonight we'll tie one on. You and me, and a bottle of champagne. How's that sound?"

"Well . . ." Her eyes sparkled mischievously. "I suppose it's worth consideration, unless I get a better offer."

"You let me catch you flirting and I'll really give you something you won't forget."

"Listen, wise guy!" She shook a tiny fist under his nose. "You try any rough stuff and I'll box your ears good. How d'ya like them apples?"

There was a rap on the door. Earl chuckled as Monte pulled back her fist and assumed a more ladylike stance. He called out and the door opened a crack. Virgil stuck his head inside.

"Not interrupting anything, am I?"

"No," Earl said quickly. "We were just hashing over some business matters."

Virgil grinned. "Sounded a little domestic from out here."

"Come on in," Earl said, ignoring the gibe. "What brings you to our den of iniquity?"

"Somebody you haven't seen in a spell."

Virgil moved through the door, then stepped aside. Behind him, Clint eased into the office with a look of undisguised discomfort. His eyes locked on Earl momentarily and quickly shifted away. He took a halting step forward.

Monte caught the byplay. She saw Earl stiffen, his normal composure sharply rattled. In that instant, she sensed that the man was Earl's younger brother. The family resemblance was readily apparent, and the tension between them seemed to cloak the room in stillness. She recalled the story of their falling out and the bitterness of their parting. She abruptly decided it was a good time to leave.

"Excuse me," she said, moving past Virgil. "I just remembered an errand."

The door closed with a soft click. For a moment, the three brothers were enveloped in a cone of silence. Earl felt as though his eardrums were blocked, and he had to force himself to look in Clint's direction. At last, Virgil saw that neither of them would make the first move. One was immobilized by lingering guilt and the other was simply rooster-proud. He forcibly took hold of Clint's arm.

"Don't be a hardhead," he ordered. "What's past is past. Let's forget the war—start fresh."

Earl took the lead. He smiled nervously and rose from his chair. Still somewhat uncertain, he extended his hand. Clint dutifully pumped his arm up and down, then let go. Virgil nodded his approval.

"Pardon the sentiment," he said hoarsely. "But I waited a long time to see that. You boys have done the right thing."

Earl quickly bobbed his head. "I want you to know something," he said, staring at Clint. "Not a day's gone by that I haven't kicked myself for leaving Missouri. You never thought half as bad of me as I thought of myself."

Clint averted his eyes. He studied the floor, as though trying to come to grips with something inside himself. Finally, he inclined his head in a faint nod. "Like Virge says, what's past is past."

The tension seemed to melt away. Virgil grinned, aware that the younger man had compromised for one of the few times in his life. He smote Clint across the back with brotherly affection and shot Earl a hidden look. Earl took the cue, and smoothly changed the subject.

"Goddamn, Clint, we've got a lot of catching up to do. Where you been since the war ended?"

"Drifting around," Clint said without elaboration. "Looks like you're doing pretty well for yourself."

"Hit it lucky, and then some." Earl paused, struck by a sudden thought. "Say, look here, how'd you like a job?"

"Job?"

"Well, I see you're packing a gun. So the war couldn't have changed you a helluva lot. Are you still handy with your fists?"

Clint shrugged. "I generally manage."

"Come to work for me, then. Hell, I'll even give you a piece of the action!"

"Doing what, exactly?"

"Lots of money changes hands here," Earl explained. "I keep a couple of lookouts posted around the place every night. Just in case anybody gets funny ideas."

"Sort of a combination guard and bouncer. Is that the idea?"

"Yeah, something like that. Only I'd put you in charge of it. Let you take it off my shoulders."

"Thanks all the same," Clint said. "Thing is, I've got other plans just now."

"Other plans?" Earl asked. "Here in Denver?"

When Clint hesitated, Virgil took it upon himself to explain. He recounted the search for Jack Quintin and Clint's determination to kill the former guerrilla. He ended with a forceful expression of his own opinion.

"Damn-fool nonsense," he said gruffly. "It's time to get on with living, forget the killing."

Clint appeared unfazed by the argument. Earl looked at him with a curious expression and slowly nodded. "I tend to side with you. By all rights, the bastard ought to roast in hell. But from a practical standpoint, you haven't got much chance of finding him. It's a case of the needle in the haystack."

"Exactly so!" Virgil added hastily. "For all we know, he could've gone to California or Oregon. You could waste the rest of your life traipsing around the West."

"What's worse," Earl chimed in, "he might've already got himself killed. From what you told Virge, he travels in pretty rough company. You might end up tracking down a dead man."

Clint looked from one to the other. His somber resolve turned to a slow smile. "You two sound like a couple of parrots. Anybody would think you'd been rehearsing the same speech."

"Maybe so," Virgil countered. "But we're talking common, ordinary horse sense. And you know damn well it's a fact."

"He's right," Earl said emphatically. "There comes a time when a man has to take the practical outlook. You've got your own life to think about."

"Well . . . ?" Clint appeared to be wavering.

"Stay here," Virgil urged him. "We're all the family we've got now, the three of us."

Clint eyed them in silence for a time. "All right," he said in a resigned voice. "I suppose I could stick around for a while. Just so you understand it's temporary."

"Good enough," Virgil said, unwilling to push it further. "While you're thinking things over, why not come to work for me? I was fixing to hire some extra men anyway."

"I've got no head for business."

"So what?" Virgil declared. "You think Earl and me

aren't still learning the ropes? All it takes is a little get-up-and-go.''

"Guess I'll pass," Clint said firmly. "Maybe I'll have a look around town. See what gets my attention.''

"Denver's worth a look-see! You'll never find a likelier place to make your fortune. And as we used to say back home, that's puredee fact!''

"Like I said, Virge . . . I'll scout around!''

Virgil wisely let it drop. He was content for the moment that they were all together again, the old wounds healed. A handshake had absolved Earl and brought Clint back into the fold. They were a family once more, the past behind them.

It was enough for now.

12

EARL TOOK THE NIGHT off. He wasn't overly concerned about the Bella Union with Monte to keep an eye on things. She was sharper than even the best of his housemen.

The impromptu celebration was Earl's idea. In part, it was to celebrate Clint's safe return from the war. But Earl had another purpose in mind, one that was entirely personal. A mere truce with his younger brother seemed to him too little. He wanted to rekindle the bond of old.

Virgil endorsed the idea heartily. Some four years had passed since the brothers had last broken bread together. While they were apart, war had ravaged the land and taken the lives of their parents. To no small degree, time and events had made them strangers. He thought a night on the town was the very thing needed.

Under Earl's guidance, they set forth to "see the elephant." A round of drinks was followed by a tour of the sporting district. Clint was hardly a tyro when it came to hell-raising and women. Like most Missouri men, he'd been weaned on backcountry corn likker. And he had enticed many a young farm girl to share the intimacy of a haystack. Yet, for all the wild seed he'd sown, Denver was a wholly new experience. He had never before sampled a Western boomtown.

By early evening, the brothers had walked the sporting district from end to end. The dives along Blake Street were a revelation of sorts to Clint. Even as a soldier, he'd never seen anything to match the string of gambling dens and raucous dance halls. Nor was he any less amazed by Holladay Street, with its dollar cribs and fancy parlor houses. Taken as a whole, the sporting district was like a vulgar fairy tale created especially for grown men. He began thinking Denver might be worth a second look.

No celebration was complete without strong drink. Along the course of their tour, the brothers paused for an occasional libation. After the fourth saloon, their spirits took on a jocular note. At one point Clint actually threw his arm around Earl's shoulder. And Virgil, who was a sobersides by nature, looked on with a sly-eyed possum grin. Though far from drunk, none of them was in any danger from snakebite. They felt loose and easy, comfortable together. All things past were now forgotten.

Shortly before eight o'clock, they stepped into a café for supper. Nothing whets the appetite like hard liquor, and they were suddenly ravenous. While Clint flirted with the waitress, Earl studied the menu with a critical eye. As host for the evening, he insisted on the best the house had to offer. They dined on thick juicy steaks, panfried potatoes, and biscuits the size of teacups. All of them agreed that it was a meal befitting the occasion. Earl left the waitress a generous tip, and Clint gave her a friendly pat on the rump. She accepted both with giggling equanimity.

An hour later they strode through the doors of the Criterion Hall. The owner, Count Henry Murat, greeted them with genuine warmth. With the opening of the Bella Union, he and Earl were now fierce rivals for the high-roller trade. Still, their friendship went back several years, and Murat was perhaps the one gambling impresario in Denver who maintained cordial relations with Earl. As introductions were made, he shook hands all around.

"Honored," he said, pumping Clint's arm. "You bear a striking resemblance to your brothers."

The count was a bit of a dandy for Clint's tastes. He nonetheless responded with an amiable smile. "Three peas out of the same pod. All the Brannocks look alike."

"Indeed so," Murat agreed, glancing back at Earl. "And what brings you to my humble establishment?"

"We're celebrating," Earl informed him. "Clint just pulled into Denver today. Spent the last two years in a Yankee prison camp."

Murat looked properly impressed. "In that event," he said expansively, "you are my guests for the evening. I insist!"

"Why, thanks, Henry," Earl said, touched by the gesture. "Stop by the Bella Union sometime and let me return the treat."

"Never!" Murat pretended mock horror at the suggestion. "You've already lured many of my best customers away. How would it look if I went there myself?"

Earl laughed. "Let's call it an open invitation."

"Champagne!" Murat rapped to a passing waiter. "And make sure it's chilled properly. Enjoy yourselves, gentlemen."

As he waved and walked away, the brothers seated themselves at a table. The barroom was crowded, but play was only moderately heavy at the gaming layouts. Clint sat for a moment studying the ornate interior, aware of murmured voices and the clink of chips. He finally turned to Earl.

"Funny thing," he said, motioning around the room. "Something about it reminds me of your place."

Earl shook his head. "It's the other way 'round. I patterned the Bella Union on Henry's place. And to hear him tell it, the Criterion's laid out along the lines of a European casino."

"Well, you damn sure went him one better. Your place must've cost an arm and a leg."

"An arm and *two* legs!"

Earl went on to recount the story of his hot streak in Central City. He then related how he'd bought a run-of-the-mill dive and refurbished it to create the Bella Union. The only thing he omitted telling was his private arrangement with Ed Case.

"From the sound of it," Clint remarked, "you've found your niche."

Earl nodded thoughtfully. "I sort of fell into gambling as a profession. But I'd have to say it's like I heard the call. It comes real natural."

Clint grinned. "I expect it takes a little luck, too. Or have you got it worked out to a science?"

Earl threw back his head and laughed hard. "When I started, it was strictly feast or famine. One day flush and the next day stony broke. Damned near starved before I learned to play the odds."

The waiter appeared with a bucket of iced champagne. He popped the cork and poured with the deft hand of a pickpocket. After screwing the bottle back into the ice, he nodded around the table. "Compliments of the house, gents."

Earl hoisted his glass. He smiled, extending it in a toast to his brothers. "Here's mud in your eye."

"To the Brannocks!" Virgil added quickly. "And the future!"

They clinked glasses and drank. Clint wrinkled his nose at the bubbly fizz and smacked his lips. He'd never before sampled champagne, and the dry aftertaste reminded him of a green persimmon. He glanced across at Earl.

"You think the count would be insulted if I ordered some honest-to-God whiskey?"

Earl let go a snorting laugh and Virgil chuckled out loud. The waiter was summoned and shortly returned with a bottle of aged rye. He gave Clint a look all waiters reserve for the uncouth and the feeble-minded. Clint happily poured a shot glass to the brim.

After another toast, Earl fished a leather cheroot case from inside his coat. Clint declined, having lost his taste for tobacco while in prison camp. As Virgil and Earl lit up, he took an appreciative sip of whiskey. A blue haze of smoke separated them when he finally looked over at Virgil.

"Champagne and cigars," he said wryly. "You're a proper advertisement for your own goods."

"Damnedest thing," Virgil admitted. "Before I got into the business, I figured champagne was rich man's swill. Now, I've come to like the stuff. How d'you explain that?"

"Simple," Earl joked. "You sell it for a king's ransom. Before long, it'll make you a rich man yourself."

"Well, boys," Virgil said only in half-jest, "I have to say I kind of like the idea. Until I hit Denver, I never had no inklin' of what real money meant."

"Since you mentioned it," Clint mused aloud, "I've been wondering where you got the money to start with. Hope you didn't rob a bank."

Virgil chortled softly. "You're not far off the mark."

With no great elaboration, Virgil explained how he'd put together a stake. The clincher, he noted, had been the bank loan from Walter Tisdale. He concluded on an optimistic note.

"I've already paid Earl off, and your share from the farm is yours when you want it. With interest, it'll come to better than a thousand dollars."

"Not bad," Clint said jovially. "Yesterday I was flat busted and today I'm filthy rich."

"You could be," Virgil advised him. "Leave it where it is and I'll give you a piece of the business. We'll make a goddamn fortune!"

"Thanks all the same," Clint said. "I reckon I wasn't cut out to be a businessman."

"What about a farm? Hell, Earl and me would gladly stake you. And the market's already here. Denver needs all the produce you could grow."

"No," Clint said rather sadly. "After the war, farmin'

sounds pretty tame. Guess I'll see what's on the other side.''

"Other side of what?"

"I reckon it'd be the other side of sundown. I'm damn sure not headed east again.''

The statement was hardly surprising. From the time of generations past, the Brannocks had always been Westering men. As boys, the brothers had listened round-eyed to tales handed down from generation to generation. The founder of the family, their great-grandfather, had immigrated to the colony of North Carolina. A long hunter, he had joined Daniel Boone in opening the Wilderness Road westward. In 1778, he'd fought beside Boone when the British and their Indian allies besieged the frontier settlement of Boonesboro. Their grandfather had been born the day after the siege was lifted.

Some twenty years later, Daniel Boone had once more trekked westward, resettling on the Missouri frontier. Their grandfather, by then grown to manhood, had elected to remain in Kentucky. But his sons, James and Ezra, had followed in Boone's footsteps the spring of 1832. After carving farms from the wilderness, they had married and sired families of their own. At the time, Missouri was the gateway to the West, where the Santa Fe Trail and the Oregon Trail began. There the fourth generation of Brannocks had been born.

By 1860, the farmers of Missouri were divided into two factions. Those who produced cotton and tobacco were largely slave owners. Those who raised livestock and grain crops shunned slavery on general principle. James and Ezra Brannock were among the latter group at the outbreak of the Civil War. Shortly after Missouri went with the Union, James and his wife had been killed by Jayhawker guerrillas. A year later, Ezra's only son had fallen in battle under the Union standard. Unlike his cousin or his older brother, Clint had chosen to serve with the Confederacy. An idealistic youngster, he'd believed strongly in the right of men and states to determine their own destiny. Confinement in a Yankee prison had done little to alter his outlook.

Yet, now, Virgil sought to avoid argument. His one purpose was to somehow keep Clint in Denver and thereby keep him alive. He steered the conversation into safer waters.

"How were Uncle Ezra and Aunt Angeline when you left them?"

"Fair to middlin'," Clint said, then shrugged. "They're getting on in years and I suppose they're pretty lonesome."

"Lonesome?" Earl repeated quizzically. "I thought their girl, Ellen, still lived in town."

"She does," Clint acknowledged. "But she's married and her name's not Brannock anymore. She's a Dawson now."

"What's that got to do with them being lonesome?"

"Well, her kids will be Dawsons. With the only boy dead, I guess Uncle Ezra and Aunt Angeline figure there's nobody to carry on the Brannock name. Not on their side of the family, anyhow."

Earl stared at him. "When you showed up, it must've taken them back some. I recollect you were just about Ethan's age."

Clint nodded ruefully. "These are his clothes I'm wearing. They never come right out and asked, but they wanted me to stick around. I reckon they thought I could take Ethan's place."

"Only natural," Earl observed. "You ought to write them now and then. They'd like that."

"Yeah, I will." Clint was silent a moment, considering. "How would I go about getting some money to them?"

"Why would you send them money?"

"It's owed," Clint said simply. "Little as they had, they staked me to a hundred dollars. I'd like to pay it back."

Earl's mouth lifted in a quick smile. "Virgil could arrange a bank draft. Him and the banker are regular bosom buddies."

"No problem," Virgil said. "I'll see to it first thing in the morning."

"Thanks," Clint said. "I'll send a note along with the money. Let 'em know how you boys have made your fortune."

Virgil scratched his jaw with a thumb. "Something you said a while ago stuck with me. I'm talking about Ethan getting killed and Ellen marrying a Dawson."

"What about it?"

"Well, just stop and think a minute. Ellen's kids won't carry the family name. We're it—the last of the Brannocks!"

"Don't sound so miserable. Worse things have happened."

"Like hell!" Virgil said vigorously. "We've got an obligation to the family. We can't let the name die out."

Earl gave him a smirky grin. "Maybe you ought to find yourself a woman. A passel of kids would be right down your alley."

"How about you?" Virgil demanded.

"*Me!*" Earl rolled his eyes. "You'd better tend to it yourself. I'm not the marrying kind."

Virgil's gaze slewed around to the youngest brother. "Don't look at me," Clint warned him. "It's not my style, either."

"Goddammit to hell anyway! You boys have got the wrong attitude. What we're talkin' about is family and tradition— and . . ." Virgil faltered, searching for an impressive-sounding word.

Earl cocked one eye in a sardonic look. "What we're talking about is that old death-do-us-part malarkey. I'm too young and nimble-footed to get tied down just yet."

"And besides that," Clint added, "it could sure put a damper on things. Not many married men get to see the other side."

Virgil groaned. "Don't start that other-side stuff again. Whatever's beyond sundown wouldn't be a helluva lot different than what you've got right here."

"How do you know till you been there?"

"Godalmightydamn! You two sure try a man's patience."

Earl laughed. "Sounds just like Pa, don't he?"

Clint nodded. "Spittin' image if ever I saw it."

They toasted one another with wide grins and quaffed their

drinks. Virgil smiled his sly, possum smile and poured himself a glass of champagne. He'd given them the last laugh and, in doing so, watched as their bond of old was formed anew. He told himself that it had worked out better than he'd dared hope.

Once more, as though the three of them had joined hands, they were brothers again. The Brannocks.

13

A WEEK WENT BY all too quickly. On the following Friday, Clint came out of the hotel and paused in the warm July sun. He stood watching the throngs of people milling about on the street.

After a moment, he turned and strolled off through the business district. Only that morning, over breakfast, he'd decided that Denver wasn't for him. It put him in mind of an anthill, with all the scurrying and hectic rushing about. The comparison struck him as more truth than fancy, an honest observation. People in Denver, like worker ants, seemed intent on building an ever-larger hill.

Crowds bothered him. Whenever he walked the streets, he felt vaguely uncomfortable, somehow ill-at-ease. There was a sense of being surrounded, partially blind, with masses of people at his back, and too close for comfort. Then, too, he felt distinctly out of place, wandering aimlessly where he didn't belong. While he was the outsider, it was nonetheless Denver that seemed foreign. He halfway expected people to start speaking another language.

Nor was he any more taken with the mining camps. Earlier

in the week, he had accompanied one of Virgil's drivers on a routine haul to Black Hawk. The following day, he'd saddled the dun gelding and ridden off on his own to Central City. He found the camps to be grungy eyesores, dung heaps that could be scented a mile or more downwind. As for the miners, he pegged them as the largest single collection of dimdots he'd ever come across. They grubbed and scrounged, busting their butts from dawn to dark for a thimbleful of gold dust. And then witlessly tossed it away on boozy whores and crooked card games.

As a matter of curiosity, Clint had spent an afternoon wandering around the gold claims. Miners he talked with were fond of saying, "Iron rides a gold horse." Always alert to color, they searched the streambeds for the metallic rusty brown of iron, which indicated a likely place to start panning. The color generally led them upstream, to what they hoped was the origin of a lode. There, with pick and shovel, they began work in earnest.

A flat metal pan was the miner's principal tool. With it, he scooped a mixture of sand and water from the streambed. When he whirled it around, lighter minerals spilled over the pan's rim while iron particles and gold settled to the bottom. The process was tedious and time-consuming, with most men unable to work more than four or five pans an hour. Unless nuggets were found, a miner might pan the entire day for a teaspoon of gold dust. Often as not, a full day's labor amounted to nothing.

Other methods were employed on the more promising claims. One, known as a cradle, was essentially a boxlike strainer that separated stones and sand, and finally any particles of gold. Another was the Long Tom, which allowed six to eight men to work gravel and water through a trough and trap the gold in a riffle box. The more ambitious projects used the sluice, which was a series of connected riffle boxes. With a large team of miners, upward of a hundred cubic yards of gravel could be processed daily. Their reward, when split into shares, was sometimes less than a day's panning would have brought.

A few hours convinced Clint that gold fever was really a form of madness. The work was backbreaking and hard, performed under conditions so cruel that most men eventually lost their health. The miners lived in primitive quarters, often no more than canvas shanties, and subsisted on a diet of salt pork and beans. Only the very fortunate were able to elude the twin maladies of scurvy and dysentery. The fact they spent their nights whoring and swilling rotgut seemed to Clint all part of the lunacy. For most of them, the night was a time to forget what awaited them tomorrow.

By the end of the afternoon, Clint had seen enough. Whatever thoughts he'd had about taking a fling at prospecting were quickly shunted aside. His interest in the mining camps was limited solely to the night he spent in Central City. After dark, the saloons and dance halls became galvanized with life. One tour of the main street dives confirmed what he'd only suspected before. Nowhere had he ever seen a greater assortment of ruffians and cold-eyed hard cases. The camp, from all appearances, was a magnet for the frontier's rougher element.

All in all, Clint thought it a promising hunting ground. He'd by no means put aside his resolve to dance on Jack Quintin's grave. Despite the pressure from Virgil, he fully intended to carry through with his original plan. Some men were peaceful by nature and looked upon retribution as an act relegated solely to God. But Clint wasn't all that confident about divine intervention. He questioned whether the Almighty became directly involved in meting out justice to the world's lowlifes and murderers. He thought such matters were perhaps delegated to men who took an interest in seeing a wrong put right. Where Quintin was concerned, he figured he'd been tapped for the job.

For all that, Virgil had nonetheless made a telling point. The former Jayhawker could very well have made a beeline for California or Oregon. Or points in between, not excluding New Mexico, Utah, and other sparsely populated territories. The West was indeed a vast land, with parts of it still unmapped. To wander aimlessly across the mountains and plains could easily consume a lifetime. Worse, such a search depended largely on happenstance and chance encounters, simply getting lucky. And no assurance that the luck wouldn't fall to Quintin instead.

Upon reflection, Clint concluded that he'd made the wisest choice. Colorado was a natural stopover on the way to somewhere farther west. Equally significant, Quintin was unknown and unwanted in Colorado Territory. A former guerrilla turned horse thief was of interest only to the Kansas authorities. So it made sense that Quintin would delay, however briefly, in the fastness of the mountains. The idea had even greater merit since the mining camps were a gathering place for desperadoes and renegades. Forced to choose a likely hunting ground, no better spot existed.

Upon returning to Denver, Clint felt it was only a matter of time. He'd inquired about Quintin in both Black Hawk and Central City. While the name had sparked no response, he wasn't particularly concerned. A man like Quintin, unless he was dodging a hangman's rope, was too vain to assume an alias. Moreover, Quintin was accustomed to the limelight, and he wouldn't be content to remain in the shadows. Sooner or later, he would surface, draw attention to himself. Habitual troublemakers wallowed in their own notoriety.

Clint decided to give it a month. A regular jaunt through the mining camps would serve to keep him informed of new arrivals. At the end of a month, if he'd uncovered nothing about Quintin, he would then extend the search farther westward. All of which solved one problem and presented him with a more immediate concern: his funds were running low and he needed a temporary source of income. Virgil had insisted that he take his share from the sale of the family farm, but he'd squirreled that away for the future. However long it took, he meant to have the wherewithal to run Jack Quintin to earth. Meanwhile, he wasn't about to sponge off his brothers.

Nor would he consider going to work for them. Though he was proud of them, he in no way envied the lives they led. Virgil was absorbed with his business, bursting with plans for future expansion. Even more remarkable, he'd been accepted by the uptown crowd and seemed assured of making his mark in the world. Still, Clint had nothing in common with such people, and he was bored stiff by the thought of working in a warehouse. He figured there had to be a better way.

The alternative was Earl's gambling dive. For the most part, Clint was willing to put their past differences aside. He even admired Earl, for the gambling trade was a tough business, no place for the faint of heart. As for Earl's partner and bedmate, he'd found Monte to be his kind of woman. Like most of the sporting crowd, there was nothing phony or artificial about her. In fact, given the choice, he much preferred Earl's associates to Virgil's more respectable friends. Yet, in his mind, none of that altered what seemed the sticky point. He wouldn't allow himself to get bogged down in any job, and brothers had a way of making a man feel beholden. So he scratched the gambling dive off his list as well.

Not that his list was all that long. Walking along the street, it occurred to him that he was a man without a trade. Apart from working a farm, he'd done nothing but soldier and learn how to survive in a prison camp. None of those skills was in any great demand, particularly in Denver. As he approached the intersection separating the business district from the sporting district, he found himself in something of a quandary. However ill-suited he was to city life, he still needed a job. The trouble was, he hadn't the least idea where to start looking.

Nearing the corner, he saw the storefront sign of the *Rocky Mountain News*. Then, his interest whetted, he took a closer look at two men loitering outside the newspaper. One was a bruiser, heaving-muscled, with a thick neck and powerful shoulders. The other man was shorter and whipcord lean, with a face like a hatchet blade. Both of them were unkempt and unshaven, and looked as though they belonged in the sporting district. He thought they also looked vaguely suspicious.

A small bespectacled man emerged from the newspaper office. He was dressed in suit and hat, and appeared in something of a hurry. As he turned uptown, the bruiser suddenly grabbed him by the shoulder and spun him around. Without a word, the bigger man unleashed a haymaker and knocked his victim sprawling on the boardwalk. Then, joined by his hatchet-faced confederate, they proceeded to stomp and kick the fallen man. Their intent, clearly, was to maim and cripple.

Clint instinctively jumped into the melee. He spun the bruiser around and clouted him between the eyes with a hard clubbing blow. The man went down like a poleaxed steer, flat on his back. As the shorter one whirled to help his partner, Clint hit him with a splintering left hook. His mouth spurted blood and he crashed into the office door, sliding down on his rump. A flash of movement caught Clint's eye and he turned back toward the bigger man. He saw the bruiser digging at a pistol stuffed in his waistband.

For what seemed a sliver of eternity, Clint fumbled with the flap-top holster. His Colt cleared leather as the bruiser raised himself up on one elbow and fired. A bullet plucked at his sleeve, and a split second later the report of his own shot echoed up the street. The slug struck the other man slightly below the breastbone, and Clint placed a second shot within a handspan of the first. The big man collapsed, his boot heel drumming the boardwalk in a spasm of afterdeath. His eyes stared sightlessly into the sun.

A low groan diverted Clint's attention. He turned as the bespectacled man wobbled upright and propped himself against the storefront. One lens of his wire-rimmed glasses was broken and blood oozed down over his cheekbone. Faces appeared from doorways along the street, and several bystanders to the shooting cautiously edged forward.

Clint holstered his gun, moving across the boardwalk. He took hold of the man's arm. "You all right?"

"I think so," the man said in a reedy voice. "Nothing feels broken."

"Why'd they jump you?"

"The one you killed—I wrote an editorial about him, accused him of murdering a prostitute."

"You're a journalist?"

"William Byers," he nodded. "I own the newspaper. I want to thank you, Mr.—?"

"Brannock," Clint said. "Clint Brannock."

Byers blinked, licked his lips. "Any relation to Virgil Brannock?"

"He's my brother."

"We're good friends, your brother and I. I'll have to tell him you saved my life."

Clint stepped back as the hatchet-faced man uttered a ragged moan. He walked to the doorway, and after a quick search, he relieved the man of a hideout pistol. He looked around at Byers.

"You want to hold this one for the marshal?"

"I would," Byers said with a weak smile, "but we don't have a marshal. He quit last night."

"Quit?"

"Not only quit," Byers added, "he left town."

"Helluva note," Clint muttered. "I suppose you do have a jail?"

Byers pointed upstreet. "In the basement of city hall. I understand it's empty now."

"Well, that's no problem. We'll just let this runt have his choice of cells."

Clint bodily jerked the man to his feet. Holding him by the scruff of the neck, he marched him off along the boardwalk.

A low murmur of approval swept through the crowd of onlookers.

William Byers stood watching with an expression of mild
astonishment. A moment passed, and then, as though jarred
awake, he seemed to recover his wits. He took off after Clint.

14

THE JAIL WAS DANK as a cavern. Located in the basement of city hall, it consisted of an office and a lockup with six barred cells. Spotty rays of sunlight filtered through small above-ground windows.

There was an outside door, situated on the north side of the building. Clint hustled his prisoner down narrow stone steps and into the office. By now, the man was fully alert and simmering with hostility. His bottom lip was puffed and the corner of his mouth was caked with dried blood. His eyes were murderous.

"Goddammit to hell!" he raged. "You got no right to arrest me!"

Clint ignored the protest. He found a ring of keys hanging on a wall peg and unlocked the door to the lockup. Shoving the man ahead of him, he entered a dim corridor and saw that the jail was indeed empty. He halted before the open door of one of the cells. He motioned inside. "Don't give me any trouble."

The man glowered at him. "Mister, you got lots of balls, but no brains. You're gonna be sorry you butted in like that."

"I take unkindly to threats."

"Tough titty! I got friends that'll take unkindly to you lockin' me up. 'Specially since you ain't no lawman!"

"Give your friends a message," Clint said flatly. "Anybody who messes with me will wish he hadn't."

The man began a sputtered retort. Clint took a fistful of shirt and flung him backward into the cell. Then, slamming the door, he locked it and turned away.

As he entered the office, William Byers came through the outside door with another man in tow. The editor grinned broadly. "Mr. Brannock," he said, motioning to the other man, "I'd like you to meet our mayor, Amos Stodt."

Stodt held out a stubby-fingered hand. "An honor and a pleasure, Mr. Brannock. I understand you saved Will's life."

"Way it worked out," Clint said, shaking his hand, "I sort of pulled my own fat out of the fire."

"You are too modest, sir. Anyone who locks horns with Sam Baxter deserves our fullest commendation."

"Baxter?"

"The man you killed," Stodt explained.

"Not to mention Purdy," Byers added. "He's the little weasel you just locked up. And vicious as they come!"

Clint hung the keys on the wall peg. He gestured back toward the cells. "I reckon he's where he belongs, then. A stretch in that cage might teach him some manners."

Byers and Stodt exchanged a quick look. Stodt was an elegantly groomed man with a pencil-thin mustache and a politician's convivial manner. He wore a hammer-tail coat and vest that fitted snugly over his rather broad waistline. He favored Clint with a neighborly smile.

"Well, now," Stodt said genially. "Will tells me you're Virgil Brannock's brother."

"Virge and Earl," Clint replied. "You know Earl, don't you? Owns the Bella Union."

"We've never met," Stodt said. "However, I know Virgil quite well. Everyone admires him greatly."

"Yeah, he's a go-getter, all right."

"Apparently it runs in the family. You certainly didn't hesitate when those ruffians attacked Will."

Clint glanced sideways at the newspaper editor. He thought it peculiar that Byers had run straight to the town's mayor. Somewhat bemused, he wondered where the conversation was leading.

"No big thing," he said. "I just figured somebody ought to lend a hand."

"Well put," Stodt said, eyeing him keenly. "Perhaps you might consider doing the same thing for the town?"

"I don't follow you."

Stodt ducked his chin at the newspaperman. "Will thinks you're a candidate for the job of marshal. From the way you handle yourself, I rather think so, too."

Clint looked amused. "You're offering me the marshal's job?"

"I'll be frank with you," Stodt said. "Our marshal resigned somewhat unexpectedly. We need a replacement now—today."

"Why'd he quit?"

"Personal reasons," Byers said lightly. "Someone threatened his life and he took it to heart."

"I thought lawmen got used to that kind of thing."

"Not in our experience," Byers remarked. "We've had six marshals since the spring of '61. None of them lasted a year on the job."

Clint studied him inquisitively. "What did you do for law before that?"

Byers tried to downplay the problem. In 1859, he explained, a vigilance committee was formed by the town's more responsible citizens. Violence was rampant, with killings and shootings an everyday occurrence. To restore order, the vigilantes pursued and apprehended anyone accused of murder. After a citizens' trial, which usually resulted in a death sentence, the condemned man was hanged. These public executions, lasting through 1860, served as a damper on the lawless element.

Then, in 1861, the vigilance committee was disbanded. The town leaders felt it was time to create stability through a more orderly process of law enforcement. Local ordinances were passed by the city council, all of them designed to put the rowdier element on warning. But lax enforcement of the laws, abetted by a speedy turnover in the marshals, brought a steady erosion of peace and order. The past four years had been a time of trial and error where marshals were concerned.

"In a nutshell," Byers concluded on a jocular note, "none of them had any real aptitude for the job."

"Aptitude?" Clint repeated slowly. "What's that mean, exactly?"

Byers smiled. "They lacked the necessary intestinal fortitude. None of them seemed inclined to meet force with force."

"Why not bring back the vigilantes? From what you say, hanging worked pretty well."

"That's true," Byers admitted. "Hanging was a persuasive deterrent. We had more law and order with the vigilance committee than we've ever had with marshals."

"Why'd you stop, then?"

Stodt cleared his throat. "A civilized community," he said in an orotund voice, "doesn't resort to vigilantes. The outside world views that as mob rule, somewhat barbaric. It creates a bad image for the town."

A ghost of a smile touched Clint's mouth. "What've all these marshals done for your image? Sounds like an open invitation to troublemakers."

"Precisely!" Byers said, staring at him earnestly. "And that's why I've asked the mayor to offer you the job. We need a man who's willing to go head to head with the rougher crowd."

"And a man," Stodt intoned hastily, "who believes in the

sanctity of the law. We simply cannot condone violence on our streets.''

"Well . . .'' Clint said doubtfully. "What makes you think I'm your man? I've never had any experience enforcing the law.''

"Perhaps not,'' Byers said with conviction, "but you've demonstrated what I mentioned a moment ago—an aptitude for the work. Not one of our previous marshals so much as *drew* his gun.''

"Are you saying you want men shot instead of hung? Appears to me that's six of one and half a dozen of another.''

"No,'' Stodt said quickly. "We want our streets safe and orderly, nothing more. We have no intention of pinning a badge on a hired killer.''

"On the other hand,'' Byers said eagerly, "we won't quibble over methods. Whoever we hire will have the full support of the town council. Isn't that correct, Amos?''

"Absolutely,'' Stodt affirmed. "Our full and unanimous support, no strings attached.''

Clint mulled it over a minute. "How much does the job pay?''

"Salary plus fees,'' Stodt replied. "One hundred and fifty a month plus ten percent of all court fines.''

"When do you need an answer?''

"As fast as possible. Someone has to be on the streets by tonight.''

"I'll let you know.''

Clint walked to the door. As it closed behind him, Stodt's forehead wrinkled in a frown. He glanced around at Byers.

"I hope you're right about that man.''

"Trust me, Amos. He's a natural.''

Clint went directly to the warehouse. News of the shooting had already spread through town, and Virgil pressed him for the details. The story was simply told, requiring no elaboration. Virgil agreed completely with what he'd done.

The matter of the marshal's job was altogether different. As Clint related the conversation with Byers and Stodt, Virgil's expression turned pensive. He understood, from the tone of Clint's voice, that his advice was being sought. He listened without interruption or comment.

"That's it," Clint said finally. "They want an answer by tonight."

Virgil looked troubled. "Aren't you rushing into something sort of willy-nilly?"

"What's to be gained by waiting? Tomorrow or the next day wouldn't change the shape of it none."

"Maybe not," Virgil allowed. "But law work isn't a casual occupation. You ought to give it some serious thought."

Clint returned his stare. "You're not worried about me getting myself killed, are you?"

"I'd say it's a consideration. After all, six marshals in four years tells you something. Denver's still a damn rough town."

"What the hell," Clint said, grinning. "I've got a few rough edges myself."

"Don't joke," Virgil said sternly. "We're talking about a job where kill-or-get-killed is ordinary stuff. Are you prepared to face that every night?"

"The war wasn't exactly a Sunday-school picnic. We've both killed our share of men, Virge. I reckon neither one of us has lost any sleep over it."

"Speak for yourself. I stopped carrying a gun the day I was mustered out. I've seen all the killing I want . . . and more."

"Well, I reckon that's what makes horse races. Nobody sees anything exactly the same."

Virgil was silent a moment. "I thought Denver was just a stopover. Why would you get involved in anything permanent?"

"Nothing says I couldn't quit whenever I took a notion."

"Why sign on in the first place, then? I don't see the sense behind it."

Clint stared off into some thoughtful distance. Finally, as though he'd found the right words, his gaze swung around. "Wasn't it you that told me to use the law to get Quintin?"

"Quintin?" Virgil fixed him with a dour look. "I don't see the connection. You'd have no authority in the mining camps."

Clint cracked a smile. "Any badge is better than no badge at all. Besides, who knows? Quintin might get an itch to see the big city. Denver's not that far from the camps."

"By Judas," Virgil murmured uneasily. "Once you get your mind set, you just don't give up, do you?"

"Any reason I should?"

"None you haven't heard before."

"No need to rehash it, then, is there?"

Virgil gave him a searching look. "You've already made up your mind, haven't you? You plan to take the marshal's job."

"Yeah, I do."

"Then why bother asking for my advice?"

"Old habits are hard to break."

Clint smiled and walked from the office. Virgil watched him out the door, wondering where it would end. He turned back to the desk and began fussing with a stack of invoices. Then, as though answering himself, he nodded silently.

It would end with still more killing.

15

THE BELLA UNION OPENLY courted high rollers. House limit on faro, roulette, and twenty-one was five hundred dollars. Other games, such as Spanish monte and chuck-a-luck, were routinely played with no limit. Three poker tables, operated by house dealers, were table-stakes games.

There was an underlying purpose to the betting policy. Earl reasoned that high rollers preferred the company of other high rollers. So he created an atmosphere where they could congregate and pursue their favorite games. For the average bettor, it was an opportunity to rub shoulders with the gambling elite. The high rollers became, in effect, an attraction for the house.

On another level, Earl's decision was even more calculated. He purposely set out to lure the high rollers away from Denver's established gaming parlors. While his goal was not publicized, it was hardly a secret to the other owners. Yet, even though many of them raised their betting limits, they were a step behind from the outset. The Bella Union's policy of honest games—and the $10,000 reward—was a first for Denver. No one could duplicate the offer without appearing to be a sleazy imitator.

Still, taking business from the other dives was a risky proposition. Other owners, suffering a loss of play from high rollers, would like nothing better than for the Bella Union to go busted. A run of bad luck or one crooked game could conceivably break the house. As a result, Earl was constantly on guard against an outside setup. Specifically, he was alert to a high roller possibly financed by another house, who was working in collusion with a turncoat dealer. A single game, properly rigged, could put him out of business.

The Bella Union's bank, on any given night, contained upward of fifty thousand dollars. Should the house be tapped out, Earl would have no choice but to close the doors. No reputable gambling impresario would continue to operate unless he could cover all bets and, if necessary, pay off on the spot. Having once closed the doors, Earl was well aware that he would never again reopen. No one in Denver would bankroll him the second time around. Nor would they shed any tears over his downfall.

Earl's concern turned to reality on a Friday night. Halfway into the evening, a well-dressed man took a seat at one of the faro tables. He was soft-spoken, urbane, and quite obviously an experienced gambler. He bought an initial five thousand in chips and began betting the house limit from the start. Though he lost occasionally, he exhibited an uncanny sense for predicting the turn of the cards. By midnight, he was something more than twenty thousand ahead.

Faro, by its nature, was widely considered immune to cheating. An old and highly structured game, it had originated a century before in France. The name was derived from the king of hearts, which bore the image of an Egyptian pharaoh on the back of the card. All betting was against the house, known in Western parlance as "bucking the tiger." After being shuffled and cut, a full deck of cards was placed in a small wooden box, positioned directly before the dealer. Cards were then drawn in pairs, faceup, from a narrow slot in the box.

A cloth layout on the table depicted every card from deuce through ace. Before the turn of each pair drawn, players placed bets on the card of their choice. The first card out of the box was a losing bet, and the second was a winner. If there were no wagers on either card, then all bets were canceled out. Since no wagers were allowed on the top and bottom cards in the box, there were twenty-five betting turns in a deck. The dealer then shuffled and began a new game.

The dealer collected losing bets and paid off winners on each turn. As the pairs were drawn, an abacuslike casekeeper was used to keep track of the cards already out. By watching the casekeeper, players were able to calculate the odds on remaining cards as the game progressed. On either card drawn in a turn, the players could bet win or lose on the layout. To wager on a losing card, they "coppered" their bet by placing a copper token on their chips. A daring player or a confident high roller would bet both win and lose at the same turn. The practice gave rise to the saying "get a hunch, bet a bunch."

Like any working professional, Earl was only too aware that faro could be rigged. All it required was a clever dealer, with the skill and audacity to manipulate a deck of cards. The most common method was to use "strippers," a deck with certain cards trimmed slightly along the edges or on the ends. A dealer with sensitive fingers could then "read" the cards before slipping them from the box. By dealing "seconds"— holding back the top card and dealing the one below—he could determine the outcome of bets on the layout. To rob the house, of course, he needed a confederate on the other side of the table.

Shortly after midnight, Earl began wondering if he'd been gaffed. The affable high roller was winning consistently, still betting five hundred a turn. From a discreet distance, Earl observed the game, looking for any irregularity. He saw nothing to indicate either marked cards or crooked dealing. A talk with the floor lookout merely confirmed his own judgment. Nothing appeared out of order.

Finally, Earl exercised a prerogative of the house. He put a new dealer at the table and ordered a fresh deck of cards. A groan went up from the crowd of onlookers, but no one complained too strenuously. Even the well-groomed high roller agreed that the house was within its rights. His luck seemed unaffected by either the new dealer or the fresh cards. He won the first turn out of the box.

As play resumed, Earl had the old deck brought to his office. He examined the cards closely, looking for shaved edges or needle pricks, which was another method of marking a deck. The cards were unaltered, and he decided there was no need to talk with the dealer. The game was on the up and up, and the high roller was apparently enjoying a hot streak. Luck was a capricious thing, as Earl well knew, and even as it served some men, it turned on others. Tonight might well be the night he went busted.

A pleasant surprise awaited him when he returned to the game room. Where the high roller had been winning three out of four turns, he was now losing by the same ratio. Earl had no idea whether fresh cards and a different dealer had reversed the game. But it was clear, as gamblers were fond of noting, that "the worm had turned."

In the space of an hour, the high roller lost back something more than ten thousand dollars. No fool, he realized his luck had gone sour. He called it a night. Collecting his chips, he moved across the room to the cashier's window. The final count put him almost ten thousand ahead for the evening. After stuffing his pockets with money, he turned toward the door.

Earl was waiting just inside the entranceway. He smiled, extending his hand. "I'm Earl Brannock, the owner."

"Mr. Brannock." The man nodded, accepting his handshake. "I'm George Devol."

"Devol?" Earl sounded surprised. "George Devol, the riverboat gambler?"

Devol laughed. "Formerly a riverboat gambler, Mr. Brannock. I fear the railroads are fast writing an end to a very pleasant era.''

"Well, I nonetheless admire your style of play, Mr. Devol. Your reputation hasn't been harmed any here tonight.''

"Nor yours," Devol said. "You run a very professional operation, Mr. Brannock.''

"Perhaps you'll give me a chance to recoup. I've heard it said that you play a shrewd game of poker.''

"Unfortunately, I'm only passing through. I leave on the morning stage.''

"Too bad," Earl said genuinely. "I would have enjoyed playing against a man of your caliber.''

"Perhaps another time," Devol replied. "Just now, I'm off to test the waters in San Francisco.''

"I've always had a yen to see the Barbary Coast myself.''

"Indeed? Well, if ever you journey west, be sure to ask for me. I intend to stay awhile.''

"I'll do it," Earl said cordially. "Until then, I wish you luck, Mr. Devol.''

Earl made a show of walking him to the door. Then, after returning to the gaming room, he began spreading the word. By morning, every gambler in Denver would hear the story. George Devol, the fabled riverboat high roller, had selected the Bella Union for his night in town. And bucked the tiger for a cool $10,000.

Apart from the prestige, Earl saw it in a practical light. He knew the mentality of gamblers, and the story would enhance the idea of winning—or losing—at the Bella Union. He figured it was the best ten thousand he'd ever spent.

The upstairs suite was a private world. There Monte and Earl dropped the facade they put on during business hours. The time spent there was personal time, their favorite time. When they were alone, together.

Late that night, after closing, Earl strolled from the parlor through the bedroom. He was in shirt sleeves and carrying a large snifter of brandy. He halted in the doorway of the bathroom, which was dominated by a huge porcelain tub. One eye cocked askew, he grinned. "You look like the Queen of Sheba."

Monte was lazed back in the tub. A nightly ritual, she had buckets of hot water brought from downstairs and fixed herself a frothy bubble bath. Then, luxuriating in the steamy water, she revitalized herself for the moment they went to bed. She looked up at him now with a catlike smile. "What kept you, lover?"

"Brainwork," he said with mock seriousness. "I've been stewing on an idea."

"Oh," she inquired. "Anything worth telling?"

"Well, Devol showing up tonight put me to thinking. Maybe it's time we broadened our horizons . . . expanded."

"Expanded what?"

"The operation," he said with a wave of the snifter. "What's to stop us from branching out, going big-time? A Bella Union in Central City and another in Black Hawk."

"Omigawd!" she yelped. "You're really not serious, are you?"

"Why the hell not? We could wind up the gambling czars of Colorado."

"Or dead broke," she scoffed. "Too much ambition can be a bad thing, lover. We're not out of the woods here . . . not yet."

"Maybe so," Earl conceded. "But we've got ourselves a damn nice piece of the action. I'm just saying it's time to look to the future."

"What's your hurry? The future won't run off and leave you."

"Very funny," Earl said dryly. "You ought to be a comedian."

"I could definitely show you something that would tickle your funny bone."

"And what might that be?"

Monte laughed and tossed her head. "Why don't you join me in the tub and find out?"

Earl took a long swig of brandy. He studied her a moment, as though weighing the invitation. Then, with a matter-of-fact shrug, he set the snifter on a nearby commode. He smiled and slowly began undressing.

"Don't mind if I do."

16

IT WAS LATE EVENING.

Blake Street resembled a carnival without the tents. Knots of men clogged the boardwalks and music blared from inside the brightly lit dives. An air of rowdy celebration boosted the noise level to a deafening pitch.

Clint was no longer a stranger to the sporting district. After three nights on the job, he'd become a familiar figure along Blake Street. He made the rounds several times every evening, careful to avoid a set pattern. No one knew when he would appear, or where, and the element of surprise tended to keep people on their toes. All the more important, it gave him the edge whenever trouble developed.

Quite quickly, Clint had discovered what any veteran peace officer already knew: saloons were fairly tame places, for whiskey alone was seldom the culprit. Instead, it was the volatile mix of liquor and women that provoked trouble. Fistfights and knock-down-drag-out brawls occurred most frequently in dance halls and whorehouses. All such establishments had resident bouncers, but the donnybrooks some-

times got out of hand. He made it a practice to be
johnny-on-the-spot.

So far, he'd arrested fourteen men for disturbing the peace.
Those who resisted arrest, obstreperous drunks and hard-ass
troublemakers, were unceremoniously cold-cocked. At first,
he had used his fists, but skinned knuckles on a nightly basis
seemed impractical. Switching to something more substantial,
he now laid the barrel of his Colt across their skulls. It was
fast and persuasive, and left an indelible impression on bystanders. For the first time in the town's history, the jail had
a regular clientele. And in three nights, he'd earned twenty-
eight dollars in court fees.

Yet none of the altercations had turned serious. The businesslike manner in which he'd killed Sam Baxter was the talk
of the sporting district. His reputation, rather than the badge
pinned on his shirt, served as a deterrent. People spoke of his
cool, no-nonsense attitude and rated him very sudden with a
gun. The men he had arrested thus far appeared reluctant to
carry it beyond fisticuffs. Still, he had no illusions on that
score. He knew it was only a matter of time.

The war had taught Clint an essential lesson: where rough
men congregate, there was a certain daredevil mentality. Inevitably, the bull-of-the-woods felt compelled to try himself
against the cock-of-the-walk. Sooner or later, the same thing
would happen in the sporting district. Someone would work
up the nerve to test Clint not with fists, but with a gun. The
lure of it was irresistible, and eventually some self-styled
tough nut would challenge him. When it happened, he
planned to kill the man swiftly, without a moment's hesitation. He figured an object lesson would serve to put the sporting crowd on notice.

Tonight, strolling along Blake Street, he had only one res-
ervation. While he liked the job and actually enjoyed the duties of a peace officer, there were aspects of the sporting
district beyond his control. In talking with Earl, he'd learned
that a man named Ed Case was undisputed boss of the neth-
erworld. Further, though it was unstated, he sensed that a

certain animosity existed between Earl and Case. Apparently it had something to do with the payoffs that Case's goons collected every week.

To date, Clint hadn't had occasion to call on Case. The Progressive Club and the Palace, both of which were owned by Case, were among the quieter dives on Blake Street. Insofar as Clint was concerned, it was just as well. He wanted nothing to do with the payoffs or the politics of the sporting district. In his view, that was the business of Case and the crowd in city hall.

All the same, he wondered whether Case would be satisfied to live and let live. He'd already decided that he wouldn't brook any interference with respect to his job. Nor would he be influenced by Case, or the uptown politicos, when it came to enforcing the law. To his way of thinking, everybody danced to the same tune, regardless of connections. He thought Case would be wise to leave the matter there.

Turning a corner, he walked over to Holladay Street. Named after Ben Holladay, owner of the Overland Stage Line, the street was known locally as the Row. Here, along three city blocks, the "brides of the multitude" practiced the oldest profession. Some estimates put the number of working whores at five hundred, but the true count was anyone's guess. Holladay Street was a world unto itself.

Denver's original whoresville was a cluster of log cabins on the south bank of Cherry Creek. Shortly after the outbreak of the Civil War, the girls jumped the creek and moved six blocks north, staking claim to Holladay Street. There the parlor houses and lowly cribs flourished as the town experienced an ever-greater influx of men. Lust was a whore's stock-in-trade, and sin for sale never went begging on the frontier. Only recently had the number of decent women in town surpassed the number of Jezebels.

Holladay Street was governed by a social structure all its own. On the lower end of the street were the cribs, each one fronted by a door and a narrow window. Comprised of two tiny rooms, the crib had a sitting room up front and a bedroom in the rear. The tariff for a quick trick was four bits, and landlords charged the girls three-dollars-a-day rent, collected daily in cash. Attired in knee-length dresses and black stockings, the girls stood in doorways and openly solicited business. A form of live advertisement, it allowed their customers to inspect the wares before making a selection.

The upper end of the Row was reserved for the elite of whoredom. There, along a one-block stretch, were the more refined parlor houses. Generally constructed of brick and two or three stories high, the parlor houses were staffed by young lovelies who commanded top dollar. Their expertise in the boudoir was renowned, and any man with the price was treated to all sorts of exotic high jinks. The madams euphemistically referred to their brothels as "young ladies' boardinghouses." The girls, among other things, were known as "soiled doves" and "fallen sparrows." A local wit, tongue in cheek, had tagged them the *filles de joie*.

Clint was vaguely uncomfortable about the Row. He had no moral objections to whores, and back home he'd been known as something of a ladies' man. But he had never understood women or what made them tick. They were strange creatures who abhorred logic and reason, and operated instead on an emotional level that defied comprehension. An angry woman was to him some curious crossbreed of buzz saw and wildcat. Every evening, when he walked over to Holladay Street, his nerves took a sharp upturn. He dreaded the night he'd be forced to separate two clawing, hot-eyed whores.

Tonight, by the sound of things, appeared to be the night. As he passed one of the parlor houses, he heard screams and the crash of furniture from inside. Grumbling to himself, he pushed through the front door and entered a small alcove. To his left was a flight of stairs and to his right was a wide, arched doorway. He moved to the doorway and halted, momentarily taken aback. The parlor was a scene of screeching chaos.

Across the room, one man had another pinned in a corner.

The one in the corner was propped upright by a hand around his throat while a sledgehammer fist methodically reduced his features to a pulp. The one administering the punishment was a burly man, heavily built, with a square, thick-jowled face. Straddling his back was a squealing girl who had him locked in a stranglehold. All around him were several other girls, alternately pounding on him and shrieking at the top of their lungs. Neither the girls nor the noise seemed to distract him from pummeling the other man.

Clint sized up the situation at a glance. From the girls' hysterical behavior, the one pinned in the corner was clearly the house bouncer. The one handing out the beating was just as clearly not a member of the family. His determined attitude indicated as well that he was a man gone crazy with rage. Once he finished with the bouncer, he probably had similar ideas for the girls.

The parlor was littered with broken tables and overturned chairs. Clint picked his way through the debris and swiftly crossed the room. Using both hands, he waded into the squalling pack of girls. The decibel level of their screeching increased as he flung them aside, right and left. Finally, with a mighty heave, he plucked the girl off the man's back. She let loose a shrill curse as he dropped her on the floor.

There seemed nothing to gain by trying reason on the man himself. Clint pulled the Colt and his arm lashed out in a fast shadowy movement. The dull thunk of metal striking skull bone put an immediate end to the beating. The man grunted a surprised woofing sound, then released his hold on the bouncer and collapsed as though he'd been hit by lightning. The bouncer, who was already out cold, slumped down in the corner.

Holstering his pistol, Clint turned to survey the damage. All around him, like wilted flowers, the floor was littered with sweaty women. They stared up at him as though some Olympian god had suddenly appeared in their midst. Their eyes were round with a mixture of fright and amazement, and their bosoms heaved in unison as they tried to catch their breath. To his great relief, all of them had stopped screaming.

The one he'd pulled off the man's back slowly got to her feet. She was a blond tawny cat of a girl, with a sculptured figure and bold amber eyes. She appeared to be in her late twenties, and up close, she smelled sweet and alluring. She looked him over with an inquisitive, saucy expression.

"You must be our new marshal?"

Clint tipped his hat. "The name's Brannock."

"So I've heard," she said softly. "Well, thanks a load, Marshal. You got here just in the nick of time."

"Pleased to be of service, ma'am. I take it you're the, uh, proprietor?"

Her laugh was a delicious sound. "Yeah, you take it right. I own the joint."

"What happened here, Miss—?"

"London," she said, dusting off her skirt. "Belle London."

Clint nodded. "The one in the corner your bouncer?"

"Poor devil," she said, glancing past him. "He tried to stop that bastard from pawing one of my girls. Probably would've gotten himself killed if you hadn't shown up."

"If I was you," Clint advised her, "I'd get a sawbones over here. He looks hurt pretty bad."

"Thanks, I will. What about that tub-of-guts on the floor?"

"I'll cart him on down to jail. You can drop by in the morning and sign a formal complaint."

"How about attempted murder? It's the least the sorry s.o.b. deserves."

"Sounds fair to me."

Clint stooped down and took hold of the man's legs. A boot heel under each arm, he began dragging the man across the room. The girls scattered, clearing a path, darting venomous looks at his prisoner. Belle London called out as he neared the doorway.

"Marshal!"

Clint turned back. "Something else?"

She gave him a bright, theatrical smile. "I just wanted to say, don't be a stranger. You're welcome here anytime."

"Much obliged, Miss London. I'm liable to take you up on that."

Clint hauled the man out through the alcove. On the street, he paused a moment to get his breath. Staring back at the house, he was struck by a sudden thought. He pondered how a woman so young—and so pretty—got to be a whorehouse madam.

He figured it might be worth his while to find out.

Clint turned back. "Somethin' else?"

She gave him a bright, theatrical smile. "I just wanted to say don't be a stranger. You're welcome here anytime."

"Anytime, huh," Clint replied. "I'll have to take you up on that."

Clint hurried the men out through the alcove. On the street, he paused a moment to get his breath. Staring back at the house, he was struck by a sudden thought. He conceded now Lucille was young—and so pretty—not to be a Wilbanks widow.

He feared it might be worrisome while it lasted.

17

"GOOD MORNING, AMOS."

"Well—good morning, Ed."

Amos Stodt looked a bit startled. Seldom was Ed Case up and about so early in the morning. Nor was he in the habit of dropping by the mayor's office. Their business was generally conducted somewhere else than city hall.

Case closed the office door. His features were drawn and he appeared somehow preoccupied as he crossed the room. When he stopped before the desk, Stodt experienced a vague sense of uneasiness. Something about the unannounced visit was all wrong.

"Have a seat," Stodt offered. "Take a load off your feet."

"I'll stand," Case said shortly.

"You sound a little out of sorts. Anything wrong?"

"We have to talk."

"About what?"

"The Brannock brothers."

"The Brannocks!" Stodt echoed. "What about them?"

"I think they're out to get me."

"I beg your pardon?"

"You heard me," Case snapped. "I think they've got plans to take over the sporting district."

Stodt blinked with disbelief. He could hardly credit his ears, and yet he knew the accusation was made in dead earnest. Staring across the desk, he warned himself to proceed with caution. He owed his political existence to David Hughes, Denver's chief power broker. But he dared not offend Ed Case.

To Stodt, it was like walking a tightrope. Some years past, at Hughes' order, he had formed a political alliance with Ed Case. The deal gave Case control of the sporting district and allowed him to operate without interference from city hall. In return, Case was obliged to deliver the sporting crowd's vote at election time. As Case consolidated his position, however, he'd become increasingly independent. By controlling the swing vote, he could now make demands on city hall and the political hierarchy. It was, at best, an extremely sensitive arrangement.

"Frankly, I'm amazed," Stodt said at length. "What makes you suspicious of the Brannocks?"

"Everything!" Case said crossly. "For openers, I hear Virgil Brannock's gotten awful clubby with Hughes."

"I wouldn't term it clubby. Walter Tisdale introduced them, and Hughes was rather impressed. He thinks Brannock has potential."

Case gave him a sidelong look. "Potential for what?"

"I have no idea," Stodt said vaguely. "You know how Hughes operates. He collects people who might be of some use."

"Yeah, that's my point."

Stodt appeared confused. "What do you mean—your point?"

"Funny thing," Case said with heavy sarcasm. "Virgil shows up out of nowhere and worms his way in with Hughes. Then Earl Brannock opens the Bella Union and sandbags me into a special deal. How's that for coincidence?"

"I fail to see the connection. Exactly how were you sand-bagged?"

"What's the difference?" Case said curtly. "The point is, I had to give Earl a break on the payoffs. It was that or risk a revolt with the sporting crowd."

Stodt shook his head, as if confronted by a testy child. "Ed, you aren't making a great deal of sense. I don't understand any of this."

"Wise up," Case growled. "Earl Brannock opened the fanciest gaming parlor in town. And he's made himself a reputation by operating square games. Doesn't that strike you as the least bit peculiar?"

"No, it doesn't. Offhand, I'd say it's shrewd business."

"You goddamned fool! He's trying to undercut me in the sporting district. It's just the first step."

Stodt gave him a quick, guarded glance. "First step in what?"

Case rolled his eyes to the ceiling. He stumped across to the window and stood for a moment staring out at the street. When he turned back, he peered suspiciously at Stodt. His gaze was sharp, somehow cunning, like a watchful animal.

"Why'd you hire Clint Brannock?"

"Why?" Stodt said, astounded. "Because Will Byers twisted my arm. You may recall he saved Byers' life."

"So what?"

"Oh, come on, Ed. We needed a marshal. And we also need the continued support of Byers and his newspaper. Why shouldn't I hire Clint Brannock?"

"I'll tell you why," Case said with wintry malice. "There's a conspiracy going on here, that's why!"

"Conspiracy?"

"You heard me! One Brannock gets chummy with Hughes. Another puts himself in position to challenge me downtown. And the third just happens to get himself appointed marshal. What would you say they've got in mind?"

"You tell me, Ed."

Case stared at him with open contempt. "They've rigged it. Political connections, the law on their side—it's pretty damned obvious. Earl's been slotted to push me out."

Stodt dismissed the idea with a wave of his hand. "You're imagining things, Ed. I assure you there's no conspiracy involving the Brannocks. You have my word on it."

"Do I?" Case said scornfully. "What makes you so certain?"

"I'm the mayor," Stodt reminded him. "I decide who runs what in this town."

"No, you don't," Case replied with cold hauteur. "Hughes decides and tells you what to say. You're his polly parrot."

"In the end," Stodt observed woodenly, "it amounts to the same thing."

Case's tone was harsh, roughly insistent. "Then you'd best carry a message back to Hughes. Tell him I won't be pushed out. Not by the Brannocks or anybody else. And I've got the muscle to make it stick."

Stodt pursed his mouth as if his teeth hurt. "You're whistling in the graveyard, Ed. There is no conspiracy."

"Just deliver the message, Mr. Mayor."

Case stormed out of the office. Stodt reflected on it a moment, wondering if he should actually deliver the message. Then, with a politician's instinct for survival, he decided he had no choice. For, as Case had so aptly put it, he was indeed David Hughes' polly parrot.

Virgil walked with his head down. He was lost in thought, unaware of passersby or street traffic. His destination was the First National Bank.

Only that morning he'd formulated the last part of his plan. All the pieces had fallen into place, and he now had a strategy for buying out the icehouses one by one. He wanted to solicit Walter Tisdale's opinion, ask the banker's advice. Then, assuming a favorable response, he would ask for another loan. He calculated ten thousand would do the job nicely.

Unwittingly, his mind jumped from father to daughter. Over the past few weeks he'd escorted Elizabeth to several church socials and a boring music recital. She welcomed his attention and evidenced genuine interest in him. Yet her attitude toward him was one of coy playfulness, like a flirtatious schoolgirl. Still, for all that, he sensed she was an intelligent and rather insightful woman. Why she pretended otherwise seemed to him a full-blown enigma. He'd never met anyone like her, and perhaps that was the reason for his mystification. She was, in a word, a paradox.

"Virgil!"

The sound of his name broke his reverie. He turned back and saw Will Byers in the doorway of the newspaper. As he approached, he saw that Byers was in high good humor. The editor pulled him into the front office.

"I'd like you to look at something."

"Oh, what's that?" Virgil asked.

"You told me you'd worked a farm most of your life—"

"All of it, except for the war."

"Then you're the very man I need. I want a farmer's honest reaction."

Spread out on Byers' desk were several sheets of paper. Some were covered with printing and others were rough sketches of the town and the surrounding countryside. He explained that the sheets represented a dummy layout for a brochure.

"What sort of brochure?" Virgil inquired.

"A sales brochure," Byers said with cheery vigor. "I intend to sell Colorado as the undiscovered Promised Land."

Looking closer, Virgil saw that the sketches depicted flatland rather than mountains. Before he could ask, Byers leapt into an enthusiastic monologue. Gesturing wildly, the editor outlined his plan to promote eastern Colorado as prime farmland. The future growth of Denver, he declared, was dependent on a stable economy. To achieve that and entice the railroad into Denver, it was necessary to create an agricultural base. Farms, not gold, were the building blocks for permanence.

The key, as Byers saw it, was the Homestead Act. Enacted in 1862, the legislation allowed any head of family to claim 160 acres of surveyed public land and gain title after five years' residence. A later amendment permitted Civil War veterans to apply their years of military service toward the residency requirements. The promotional brochures, Byers noted, would be sent to Eastern newspapers and resettlement organizations. Immigrants, who were flooding in from Europe, as well as western-bound settlers were eager for information. By publicizing itself, Denver would benefit greatly from the westering migration.

"Homesteaders are the wave of the future," Byers concluded grandly. "There's no reason why Colorado shouldn't claim its fair share."

Virgil appeared dubious. "I crossed the plains east of here on my way to Denver. It looks to be a pretty harsh land. Not a helluva lot of rainfall."

"Enough for farming," Byers said stoutly. "But you've touched on the salient point, Virgil. People back East have been told the plains are the Great American Desert. We have to change that image now—starting today!"

The editor's zealotry was infectious. Virgil nodded vigorously, studying him a moment. "Tell me something, Will. Are you promoting Denver or Colorado Territory?"

The question was searching and deceptively astute. Denver's chief rival was the town of Golden, located some ten miles to the west. As the capital of Colorado Territory, Golden held a slight edge in the race for dominance. Community leaders in Denver were determined to reverse the situation.

Byers removed his glasses and began polishing them with a handkerchief. When he spoke, his voice was almost dreamy. "Virgil, we have to harness all our resources to bring about increased development. Otherwise Golden will remain the territorial capital and steal our thunder. In that event, the future of Denver could only be characterized as grim.''

"Hmmm." Virgil considered that a moment. "Are you saying there's some plan afoot to make Denver the capital?"

Byers permitted himself a sly smile. He fixed the spectacles over his ears and tucked away the handkerchief. "Suffice it to say there are forces at work at this very moment. Apart from that, I'm not at liberty to divulge the particulars. However, I'm confident you can draw your own conclusions."

The conversation ended there. Out on the street again, Virgil turned uptown and walked toward the bank. He knew that Byers had stopped short of betraying a confidence. Yet, as one friend to another, a message had been imparted. And the conclusion was inescapable.

Men of vision and sturdy pragmatism were at work. Denver, as the territorial capital, would make them rich and influential. He saw no reason why he shouldn't join the club.

18

DAVID HUGHES WAS A man of meticulous habit. Every morning, on the stroke of eight, he walked through the door of his law office. His male secretary was already hard at work.

Nodding brusquely, he crossed the outer office. His secretary was accustomed to the silent greeting and merely smiled. Hughes' morning routine was by now an established ritual, and seldom broken. The first hour was devoted to ordering his thoughts, structuring the day ahead. He rarely spoke to anyone.

The inner office was comfortably furnished. Hughes hooked his hat on a hall tree and moved behind a large walnut desk. Awaiting him was a stack of legal correspondence as well as a schedule of the day's appointments. He briefly scanned the correspondence, then pushed it aside. His gaze went to the appointment schedule, lingering there a moment. Something in his expression changed, and he swiveled around in his chair, staring out the window. His eyes were remote, and hard.

Mayor Stodt and Luther Evans arrived precisely at nine o'clock. Theirs was the first appointment of the day, and neither of them thought it prudent to keep Hughes waiting. The secretary ushered them inside and they took seats before the desk.

When the door closed, Hughes finally turned from the window, acknowledging their presence. He came straight to the point. "We've got troubles," he said. "Yesterday I received a letter from my man in Washington. The news is all bad."

Neither man questioned why he had delayed sending for them. Hughes rarely sought anyone else's counsel, and he'd obviously taken overnight to assess the situation. Nor were Evans and Stodt unaware of why they'd been summoned here today. Anything originating out of Washington almost certainly dealt with the railroad.

"I have it on good authority," Hughes went on, "that Denver will be bypassed. The Union Pacific plans to build through Cheyenne."

Stodt appeared visibly startled. "What does Wyoming have to offer that we don't?"

"An easier route," Hughes replied, "and a more direct route. Building through Cheyenne will speed completion of the line."

"Is it final?" Evans asked. "No chance we could get the decision reversed?"

"No chance at all."

Stodt let out a gusty breath. "Without a railroad, we're ruined. All our plans will come to nothing."

The statement merely underscored their problem. All three men had heavily invested in Denver real estate. Their holdings were funneled through Evans' land company and bought without any great fanfare. Yet their belief in Denver's future was tied directly to the railroad. No town prospered without a link to the Eastern markets.

A transcontinental railroad line was no longer a pipe dream. While the Union Pacific built westward, the Central Pacific, which originated in California, was laying track eastward. One day the lines would join, connecting the nation's distant shores with a ribbon of steel. Any town located along the right-of-way would be linked to an artery of commerce and trade.

"What happened?" Evans said at length. "I thought we had firm assurances from the Union Pacific people."

Hughes seemed to look through him. "Whatever we had, we don't have it now. Cheyenne will definitely get the railroad."

"Good God," Stodt said gravely. "We'll lose any chance of getting the capital moved from Golden. The railroad was our best hope."

"It still is," Hughes informed them. "However, we'll have to revise our plan."

Evans and Stodt stared at him. When neither of them spoke, Hughes lifted his hands in a shrug. "If the railroad won't come to us, then we'll go to the railroad."

Evans angled his head critically. "Are you saying what I think you're saying?"

"Exactly," Hughes said in a dry cold manner. "We'll organize our own railway line and lay track to Cheyenne."

"You're not serious!" Stodt said. "It's more than a hundred miles to Cheyenne. Where would we raise the money?"

Hughes' smile was cryptic. "I have reason to believe Congress will award a land grant along our right-of-way. Something on the order of a million acres."

"What, then?" Evans inquired. "A land grant isn't cash in hand."

"Suppose we call it an asset," Hughes said. "An asset to dangle before investors."

"What investors?"

"The people of Denver."

"You propose to raise the money locally?"

"Who has a better stake in the future of Denver? We'll form a corporation and promote sale of the stock. I suspect it won't be all that difficult."

Stodt looked worried. "Will this corporation be on the up and up?"

"Of course," Hughes replied loftily. "I won't say as much for some sideline ventures I have in mind. But that's a discussion for another time."

Evans' eyes narrowed. "What is it we're discussing right now?"

"First things first," Hughes noted. "Denver needs a board of trade, similar to the one in Chicago. Such an organization could rally the people, get them behind the railroad. Particularly if it were headed by the right man."

"And you have someone in mind"—Evans hesitated, watching him—"don't you?"

Hughes laughed suddenly, a harsh sound in the closed room. "I have just the man we need. Honest and reliable, a man of the people."

Stodt shook his head. "I don't get it. If everything's on the up and up, why do we need a front man?"

"Just in case."

"Just in case of what?"

"In case anything at all"—Hughes paused to underscore the words—"should go wrong."

Late that afternoon Hughes entered the First National Bank. Walter Tisdale and Virgil Brannock were waiting in the banker's office. Hughes shook their hands warmly before taking a seat.

"Gentlemen," he said, looking from one to the other, "I appreciate you seeing me on such short notice."

"Happy to oblige," Tisdale said. "Although I must admit, your message has me curious. You said it was a matter of the utmost importance."

"Nothing less," Hughes affirmed. "I think it's fair to say we're faced with an emergency."

"Indeed?" Tisdale peered across the desk at him. "What sort of emergency?"

"Allow me to explain."

Hughes recounted the problem in some detail. He told of the Union Pacific's decision to bypass Denver and build instead to Cheyenne. In a somber tone, he went on to relate how the decision affected Denver's rivalry with Golden. Then he outlined the one countermove that might yet save the town. A railroad, incorporated and financed locally, to provide a link with the Union Pacific.

"Either we do it ourselves," he concluded, "or Denver faces a very uncertain future."

Tisdale eyed him keenly. "You haven't mentioned the Kansas Pacific. I understood they also planned on building to Denver."

"I regret to say," Hughes confided, "the Kansas Pacific has stumbled on hard times. At last word, the line was stalled in eastern Kansas, trying to raise additional capital." He stopped, let the idea percolate a moment. "Our one hope is to establish a direct link with Cheyenne."

"Quite an undertaking," Tisdale observed. "You're talking about a great deal of money."

"*Progress!*" Hughes invested the word with import. "That's what we're talking about, and it doesn't come cheap. However, I have every confidence that the people of Denver will give it their support."

"Perhaps," Tisdale said rather formally. "How would you proceed?"

Hughes outlined his plan for a board of trade. An instrument of civic betterment, it would be presided over by responsible business leaders. The purpose of the board would be to organize the people behind a community effort, namely the railroad. To that end, the board president had to be someone the entire town would accept. A man of vision and bold thinking.

"In my mind," he said finally, "our young friend here fits the bill perfectly. How would you feel about it, Virgil? It's an important job."

Surprise washed over Virgil's face. "You want me to head up the board?"

"Why not?" Hughes laughed indulgently. "You've shown yourself to be an astute businessman. I hardly think the town could do better."

"Well . . ." Virgil sounded flattered. "I don't know what to say."

"Of course," Hughes went on smoothly, "we could only recommend your name. The townspeople would have to approve."

Virgil smiled broadly. "I'd consider it an honor."

"Then it's settled," Hughes said, turning back to the banker. "Unless you have anything to add, Walter?"

Tisdale's look betrayed nothing. Yet he viewed the offer with mixed feelings. He was aware that Virgil and his daughter were in the initial stages of courtship. Privately, he'd already given the union his blessing and therefore took a personal interest in Virgil's affairs. He thought the younger man's prospects would be greatly enhanced by serving on the board of trade.

Still, he was always cautious where David Hughes was concerned. He accepted Hughes as Denver's power broker, for it was an unavoidable fact. In a sense he even admired Hughes, for it took nerve and skill to exercise control over the town's political apparatus. But he was nonetheless aware that powerful men sometimes justified unconscionable deeds in the name of noble ends. He wondered if the railroad was just such a scheme.

For all that, he was himself a pragmatic man. Denver would wither and die unless it was infused with the lifeblood of a railroad. In the end there was no alternative for him or the townspeople. Nor was it a time to dither and hesitate as to Virgil's involvement. There were, quite simply, no alternatives to David Hughes.

"One question," he said at last. "How will you proceed with respect to the board of trade?"

Hughes gestured forcefully. "I suggest we organize a public meeting. The town has a right to vote yea or nay."

"And if they vote nay?"

"They won't," Hughes said with a measured smile. "Not after Virgil gives them a stem-winder of a speech. Isn't that right, Virgil?"

Virgil grinned, knuckled one side of his mustache. "I'll do my damnedest, Mr. Hughes."

"I know you will, Virgil. I'm counting on it."

Looking on, Walter Tisdale experienced an uncomfortable moment. He was reminded of himself when he was young and ambitious, and not quite so cynical. He made a mental note to have a talk with Virgil. A word to the wise would work to everyone's benefit.

19

A LAZY FORENOON BREEZE stirred swirls of dust on Larimer Street. The town's main thoroughfare was baked hard as flint by the hot August sun, and wagon traffic moved at a sedate pace. All the business district seemed somehow slowed by the midday heat.

Clint emerged from a café. He stood for a moment with a toothpick wedged in the corner of his mouth. As was his custom, he had awakened late and shaved with dulled concentration. His routine was now geared to life in the sporting district, which meant starting his day around noontime. After a breakfast of steak and eggs, he felt prepared to get on with business. He tossed the toothpick away and turned upstreet.

The town jail was his first stop. A month on the job had brought about several changes in the marshal's office. All court cases were now scheduled for the afternoon, which allowed him the mornings to himself. With the increased number of arrests and fines, he'd also convinced the city council to hire a jailer. These days he no longer concerned himself with feeding prisoners and swamping out cells. He devoted his time instead to policing Denver.

Lately, he'd devoted a good deal of thought as well to the job itself. Law enforcement, like soldiering, had certain tricks of the trade. Foremost was the matter of equipment, which for a peace officer centered on his sidearm. Without a reliable pistol, no lawman could expect to survive the job. Yet, as Clint had discovered, reliability was an uncertain thing. No gun could be trusted completely.

Outside town, he'd begun practicing with the Colt on a regular basis. He found that accuracy was greatly increased when the pistol was kept clean. Fouling from black powder and leading in the barrel made reliable functioning a very iffy proposition. A clean gun, well oiled and properly loaded, allowed him to keep all shots on a playing card at twenty paces. When dirty or fired with old loads, the Colt was prone to malfunctions and misfires. The difference seemed to him worth considerable thought and effort.

From trial and error, Clint had gradually found a method that worked. His morning ritual, which he followed religiously, varied only by degree. If he went for a practice session and fired the Colt, he then swabbed it out thoroughly before reloading. On those mornings when the pistol wasn't fired, he followed another routine. Before leaving the hotel, he would draw the old loads and reload with fresh powder and new caps. While tedious, the care and cleaning had reduced misfires to a negligible factor. He looked on it as a form of insurance.

The practice sessions had confirmed another problem as well. His dissatisfaction with the old military holster had started the day he'd killed Sam Baxter. He recalled fumbling with the flap-top simply to get a grip on the Colt. One solution would have been to cut the flap-top away, but that created still another problem. The holster itself was not a snug fit, and when left open on the top, the pistol could easily be dislodged. Moreover, with the pistol butt turned forward, it still required a corkscrew motion to draw and clear leather.

All things considered, the military holster was a distinct liability for a lawman.

Today, after leaving the jail, Clint walked west on a side
street. Only last week, with a solution in mind, he'd paid a
call on the local saddlemaker. Together, they had designed a
whole new rig, one suited to a lawman's needs. Whether or
not the idea would work remained to be seen. Charlie Webb,
the saddlemaker, had promised the holster for today, but with
no guarantees. He'd never before attempted anything quite
like it.

Webb looked up from his workbench as Clint entered the
shop. The saddlemaker was a slender man with heavily mus-
cled forearms and hands stained dark from working with
leather. He put aside a hammer and punch and nodded affa-
bly.

" 'Mornin', Marshal.''

"Charlie," Clint said, returning the nod. "How're
things?''

"Fair to middlin'," Webb allowed. "Guess you'd like to
see your new holster?''

"Yeah, I would.''

Webb opened a drawer underneath his workbench. He removed a small bundle wrapped in an oiled cloth. After peel-
ing away the cloth, he proudly handed the holster to Clint.
His mouth split in a wide grin. "I think you're gonna like
it.''

The holster was fashioned of medium-weight leather. Unlike the old military rig, the top was open and cut on a slant
to cover the pistol cylinder and trigger guard. On the bottom
side, the belt loop was stitched to cant the pistol slightly forward, with the hammer facing forward and the butt to the
rear. After being formed, the holster had been soaked overnight in a pail of water. Then a well-greased .36 Navy Colt
had been placed in the saturated holster and allowed to dry
in strong sunlight. The end result was a molded, glove-tight
fit.

"Damn nice," Clint said with undisguised admiration. "You've got a way with leather, Charlie."

"Tell you the truth, it turned out better'n I expected. Fits so tight it's pretty near like a second skin. You can turn it upside down and the gawddamn gun still won't shake out."

"How's it do on the draw?"

"Pops out slick as spit. Whyn't you give 'er a try and see for yourself?"

Webb hauled out a gunbelt that he'd fashioned specially for the holster. Clint removed the old military flap-top and laid it on the workbench. He then strapped on the new rig and buckled it to ride just below his pants' belt. The holster was positioned over his hipbone and canted forward at a slight angle. When he shoved the Colt into the open top, the molded leather closed on the metal like a pliable vise. The gun butt was fixed at waist level, quick to hand.

Gingerly, for the Colt was loaded, Clint tried a few slow-speed draws. A slight tug popped the gun loose and the arm's forward motion brought it level. Only a few tries convinced Clint that the hammer could be cocked even as the gun was being drawn. The natural balance of the Colt made pointing it almost instinctive, and alignment, with the forearm extended at waist level, was something sensed by feel alone. He tried one last draw, taking it a shade faster.

"Feels good," he said, holstering the Colt. "Damn near jumps into your hand."

Webb nodded. "Wasn't that what you wanted?"

"What you want and what you get aren't always the same. You pulled it off in spades, Charlie."

"Then mebbe you won't mind if I ask you a question?"

"Ask away."

Webb gave him a scrutinizing look. "Got to wonderin' if you aim to be a lawman all your life?"

"Hard to say," Clint said impassively. "Hadn't given it much thought. What makes you ask?"

"Well . . ." Webb tried for an offhand tone. "There's talk around town. Folks say you're a cool one."

An ironic smile touched Clint's face. "Some people probably say worse than that."

"Yeah, they do," Webb said with a graveled chuckle. "There's them who tend to believe you piss ice water."

Clint's smile broadened. "I reckon they're the ones with knots on their heads. Drunks and rowdies always take things too personal."

"I suppose so," Webb said, suddenly serious. " 'Course, most of the talk has to do with Sam Baxter, the way you killed him."

Clint's features took on a hard cast. "What about it?"

Webb eyed him obliquely. "They say you do it awful easy—sorta natural."

"That a fact?" Clint said, no timbre in his voice. "So what's that got to do with me being a lawman all my life?"

There was the merest beat of hesitation. Webb told himself he'd overstepped some invisible boundary. The marshal was clearly prodded by strange devils all his own and would tolerate few questions about the men he'd killed. Discretion abruptly seemed the wiser course.

"Just curious," he said casually. "You was mighty particular about that gun rig. Figgered you had a reason."

"You figured right," Clint said stolidly. "I had my reasons."

The conversation ended on that cryptic note. An hour later, however, Clint's reasons would have become apparent to even the most casual observer. At the hotel, he collected a powder flask and a bag of .36-caliber balls he'd molded himself. Then, behind a saloon, he gathered a gunnysack of empty whiskey bottles. The sack over his shoulder, he walked toward the outskirts of town.

The river was molten with sunlight. He stopped where driftwood and flotsam were snagged on a bend in the shoreline. Emptying the gunnysack, he stood a line of bottles on the trunk of an uprooted tree. Turning away, he stepped off ten paces and halted. His arms loose at his sides, he faced the bottles.

On a silent count of three, his hand moved. The Colt popped out of the holster and there was a metallic whirr as he thumbed the hammer. His arm leveled and the pistol belched a dense cloud of smoke. Fanned by the breeze, the smoke drifted away as he worked the hammer and feathered the trigger. One after another, five bottles exploded in a shower of glass.

Satisfied with the results, he set about reloading the Colt. The process was time-consuming, and several minutes passed before cap and ball were properly seated. Holstering the pistol, he walked at a measured pace toward the uprooted tree. Gunmetal flashed in the sun and a bottle blew apart. He continued to advance, holstering the Colt, then drawing and firing each time he took another step. A few paces from the tree, the last bottle erupted in glittery shards of glass.

The holster served the purpose he'd intended. He figured that within the span of a couple of heartbeats he was able to draw the Colt and get off an accurate shot. Even in a tight situation—where he was shooting at a man instead of bottles—it was quick enough to get the job done. When the chips were down, no one could ask for more.

As he walked back to town, his thoughts turned to Belle London. On occasion, he had dropped by the parlor house and spent a few minutes in idle chitchat. She'd made it plain that he was welcome to one of the girls, but he had let the offer pass. His interest was in her, even though madams never socialized with customers. Or lawmen.

Still, he'd made it his business to ask around. Madams generally socialized within the sporting crowd, taking a gambler or a grifter of some sort as their lovers. Yet, so far as anyone knew, Belle London had no gentlemen friends. He found that the least bit odd, for she was an attractive woman. He also saw it as a challenge, an added enticement. A madam who was choosy was a woman worth the chase.

On Blake Street, he passed a handbill tacked to the wall of a building. The announcement, in bold type, urged everyone to attend a public meeting being held that night. He was reminded of the conversation he'd had with Virgil yesterday evening. While he'd only listened, he was disturbed by what he heard. Virgil was being drawn ever deeper into the town's affairs. Worse, he was beginning to form alliances with the big muckamucks of Denver.

Word around the sporting district told the story. A sometimes lawyer, David Hughes was in fact the town's chief puppet master. He pulled the strings and Mayor Stodt danced accordingly. In turn, the mayor delivered orders to Ed Case, and Case delivered the sporting district vote. It was a cozy arrangement, one hand washing the other down the line. Yet, where politics were concerned, such things generally worked out to be an alliance of thieves. And men with a mutual interest in shady deals inevitably played rough.

Last night, Clint had kept his opinion to himself. Virgil wasn't much on taking advice, particularly when he was running red-hot with ambition. But now, studying the handbill, Clint wished he'd gone ahead and spoken his piece. Quite probably, he told himself, it would be a waste of breath. But then again, nothing ventured, nothing gained.

He walked off toward the warehouse.

20

THE PUBLIC MEETING WAS held at Cole's Hall on Larimer Street. Soon after dark that night a crowd began congregating outside on the boardwalk. By seven o'clock, almost a thousand people packed the large central gallery.

Cole's Hall was used for civic gatherings and community social affairs. Tonight, however, the throng was composed entirely of men. No women were in attendance for the simple reason that Denver's business, whether uptown or downtown, was a male domain. Merchants and storekeepers, as well as gamblers and dance-hall operators, were wedged shoulder to shoulder in the hall.

Smoke from cigars and pipes hung thick over the crowd. The warm night air, compounded by the press of bodies, quickly turned the hall stifling. Some men fanned themselves with their hats while others mopped sweat with their kerchiefs. The hum of conversation was filled with curiosity and an undercurrent of mild apprehension. Wild rumors circulated freely, and most of them had to do with the Union Pacific. No one thought the meeting had been called to announce good news.

Earl arrived shortly after seven. He found Clint posted at the rear of the hall, where he could keep an eye on the crowd. Halting beside him, Earl nodded just as an expectant hush fell over the assemblage. Down front, several men mounted a raised platform and took chairs behind a speakers' podium. Among the dignitaries were Mayor Stodt, Walter Tisdale, David Hughes, and Luther Evans. Virgil, who was dressed in his new suit, was seated beside Hughes. Behind them, like owls on a perch, were the ministers of various local churches. The clergy, obviously, had been enlisted to lend an upright air to the proceedings.

The mayor walked directly to the podium. He raised his arms overhead. "Friends and fellow citizens!"

Silence descended on the crowd. He paused a moment for effect, staring out across the room. "We gather tonight," he said in a booming voice, "because our community is at a critical juncture. What we do here may well determine whether Denver endures—or withers away!"

A startled murmur swept through the onlookers. Timing it perfectly, Stodt moved away from the podium as they settled down. He began pacing back and forth across the platform, encompassing them all with a baroque sweep of his arms. His voice was pitched an octave below a shout and filled with urgency. The crowd was held spellbound by his performance, listening intently.

Stodt took them step by step through past negotiations with the Union Pacific. With David Hughes' assistance, he revealed, the mayor's office had worked to bring the railroad to Denver. He interrupted his litany and took a moment to praise Hughes as a civic benefactor and a man of great public spirit. Then he railed at the Union Pacific and cursed their perfidy. The railroad, he thundered, was going to Cheyenne—not Denver!

Loud protests erupted from the spectators. Stodt moved to the edge of the platform, stilled them with upraised arms. His demeanor suddenly changed and his voice took on an optimistic note. All was not lost, he told them, for certain men believed deeply in the future of Denver. He ticked off the names of the men seated behind him, and briefly alluded to their plans for a publicly owned railroad. Speaking rapidly, he then went on to outline the need for a board of trade.

All major cities, he noted, maintained a board of trade. Community planning, as well as the actions necessary to implement those plans, was the business of such an organization. The single-minded goal, he observed, would be the growth and prosperity of Denver. But such an organization required a leader—he paused for dramatic effect—a man of dedication and selfless devotion to the town's welfare. He believed that man to be one of Denver's upcoming young go-getters, a regular fireball of energy: Virgil Brannock!

Working the crowd expertly, Stodt rammed through ratification of a board of trade. His tone almost evangelistic, he next secured a unanimous vote installing Virgil as president of the board. Striding back and forth, punctuating his speech with vigorous gestures, he urged the assemblage to rally behind the board and bring Denver into its own. Finally, calling for a vote of acclamation, he introduced Virgil. The spectators responded with a burst of applause and shouts of approval.

Virgil marched to the podium. He acknowledged the applause with a modest smile, waiting for the commotion to die down. Everyone in the hall was aware of his growing business empire and his reputation for shrewd investments. Tonight, for the first time, they recognized as well that he had the undivided support of the town's most powerful men. They stared up at him with the rapt expression normally reserved for sword-swallowers and trapeze artists. When he finally spoke, Virgil's voice was charged with vitality.

"You've honored me here tonight and I won't let you down. Together, we'll bring the railroad to Denver and put it on the map. Here's how we go about it."

In quick order, Virgil outlined the reasons for building a railroad to Cheyenne. He next revealed that incorporation papers had already been drawn for the Denver Pacific Railroad Company, with an initial stock issue of two million dollars. The men seated on the platform had invested a hundred thousand dollars of their own money and would serve as the company's board of directors. Accordingly, in a meeting held earlier, they had selected David Hughes as president of the railroad.

All that, Virgil advised them, was merely a beginning. The monumental task of financing the railroad was now ahead of them. In the weeks to come, everyone in town would be asked to throw their support behind the campaign to raise funds. Businessmen and merchants, as well as workingmen, would be urged to purchase stock in the corporation. Those who couldn't afford it now would be asked to make pledges for the future, or donate so many days' labor to track construction. The Denver Pacific, he declared, would be the people's railroad.

The statement was greeted with a fresh burst of applause. Virgil waited until the hall went quiet before he put the capper on his argument. Those who purchased stock, he observed, would one day retire wealthy men. The Denver Pacific, at least for the near future, would have a monopoly on railroad traffic into Colorado Territory. A wise man, he went on, wouldn't hesitate to invest all he possessed in such a venture. And at the same time, invest in the future of Denver!

Mayor Stodt led the applause when Virgil sat down. The next speaker to be introduced was David Hughes. His manner was restrained and businesslike, almost formal. Yet his voice had the quiet ring of prophecy, and men found themselves nodding in agreement as he spoke. He promised that the railroad would bring an era of growth and prosperity to Denver. Moreover, he announced, as a railway center Denver would overshadow Golden, its only rival. One day, the territorial capital would be located along the banks of Cherry Creek.

For a moment, there was absolute stillness. Then, as Hughes returned to his seat, a roar of approval shook the hall.

Stodt attempted to quiet the crowd, but with no effect. Others who were scheduled to speak, among them Walter Tisdale and several church leaders, conceded that it would be futile to try. Like converts to a cause, the spectators' enthusiasm was contagious, feeding on itself. Shouting over the clamor, Stodt adjourned the meeting.

Earl and Clint watched as men swarmed around the speakers' platform. Stodt and Hughes, as well as Virgil, were surrounded by groups of men eager to learn more about the railroad's plans.

After several minutes, it became apparent that Virgil would be occupied for the balance of the evening. Earl nudged his younger brother, and moved through the door. Clint followed him outside.

On the street, they turned downtown. Neither of them seemed inclined to speak, and they walked some distance in silence.

Finally, Clint shook his head with a bitter laugh. "Know what it reminded me of?"

"What?"

"A medicine show," Clint said. "Stodt looked like he was making a pitch off the back of a wagon."

"I hate to say it," Earl remarked, "but Virgil wasn't much better. He's wound up like a three-day clock."

Clint's brow puckered in a frown. "I tried to talk some sense into him last night. He got real huffy about the whole thing."

"You mean the board of trade?"

"Yeah, partly that," Clint said. "Mostly, though, I was talking about David Hughes."

Earl raised a questioning eyebrow. "What about him?"

"Way I hear it, he's the big auger around town. He says 'frog' and people tend to squat."

"Denver's no different than any other town. There's somebody like Hughes wherever you go."

"Maybe so," Clint said in a flinty voice. "Only problem

is, Hughes has got his hooks into Virge. Seems to me that makes a powerful difference.''

Earl was silent a moment. ''You think there's something fishy about this railroad deal?''

''Hard to say one way or the other. I just don't put a helluva lot of faith in politicians. They're generally the least bit slippery.''

''True,'' Earl conceded. ''But Virgil's pretty levelheaded. He'd be hard to fool.''

Clint shook his head in exasperation. ''Virge has got his sights set on big things. He'd do cartwheels to get himself accepted by the uptown crowd.''

''Nothing wrong with that. A man has to better himself any way he can.''

''No, he don't,'' Clint said, his face set in stubborn disapproval. ''Not if it means throwing in with a bunch of crooks.''

Earl's features congealed into a scowl. ''You oughtn't to say that too loud. You've got no proof that Hughes is a crook.''

Clint fixed him with a careful, observant look. ''Hughes runs city hall like he foreclosed on the mortgage. Leastways, that's how I get the story.''

''So?''

''So the mayor's his errand boy. And Stodt's thick as thieves with Ed Case, isn't he?''

''Just like that.'' Earl held up two joined fingers. ''But it doesn't especially prove anything.''

''It proves they run this town to suit themselves. How'd you like to see Virge crawl in bed with that crowd?''

''I suppose I wouldn't like it.''

''Then maybe you ought to talk to him yourself. He might listen to you.''

''What makes you think so?''

''Tell me something,'' Clint asked, his eyes grave. ''How'd Ed Case take over the sporting district?''

"The usual way," Earl said with a shrug. "He killed anybody that got in his road."

Clint was thoughtful for a time. He was tempted to ask why Earl was on the outs with Ed Case. But his brother was a private man, and he knew better than to pry. Some things were best left unasked.

"Virge will listen," he said at length. "You wouldn't be repeating secondhand stories. You were here when Hughes and Stodt made their deal with a killer. That makes them just as rotten as Case himself."

"I'll try," Earl said with no inward conviction. "Not that I ever had any great influence with Virgil."

"All he can do is tell you to save your breath."

Earl forced a wry smile. "You probably took the words right out of his mouth."

Clint nodded, then smiled a little. There seemed nothing left to say on the subject of their older brother, and neither of them pressed it further. They walked on toward the sporting district.

21

CHOIR PRACTICE WAS OVER at nine. Elizabeth avoided becoming entangled in conversation with the other ladies. She bid the choir director good night, collecting her shawl on the way out.

On the steps of the church she paused, visibly surprised. Virgil normally waited outside and walked her home. Tonight, though he'd said nothing earlier, he was standing beside a rented horse and buggy. She wondered if the change marked a celebration of his new appointment.

Virgil greeted her with a wide grin. Taking her hand, he assisted her into the buggy as if it were part of their customary routine. Then he climbed aboard, still smiling like a Cheshire cat, and popped the reins. The horse dutifully set out at a plodding trot, and they headed toward the river road. At last, Virgil glanced around at her.

"Well?" he said cheerily. "Aren't you going to ask?"

"Ask what?"

"About the meeting . . . what else!"

"Oh, that," she teased. "I'd almost forgotten it was tonight."

"Thanks a lot. You really know how to rain on a parade."

She patted his arm. "You poor dear. Now I've gone and hurt your feelings."

"You couldn't," Virgil said, grinning broadly. "Not tonight."

"I take it things went well?"

Virgil could contain himself no longer. He laughed out loud, slowly wagged his head. "You should've seen it, Beth! They like to tore the house down when Stodt proposed my name. They gave me a unanimous vote of approval!"

"Of course they did," she said airily. "After all, who else would they select? You were the logical choice."

"Not just exactly," Virgil corrected her. "Hughes could just as easily have tapped Luther Evans. He's been around lots longer than I have."

"Fiddlesticks! Luther Evans doesn't have half your ability. He never will."

Virgil gave her a sly look. "Funny you'd say that. I thought you were sweet on him once."

She stared back at him with round, guileless eyes. At one time or another, every eligible bachelor in town had camped on her doorstep. Luther Evans was simply one of many, even though he'd thought himself the front runner. In truth, no one stood out from the crowd, for she had despaired of ever finding the right man. Until now . . .

"You must be joking," she replied in an incredulous tone. "Luther was merely a friend, an occasional escort. And nothing more, thank you!"

"Glad to hear it," Virgil said without irony. "Guess I must've misread things."

"Indeed you did," she said promptly. "But let's not waste time on Luther Evans. Tell me all about the board of trade— your plans."

Virgil seemed to sit straighter. "Beth, tonight's only the beginning. Once we've got a railroad, the sky's the limit. You mark my word."

She gave him a fetching smile. "Aren't we confident? You sound like the railroad will begin operating any day now."

"Soon," Virgil promised. "Lots sooner than anyone thinks. I've got a stake in pushing it through."

"A stake?"

"As of tonight, I'm a stockholder in the Denver Pacific. Your father loaned me the money to buy ten thousand shares."

She smiled a little uncertainly. "Are you sure that's wise, borrowing money for something so speculative?"

"Ask your father," Virgil said lightly. "He bought a whale of a lot more than that."

"Yes, but there's a difference. He's a banker, and everyone looks to him for leadership. He had to set the example."

"So do I, and maybe more so. I'm the one who's going to ask people to invest every last nickel. The whole town has to get behind it."

"Will they?" she asked. "Are they so convinced it will work?"

"You should've been there tonight. You wouldn't have to ask."

"It's just . . ." She hesitated, searching for words. "Well, it's just such an enormous amount of money. I mean, mercy sakes . . . two million dollars!"

"Got a nice ring, doesn't it?"

"But will people invest so much on a hope?"

"Hope makes the world go round," Virgil assured her earnestly. "Don't worry your head about the money. I'll get every cent of it."

A horned moon slipped from behind a cloud. She studied him in the dappled light, more aware than ever of his determination and strength of character. Over the past few weeks, in what seemed quicksilver splinters of time, he had gradually revealed himself to her. She had discovered that he was sensitive and warm, while at the same time possessed of a force of will that was rocklike. He never doubted himself, never wavered.

Virgil was the first man who'd even come close to her hidden fantasies. She wanted someone who took her breath away, made her think wicked thoughts. While she'd known handsomer men, Virgil was the only one who kindled those secret yearnings and gave her sleepless nights. As for his crippled hand, it bothered her not at all, detracted nothing from what she felt. She preferred him to any man she'd ever met, just the way he was. And she wanted desperately for him to ask the only question that mattered.

"The railroad," she said in a musing tone, "it means everything to you, doesn't it?"

Virgil nodded. "Like I said, it's only the beginning. All that Eastern money will come running once we've got a railroad."

"What Eastern money?"

"I'll tell you a secret. Something I haven't told Hughes or anyone else."

"Yes, do," she breathed. "I want to be the one who shares your secrets."

Her voice had an electric effect on him. When he spoke, it was as though he saw a vision revealed. "The railroad's only a springboard. I intend to use the board of trade for bigger things. We'll lure some industrialists out here, maybe some Wall Street investors. Show them there's more to Denver than the mining camps."

"Oh, Virgil," she marveled. "You truly believe that, don't you?"

"Watch me," Virgil said confidently. "I see Denver as the great Western metropolis. One day, we'll be the biggest thing between St. Louis and San Francisco. I intend to have a hand in making it happen."

Elizabeth felt a warm glow of revelation. She saw now that her father had been right all along. He'd said that Virgil was a visionary, a man who dreamed outlandish dreams. And through sheer determination, a man who made his dreams come true. She took a silent oath to share it with him, whatever he dreamed.

"Would it embarrass you," she said softly, "if I told you a secret . . . a family secret?"

"Well, no, I guess not."

"Promise you won't get swellheaded?"

Virgil appeared somewhat baffled. "I'll do my best. Why, what is it?"

She cocked her head with a funny little smile. "Daddy thinks you're destined for great things. Your ears would burn if you heard him brag on you. He says you're a man with the golden touch."

"No kidding?" Virgil's features reddened. "He really said that?"

"Oh, that and more. He admires what he calls your 'gumption.' "

"Gumption's not worth a hill of beans by itself. Without the money he's loaned me, I'd never have got a start."

"Yes, you would," she said with utter certainty. "Daddy says you would have found a way, with or without him. I believe that, too."

Virgil glanced at her out of the corner of his eye. "Since we're trading secrets, maybe you'd like to hear another one."

"Aren't you the naughty one?" She scooted closer, put her hand through his arm. "I don't want any secrets between us, Virgil. Never ever."

Virgil appeared nonplussed. Her admonition sounded possessive and somewhat permanent. Uncertain how to reply, he went on with what he was about to say.

"I've got my eye on some land. Several acres, as a matter of fact. Just west of the warehouse."

"But there's nothing there. It's just . . . land."

"Exactly," Virgil said with a wry chuckle. "And I can get it dirt-cheap."

"Yes, but why would you?"

"Once the railroad hits town, we're in for boom times. Denver will grow and keep on growing. I intend to make a fortune on that piece of land."

She laughed happily. "Honestly, Virgil! You'll make a prophet out of Daddy yet. I know you will!"

Virgil reined into a clearing overlooking the river. Looping the reins on the footboard, he turned to face her. Sallow moonlight reflected off the water, framing her in an umber glow. Her hair was drawn sleekly back, accentuating the smooth contours of her features. There was an enchanting verve about her, a mixture of gaiety and innocence. Yet, beneath the surface, he detected something magical, the smoldering sensuality of a girl about to discover her womanhood. He found the combination irresistible.

Watching her, Virgil felt somehow starstruck, lightly drunk. He was not glib or clever, and what he'd brought her here to say seemed to defy words. His throat was parched and his mouth felt dry and pasty all at the same time. He sat for a long moment, staring at her with an odd steadfast look. Then, finally, he summoned some inner reservoir of nerve. He took her hands into his own.

"I suppose you're wondering why I rented the rig . . . brought you out here."

Her heart pounded so hard she thought it would burst. She nodded, squeezing his hands. "Yes," she said simply, fearful of saying too much. "I suppose I did."

"Beth . . ." He faltered, then rushed on in a somber tone. "I'm not much with words, so I'll just ask you straight out. Will you do me the honor of marrying me?"

"Yes, Virgil." Her voice dropped to a whisper. "I will."

"You will—!"

Virgil pulled her into his arms. Her hands went behind his neck and she embraced him with a fierce, passionate urgency. His arms tightened, strong and demanding, and he kissed her as though he would never let her go. When at last they separated, her eyes were shining moistly and her voice was breathless.

"Oh, Virgil, I thought you'd never ask."

22

BY THE SECOND WEEK in August, the Denver Pacific was an ongoing concern. The *Rocky Mountain News* trumpeted the story in every issue and the townspeople talked of little else. There was a consensus that Denver would, after all, get its railroad.

Virgil worked closely with Will Byers on the project. The editor was a member of the board of trade, and he used his newspaper to laud those who had invested in the railroad. In slightly more than a week, they had raised an additional hundred thousand dollars. Virgil devoted every spare moment to the campaign, pressing the town's merchants and businessmen to invest in their own future. The response, on the whole, had been notably positive.

Still, there was much to be achieved. Virgil was afire with enthusiasm and impatient with those who dragged their feet. The money raised to date represented only a tenth of the total funds needed. Construction was scheduled to begin the spring of '66, and that left scarcely eight months to make the railroad a solvent proposition. There seemed too little time for all that remained to be done.

Of particular concern to Virgil was the sporting district. Some saloonkeepers and gambling impresarios had invested nominal amounts in the venture. Others, despite considerable arm-twisting, had proved reluctant and oddly cautious. Hesitant to trade on blood ties, Virgil hadn't yet called on Earl. Today, however, he meant to rectify that oversight. The sporting crowd, though rolling in cash, seemed entirely too tight-fisted. He thought one of their own would do well to set the example.

Earl welcomed the visit. Until now, there had been no opportunity to raise the subject of David Hughes. He hadn't seen Virgil since the night of the public meeting, and he'd been hesitant to broach the matter too openly. Even now, he was none too confident that Virgil could be dissuaded. Yet he'd promised Clint to try, and he never went back on his word.

After Virgil was seated, Earl closed the office door. He returned to the desk and lowered himself into the creaky chair. Offering Virgil a cheroot, he struck a sulfurhead and they both lit up in a haze of smoke. He smiled amiably.

"Clint tells me congratulations are in order. When's the big day?"

"Week from Saturday," Virgil said, puffing smoke. "We're getting married at the Methodist church. You'll be there, won't you?"

"Wouldn't miss it for the world. Not every day a Brannock gets hitched to the banker's daughter."

"Sorry I didn't come by and tell you myself. I've been so damned busy I feel like a one-legged man in a kicking contest."

"So I heard." Earl flicked an ash off his cheroot. "How're things in the railroad business?"

"Good enough uptown," Virgil said pointedly. "Not so hot down here. That's what I've come to see you about."

"I don't follow you."

"Denver's been good to you, Earl. You've got a snazzy place and you're bound to be making big money."

"So?"

"So it's time to pay your dues. The town needs a railroad and everybody has to bear their fair share. I'd like to see you invest a sizable chunk in the Denver Pacific."

Earl examined the notion. "I guess I'll have to pass. I make it a practice never to take cards in another man's game."

Virgil's gaze was inquisitive, oddly perplexed. "What's that supposed to mean?"

"I've got no faith in your uptown crowd. I'd say the railroad's a pretty iffy proposition."

"You listen to me," Virgil said shortly. "David Hughes has connections in Washington. He's got a man there who's working on our behalf right now. And when the land grant comes through—"

Earl interrupted him. "What land grant?"

"A cool million acres," Virgil said, grinning. "Have you got any idea of what that'll be worth?"

"No, can't say that I do."

"Well, I'll let you in on a secret. Homesteaders and ranchers are always looking to buy more land. So we're talking about a ten- or fifteen-million-dollar windfall. Denver Pacific stock will go straight through the roof!"

"Anything's possible," Earl observed neutrally.

"Mark my word," Virgil said firmly. "Hughes will pull it off somehow. And you'd better get on the bandwagon now— or get left behind."

A note of concern came into Earl's voice. "Tell you the truth, it's Hughes that bothers me. I think you're in over your head, Virge."

Virgil looked surprised, then suddenly irritated. "Suppose you spell that out for me."

"Whatever Hughes has in mind, it's not civic virtue. He means to line his own pockets on the deal, and devil take the hindmost. You could wind up holding the bag."

"You sound like Clint," Virgil grumbled. "He's got some

wild hair about Hughes, too. Tried to tell me I'd thrown in with a fast crowd.''

''You have,'' Earl said reasonably. ''Hughes runs everything in this town. That includes the mayor and city hall *and* Ed Case. They're fast and they're crooked, the whole bunch—top to bottom.''

Virgil waved his hand as though dusting away the problem. ''Hughes does what he has to where politics are concerned. That has nothing to do with the railroad.''

''Believe what you want,'' Earl said, just a hint of reproach in his voice. ''But you're liable to wish you'd listened before it's over.''

''I'll thank you not to lecture me. I'm more than able to look after myself.''

Earl appeared saddened. ''You lie down with dogs, you get up with fleas. When you start itching, you won't have to look any further than Hughes.''

Virgil stubbed out his cheroot in an ashtray. He stood, glaring down at Earl a moment, then marched to the door. As he went out, Monte appeared in the hallway.

''Well, hello there,'' she said pleasantly. ''Congratulations on your—''

Virgil brushed past her. Somewhat taken aback, she stared after him as he stormed off down the hall. A moment elapsed, then she turned and looked at Earl.

''What's with your brother?''

''I think he just discovered an itch.''

''Itch?''

''Yeah, we've been talking about dogs and fleas.''

Earl managed a strained smile. Watching him, Monte thought it was a miserable attempt at humor. He looked like a man who'd just lost his best friend. Or an older brother.

The moon heeled over in the sky. All along Blake Street the dives were closing for the night. Drunks and stragglers crowded the boardwalks, slowly winding their way home.

Lights began flickering out in some of the small saloons.

Clint stood beneath a lamppost. Every night, as closing time approached, he positioned himself midway along the street. Stubborn drunks often refused to be turned out of an establishment, and the disputes sometimes became violent. He moved quickly and decisively when that occurred. Any man who resisted spent the night in the town cooler.

Closing time always struck Clint as strangely unnatural. As the saloons and dance halls emptied, an eerie silence settled over the sporting district. The laughter and music, all the sounds of festive revelers, abruptly stopped. When the lights were extinguished, any sense of glamour went by the boards as well. Blake Street, darkened and quiet, was transformed into a bloozy, careworn hag.

Watching things shut down was a time of waiting and boredom for Clint. Tonight, as the street slowly cleared, his thoughts turned to Virgil. Earlier, he'd stopped by the Bella Union and talked with Earl. What he heard had left him all the more troubled, and somewhat at a loss. Virgil apparently wouldn't listen to anyone, including Earl. His involvement with Hughes and his commitment to the railroad had clearly become a touchy subject. No amount of argument would faze him or change his mind.

What worried Clint most was Virgil's obsessive ambition. He knew it wasn't prompted by greed, the desire merely to accumulate wealth. By nature, Virgil was a generous man, charitable to a fault. Instead, the ambition sprang from a lifetime of hardscrabble farming, a bleak hand-to-mouth existence. Virgil was determined to better himself, gain acceptance and influence among the uptown crowd. Money was merely a means to an end, for he had his eye on a far greater goal. He wanted membership in Denver's most exclusive club.

Clint fathomed all that easily enough. He understood that marrying a banker's daughter was, for Virgil, a major step in the quest for status and prominence. Yet he failed to understand why Virgil would rashly form an alliance with Denver's political kingpin. The decision seemed foolhardy and ill-conceived, born of ambition rather than common sense. He suspected that Virgil would be used and then discarded, perhaps made to serve as a scapegoat should the railroad fail to materialize. It bothered him even more that Virgil was the key figure in the drive to raise two million dollars. So much money was bound to cause sticky fingers.

Whether or not he'd misjudged the situation remained to be seen. Still, he had already considered and rejected the notion that David Hughes was a civic benefactor. Any politician worth his salt was, at the very least, a student of corruption and graft. And two million dollars was an inducement for all sorts of underhanded schemes. Should any of the money disappear, he felt certain that Virgil wouldn't walk away clean. The greater likelihood was that Hughes and his cronies would somehow cover their tracks. Which left Virgil to be thrown to the wolves.

Shoving off the lamppost, Clint decided to call it a night. The street was quiet and almost all the dives were now dark. Up ahead, he noted a spill of light through the doors of the Acme Saloon. Drawing closer, he became aware of loud, unruly voices. He walked directly to the batwing doors and peered inside. A man was sprawled on the floor, blood leaking from his mouth. Standing over him, fists cocked and cursing fluently, was Frank Purdy. The bartender appeared to be shouting at both men.

Clint remembered Purdy well. The day he'd killed Sam Baxter, he had also performed a citizen's arrest on Purdy. Short and wiry, with the strutting arrogance of a gamecock, Purdy fancied himself a dangerous man. While he'd threatened Clint for the arrest, nothing had come of it. In fact, since the incident, he had studiously avoided drawing Clint's attention. Until tonight.

"Stand where you are!"

The whipcrack command froze everyone in the saloon.

Clint pushed through the doors and walked forward, halting at the end of the bar. Purdy turned to face him, and a moment slipped past while they stared at each other. The man on the floor levered himself to a sitting position.

"What's the trouble?" Clint asked.

"Personal," Purdy said, his mouth a zigzag slit. "Nothing that concerns you."

"I'll be the judge of that. Why'd you hit him?"

"None of your goddamn business! I done told you it was private."

On sudden impulse, Clint decided to press even harder. He'd been on the lookout for a wise-ass, someone to use as an object lesson to other troublemakers. Frank Purdy's antagonistic manner and sharp tongue made him a perfect candidate.

"Unbuckle your gunbelt," he said evenly. "Drop it on the floor."

Purdy laughed a wild braying laugh. "Hell's bells, me and this feller are friends. You can't arrest me for a little dustup that don't mean nothin'."

Clint smiled. "I'm not arresting you, Purdy. I'm posting you out of town—"

"You're *what*?"

"—for a week, starting tonight. Now, drop that gunbelt."

An evil light began to dance in Purdy's eyes. "Whyn't you back off and save yourself some grief? I ain't broke no laws."

"I'm the law," Clint said with chilling simplicity. "And I just gave you an order."

Purdy grinned ferociously. "You're gonna play hell makin' it stick." His hand eased toward the pistol holstered at his side. "I won't be bullyragged by nobody."

"Go ahead," Clint said in an ominously quiet voice. "I'd enjoy punching your ticket."

Purdy seemed to be weighing the odds. As they stared at each other, he saw that Clint's eyes had taken on a cold tinsel glitter. He marked a look that he'd seen before, the eager, curiously impersonal look of a mankiller. His mouth lifted in an ashen grin.

"Forget it," he said in an aggrieved tone. "I ain't all that hot to kill a lawman."

"Purdy, listen close—I'll only say it once more—drop your gunbelt."

A short time later Clint deposited Purdy at the Overland Stage Line office. There was an early-morning stage to Central City, and Purdy was ordered to be on it. He understood there was no choice in the matter and wisely kept his mouth shut. A week in Central City seemed the better part of valor.

From the stage-line office, Clint walked over to Holladay Street. His humor was immensely improved by the thought that he'd put in a good night's work. By morning, the story of Purdy being posted from town would have made the rounds. The sporting crowd, being quick on the uptake, would know he had sent them a message. He figured he'd earned himself a treat.

Belle London answered his knock. The house was closed for the night and she was in process of locking up. When he invited her out for a late supper—or an early breakfast—a devilish smile played at the corners of her mouth. She invited him instead to join her in raiding the kitchen larder.

The stove was still warm, and Belle put on a pot of coffee. Then she laid out cold roast beef, a loaf of home-baked bread, and a wedge of pungent cheese. Clint polished it off in quick order and finished with a slice of angel cake. When he pushed his plate away, she poured two cups of coffee and joined him at the table. She regarded him with an amused look.

"You worked up quite an appetite tonight, Marshal."

Clint stirred sugar into his coffee. "Well, you know how it goes. Some nights are busier than others."

She laughed a deep throaty laugh. "Around here we pray for Sunday all week long. I think God invented it especially for working girls."

"Speaking of that, I've decided to pass on your offer. Hope the girls won't take it personal."

"Oh?" She raised an uncertain eyebrow. "Any particular reason you changed your mind?"

"Never changed it."

"I don't understand."

Clint's expression was that of a tethered ram. He looked her over with a bold, suggestive grin. "It's you or nobody. I never was content with second-best."

They sat there a moment, sparring without words, each imagining the thoughts of the other. She watched him intently, aware that he evoked feelings she hadn't experienced in a long time. She had a weakness for a good-looking man, especially one who was assured and mildly audacious. Yet she warned herself to beware of emotional ties and promises. The man seated across from her was like a wild and spirited hawk. He would always soar free.

"Tell me," she said tentatively. "What sort of arrangement did you have in mind?"

Clint shrugged, hands outstretched. "Name your own game and we'll play by house rules. I'm easy to please."

"Are you?" Her voice had a teasing lilt. "Was that why you turned down a whole houseful of girls?"

"Easy to please," Clint said with a lopsided grin, "doesn't mean a man can't be particular. I've got an idea we're alike in that respect."

"I suppose we could try it out . . . see how we like it."

"I'm of a similar mind myself."

"Well, then . . ." A vixen look touched her eyes. "Would you care to join me in the boudoir?"

"Yes, ma'am, I surely would."

Her lips curved in a sultry smile. She snuffed the lamp and led him from the kitchen. Upstairs, she admitted him to her private bedroom, which was frilly and feminine and smelled faintly of lilac. After she closed the door and threw the bolt, she turned with her arms held wide. He took her on her own terms.

23

ON THE LAST SATURDAY of August, carriages began arriving outside the Methodist church. The wedding ceremony was scheduled for one o'clock, and shortly before the hour the church bell started to peal.

The wedding of Walter Tisdale's daughter was considered the social event of the year. Invitations were greatly coveted, and it promised to be the most heavily attended function in recent memory. Denver's burgeoning elite, comprising principally businessmen and their wives, flocked to the affair with eager anticipation.

The premier attraction, understandably, was the bride. As a banker's daughter, Elizabeth was considered the great catch of Denver. Any bachelor of reputable standing had paid her court, always with an eye to marriage. Yet, until now, she had spurned their proposals without an instant's thought. There were rumors that the bridegroom had been handpicked by Walter Tisdale. The gossip was compounded by the fact that the banker had loaned Virgil a large amount of money, as well as sponsoring him in community affairs. Everyone believed there was more to the marriage than a simple love match.

By half-past twelve, the street was clogged with carriages. Outside the church, the guests stood in long lines, slowly filing up the steps. They conversed in low voices, and a good deal of the conversation revolved around the bridegroom's selection of a best man. The choice was between his two brothers: one the town marshal and the other a gambling impresario. There was conjecture that the middle brother, Earl, had been chosen as the most acceptable to the Tisdale family. The younger brother, even though he was a peace officer, was widely looked upon as a hired gunman. The gambler, by comparison, seemed the lesser of two evils.

Inside the church, the pews on the front row were reserved for family. On one side of the aisle, seated by herself, was Mrs. Louise Tisdale. On the other side, looking distinctly uncomfortable in a new store-bought suit, was Clint Brannock. The families had formally met for the first time only last night. A prenuptial dinner, held at the Tisdale home, had brought them together in a gesture of harmony and good will. Unlike her parents, Elizabeth found her future brothers-in-law to be genuinely interesting and excellent company. The Tisdales were gracious but hard-pressed to carry on a conversation. Neither of them had much in common with either a lawman or a gambler.

A few minutes before one, the bride's party gathered in the vestibule. Smiling nervously, Elizabeth stood with her hand tucked in her father's arm. Her cheeks were flushed with excitement and her eyes positively sparkled. Janet Upton, her closest friend and the maid of honor, was positioned a few steps to the front. The organ suddenly wheezed to life, filling the church with the first strains of the wedding march. The procession moved off in slow-step tempo, and Tisdale, beaming proudly, led his daughter through the central doorway.

All the way down the aisle, the guests craned and stretched for a better view of the bride. Elizabeth was a vision of loveliness, her hair upswept and crowned by a white tiara with a long veil. Her wedding gown rose demurely to the throat and hugged the curves of her body like melted ivory. There was an aura of virginal innocence about her, and yet the swell of her breasts and the flare of her hips emphasized the ripe sensuality of a woman. She looked radiantly beautiful and ablaze with happiness.

There were whispered exclamations as the onlookers sat stunned by the sight. But Elizabeth heard none of it, nor was she aware of her mother weeping quietly in the front pew. Her gaze was fixed instead on the man who awaited her at the altar. Her eyes met Virgil's and remained locked the entire time she moved down the aisle. His regard was steady, and she saw within his eyes something intensely emotional. His features abruptly altered with a flustered smile as she drew closer.

The organ mounted to a crescendo and the wedding party slowly veered away. The maid of honor proceeded to the left, and Elizabeth's father, with a final squeeze of her hand, moved aside. Virgil, with Earl a step behind, took his place and fell in beside her. Together, they joined hands and halted before the minister. The organ went still and a moment of hushed silence fell over the church. Then, holding a Bible, the minister looked out across the assemblage.

"Dearly beloved, we are gathered here in the sight of God . . ."

A buggy, decorated with colored streamers, was waiting at curbside. The wedding guests lined both sides of the walkway as Virgil and Elizabeth emerged from the church. Shouting congratulations, everyone began pelting them with handfuls of rice. They ran for the buggy.

For their honeymoon, the newlyweds would spend the weekend in a suite at the Denver House. Anything grander, such as a trip back East, had been deferred until another time. Virgil's business interests, along with the fund-raising, required his presence in Denver. On Monday, the couple would move into a home they'd purchased only last week. There, with new furniture and a wagonload of wedding gifts, they. would set up housekeeping.

The immediate family waited beside the buggy. Elizabeth first bussed Earl and Clint on the cheek and then moved to her parents. Virgil, looking mildly embarrassed by all the attention, shook hands with his brothers. At last, amid another round of congratulations and a fresh barrage of rice, the newlyweds were assisted into the buggy. With deliberate aim, Elizabeth tossed her bridal bouquet to the maid of honor. Virgil popped the reins and they took off to a rousing chorus of cheers.

Earl and Clint watched until the buggy was out of sight. When they turned back, the Tisdales were already surrounded by a group of well-wishers. Among other prominent guests in the crowd were David Hughes and Mayor Stodt. No one took notice of the brothers or offered to include them in the conversation.

Earl jerked his chin toward town. "C'mon, let's go. Nobody will know the difference."

Clint joined him and they strolled off down the street. Once they were out of earshot, Earl shook his head with sardonic amusement. He grunted a low chuff of mirth.

"Tell you the truth," he said, "I'm damn glad they're not my in-laws."

Clint smiled. "I've got a strong hunch the feeling's mutual."

"Well, what the hell! Virge got himself a damn fine woman. I guess that's what counts."

"Yeah, she seems pretty regular. I reckon he could've done lots worse."

Earl was silent a moment. "You know what gripes me the most? Nobody had the ordinary decency to invite Monte. You'd think Virge would've said something."

"Christ A'mighty!" Clint said, laughing. "We're lucky we got invited. It's not exactly our sort of crowd."

"Too bad we can't say the same for Virge."

Neither of them laughed after that. They walked along, resigned to what seemed an unavoidable fact. Their brother was now one of the uptown crowd.

Late that afternoon, Clint returned to his office. City court had just adjourned, and all of those arrested last night had been fined or released on bond. The jail was strangely quiet.

Seated at his desk, Clint began sorting through a stack of paperwork. The jailer was off duty until six o'clock, and with the lockup empty, there were no distractions. The routine duties, checking meal vouchers and authorizing requisitions, was the part of the job he thoroughly detested. He generally put it off until the last minute.

The door suddenly burst open. Monk Boyd, resident bouncer in Belle London's house, rushed into the office. His face was flushed and he was breathing heavily, as though he'd run a long distance. He slammed to a halt in front of the desk.

"Miz Belle sent me to fetch you!"

"What's the trouble, Monk?"

"There's been a shooting."

Clint got to his feet. "Anybody killed?"

"Not yet."

"What do you mean—not yet?"

Boyd gulped a breath. "They're still at it, Marshal. They got the whole goddamn street closed down."

"Slow down," Clint ordered. "Who's still at it? What street are you talking about?"

"The Row," Boyd said, jerking a thumb over his shoulder. "Mollie May and Sallie Purple are down there takin' potshots at each other."

"Out on the street?"

"Naw," Boyd said. "They're holed up in their houses. Tradin' shots across the street."

Clint started around the desk. "When did it start?"

"Just a few minutes ago. Miz Belle says for you to hotfoot it down there."

Outside the office, Clint took off at a fast walk. Through hard experience, he'd learned never to run to meet trouble. Shortness of breath and an unsteady hand were liabilities a peace officer could ill afford. Hurrying down Larimer, he maintained a brisk, ground-eating pace. Monk Boyd fell in beside him.

A block from the Row, Clint heard the flat report of a pistol shot. An instant later the sound of an answering shot echoed through the sporting district. His stride lengthened as he covered the last block and rounded the corner onto Holladay Street. Women stood in the doorways of parlor houses; clusters of men were gathered on the boardwalks. Midway down the block the crowd abruptly thinned out, and there was a clear space of several houses. Farther away, near the distant corner, another throng of spectators was visible.

The reason for the gap separating the onlookers immediately became apparent. A gunshot sounded, followed by a second, and puffs of smoke issued from the windows of two houses directly opposite each other. Clint spotted Belle as he pushed through the last of the spectators. She was standing in the open doorway of her house, sneaking looks around the doorjamb. He squeezed in beside her.

"What the hell set them off?"

"Same old story." Her eyes sparkled with suppressed mirth. "Sallie stole one of Mollie's girls, and I guess that was the last straw. Mollie declared war."

Clint studied the street a moment. "Has all the shooting been done from the inside?"

"Of course!" she quipped. "Only men stand out in the street and blast away at one another. Women are too smart for that."

"Do tell," Clint said soberly. "Suppose you forget the jokes and give me your educated guess. Are they trying to kill each other or not?"

Belle mulled it over a minute. Mollie May and Sallie Purple were avowed enemies. Their rivalry went back several years and sprang from the fact that their parlor houses were directly opposite each other. Until now, the feud had been restricted to name-calling and one hair-pulling contest. But the great taboo of whoredom was that a madam never stole a girl from another madam. By breaking the cardinal rule, Sallie Purple had elevated the animosity to a deadly level.

"Don't hold me to it," Belle said at length, "but I'd say they're letting off steam. Neither one of them has what you'd call a vicious streak."

Clint shook his head in wonder. "I'd hate to see what happened if they really got mad."

"Well, honeybun,"—her eyes were warm with laughter—"as everyone knows, the female is the deadliest of the species."

Clint gave her a sour look. His attention was diverted back to the street by another exchange of gunfire. A window in Sallie Purple's house shattered and someone inside let loose a screeching curse. Across the street, from Mollie May's house, a cackling laugh rocketed along the Row. The laugh trailed off into a long beat of silence.

Stepping out of the doorway, Clint walked to the center of the street. He was careful to stay back out of the line of fire, and he made no move to draw his gun. He halted where he could be seen from the windows of both houses.

"Mollie May!" he bellowed. "Sallie Purple! This is Marshal Brannock speaking. Do you hear me?"

When there was no answer, he advanced another step. "You ladies better pay damn close attention! Otherwise you'll just make more trouble for yourselves."

"All right," Sallie Purple yelled. "What d'ya want?"

"I want you to lay those guns down and walk outside. The next one that fires a shot will answer to me directly."

Sallie Purple laughed a tinny laugh. "You must think I'm a half-wit, Marshal. I'm not setting a foot outta here till you've got her gun."

"You lousy bitch!" Mollie May shouted. "Who says you're to be trusted?"

"Listen, you old bag of bones, everybody knows my word is good. You just ask—"

"Like hell! You stole Emmy Lou, you goddamn thief. How's that for trust?"

"Shut your mouths," Clint roared. "I want you out of there right now, both of you. No guns and no trouble. Let's go!"

A protracted stillness fell over the street. At last, the door of Sallie Purple's house slowly edged open. She stepped into view, her hands empty. Across the street, Mollie May emerged from her house, no weapon in sight. For an instant, they stood glaring spitefully at each other. Then, screaming curses, they rushed into the street.

Clint intercepted them just short of a collision. He cuffed both women upside the ear and sent them reeling. While they were still wobbling about dizzily, he collared them both by the scruff of the neck. Hoisting them up on their toes, he turned and danced them off in the opposite direction. He looked like a puppeteer jiggling live rag dolls.

The crowd hooted laughter. Someone broke out in applause and it quickly turned to a spontaneous ovation. Women standing in the doorways shouted catcalls at the two madams, and the men added a few uncomplimentary barbs of their own. Sallie Purple and Mollie May spat back a stream of hot-eyed invective.

Clint marched them along at a brisk clip. As he passed Belle's doorway, he glanced over at her. She laughed and lowered one eyelid in a bawdy wink. Then, as he neared the corner, the applause swelled even louder. He grinned and kept on walking.

24

VIRGIL LEFT THE HOTEL early on Monday morning. Elizabeth, who was still dressed in a filmy peignoir, saw him off at the door of their suite. Her arms wrapped around his neck, she gave him a long, intimate kiss. The effects of her goodbye lingered with him all the way to the lobby.

On the street, he turned downtown. Though his step was springy, the honeymoon weekend had taken its toll. He marveled again at Elizabeth's almost total lack of inhibition. Expecting shyness, he'd found instead that her passion was wild and almost inexhaustible. Their lovemaking had been filled with the zest of discovery, and apart from meals, they had scarcely gone out of the suite. However demure she appeared in public, she had cast aside any semblance of restraint once they were in bed. He was still amazed by the fiery nature of her hungers.

Approaching the warehouse, Virgil thought it was just as well that things were back to normal. Elizabeth would spend the day supervising the move into their new home and unpacking the trove of wedding gifts. By nightfall, when he arrived home for supper, her ardor would have been dampened somewhat. At least he hoped that was the case, for he wasn't at all sure he could maintain the pace she'd set over the weekend. Once a night seemed to him sufficient, even though she had easily coaxed him into repeated unions. The memory made him smile, and then he recalled that she expected him home for lunch. He had little doubt where that would lead.

Once in the office, he quickly discovered that nothing was back to normal. The wedding and arrangements for the new house had been at the expense of business affairs. The time he'd lost had created a logjam of matters that required immediate attention. The liquor business and organizing the icehouses were dependent on his day-by-day scrutiny. There was, moreover, the pressing responsibility of raising additional funds for the railroad. Staring at the pile of paperwork on his desk, he hardly knew where to start. He was reminded of the old adage about a one-armed paperhanger. Quite suddenly, he knew the feeling.

The situation went from bad to worse. Around midmorning, David Hughes' secretary arrived with an urgent summons. Virgil dropped everything and dutifully followed the man uptown. By the time he entered Hughes' office, he felt besieged on all sides. His humor was improved somewhat by the cordial reception. Hughes warmly congratulated him on the marriage, and Luther Evans, who was already there, offered his compliments. Having observed the formalities, Hughes then waved them to chairs. He went straight to the reason for the meeting.

"I asked you here because there's been a development in our plans. In fact, it's possibly the best of all news."

Hesitating, he played the silence for effect. Virgil and Evans stared at him, waiting expectantly. After a moment, he went on with an air of understated gusto.

"Washington has agreed to award us a land grant. Barring the unforeseen, I believe we've pulled it off."

Virgil smacked a fist into his palm. "By jingo," he said

vigorously. "Nothing will stop us now. We're on our way!"

"Not so fast," Hughes cautioned. "I regret to say there's a catch in the arrangement."

"What sort of catch?"

"Well, first off, the land grant has been reduced in size. Not appreciably, but enough to merit consideration. We're to receive nine hundred thousand acres."

"That's nothing," Virgil said, somewhat relieved. "A hundred thousand acres more or less won't damage our prospects."

"No, it won't," Hughes agreed. "However, Congress has attached a condition to the grant."

"A condition?"

Hughes nodded. "To secure the grant, our railroad must connect with both the Union Pacific *and* the Kansas Pacific. Otherwise, the award will be withdrawn."

"Damnation!" Virgil swore hotly. "We'll never make it. Not with the Kansas Pacific strapped for funds."

"You're too pessimistic, Virgil. I have a piece of good news there as well."

"You do?"

"Indeed," Hughes said in his rolling voice. "I'm reliably informed that Kansas Pacific representatives are negotiating with a group of investors. Their goal is to raise something on the order of six million dollars."

"Six million!" Virgil repeated incredulously.

"A nice round sum," Hughes said, smiling. "And more than enough for them to complete the line to Denver."

Virgil slowly became aware that Luther Evans hadn't opened his mouth. So far as he could tell, Evans was singularly unsurprised by these latest developments. He got the impression that Hughes' revelations were for his benefit alone.

"All this news," he asked carefully, "when did you hear about it?"

"Just this morning," Hughes replied. "Why do you ask?"

"Seems a mite coincidental. Getting word on the land grant and the KP . . . all at the same time."

Hughes looked at him blandly. "Are you questioning our good fortune, Virgil?"

"No," Virgil said in a low tone. "Just curious, that's all."

"I'm sorry to say the coincidence doesn't end there. We've also had some bad news."

"What's that?"

"We got a flat turndown by the Union Pacific. They refuse to help defray our construction costs."

Virgil rubbed his chin, thoughtful. "So we're back to where we started. We have to raise the full two million."

"Exactly," Hughes affirmed. "Which is why I asked Luther here this morning. We have to redouble our fund-raising efforts, and I believe he can be of assistance to you. Isn't that so, Luther?"

Evans made an expansive gesture. "Fund-raising isn't all that different from selling investors on speculative real estate. I've got some ideas that ought to work."

"Speaking of investors," Virgil said, addressing his remark to Hughes, "why don't we go after some outside investors ourselves? If the KP can do it, we shouldn't have any problem."

"On the contrary," Hughes said with a vague wave of his hand. "We're small potatoes compared to the KP. It wouldn't be worth our effort."

Virgil looked at him without expression. "You never know unless you try. There's lots of money back East—Chicago and New York."

Hughes laughed, but it didn't ring true. "I'm afraid you're daydreaming, Virgil. A hope and a promise simply won't attract venture capital."

"Seems to me a nine-hundred-thousand-acre grant represents more than a hope and a promise. It's the next thing to collateral."

"No," Hughes said with finality. "I won't have outsiders

meddling in our affairs. Besides, any hint of outside investors would damage our efforts locally.''

"How so?''

"Like everyone else, the people of Denver do only what's required of them. Any mention of outside capital would cause them to tighten their purse strings and play a waiting game. Why should they underwrite a railroad if others will do it for them?''

Something stuck in Virgil's mind. He'd been talking too fast to credit it a moment ago. But now, pausing to collect his thoughts, he heard again the remark about outside investors. He wondered what Hughes meant by "meddling in our affairs.''

"I'll have to be frank,'' he said, trying another tack. "I'm not sure we'll raise the whole amount locally. People won't go into hock or risk their life savings out of civic concern—''

"You'd be surprised,'' Evans interrupted. "Appeal to their greed and they'll gladly go out on a limb. It's human nature.''

"Crudely put,'' Hughes said in a measured tone. "But Luther's point is well taken. With the land grant, Denver Pacific stock is no longer a speculative venture. We're offering them the chance of a lifetime.''

"In other words,'' Virgil persisted, "you're turning thumbs-down on outside investors. No need to raise any false hopes, right?''

"No need whatever,'' Hughes said with a faint smile. "We'll keep it in the family, so to speak. Just ourselves and the people of Denver, of course.''

Virgil sighed inwardly. His expression betrayed nothing, but he was filled with sudden misgiving. Somewhere at the back of his mind a cold premonition surfaced and took shape. Things were not altogether as they appeared with the Denver Pacific.

The meeting ended with handshakes all around. Upon leaving, Virgil discovered that he'd acquired a fast-talking colleague. Luther Evans, one arm draped over his shoulder, began enlightening him on the subtleties of wooing the public.

A late-afternoon sun dipped toward the mountains. Some miles outside Central City four men rode with the sun at their backs. Their mounts were held to a sedate walk.

Frank Purdy rode beside the man called Quintin. After being exiled to Central City, he'd spent his time loafing around saloons. Drinking heavily and feeling sorry for himself, he had told his story to anyone who would listen. His second night in town he'd found a sympathetic ear.

Jack Quintin shared his distaste for lawmen. He was generous as well and insisted on buying the drinks. By the end of the night, Purdy looked upon Quintin and his two companions as old friends. They invited him to share their room in a fleabag, and he drunkenly accepted. When he awoke next morning, he had a raging hangover and some dim recollection of having taken an oath. He found that he'd been recruited into a gang of robbers.

Sober and reflective, Purdy decided he liked the idea. He quickly learned that he hadn't been selected at random. The night before, drunk and talkative, he'd done a bit of bragging. He and his former partner, Sam Baxter, had pulled a few holdups of their own. In relating the details of Baxter's death—killed by the lawdog who had posted him from Denver—he'd spilled the beans about their form of livelihood. His newfound friends proved to be a receptive audience.

As he got the story, Quintin and his men were only recently arrived in Colorado. Their journey to the mining camps had been by way of Santa Fe and northward through Raton Pass. While their specialty was horse stealing, Quintin admitted to a stagecoach holdup in New Mexico. But he knew nothing of the mountains or the gold camps, and he needed a man with expertise in such matters. Frank Purdy seemed to fit the bill.

Purdy was under no illusions. To a man, the gang members

were cold-blooded killers. He knew he'd been recruited because he was familiar with the roads and the mountainous
terrain. Still, he would have only one chance to prove himself.
Should he steer them wrong, there was no question that his
first job would be his last. For all that, he accepted the risk
with no great qualms. He had every intention of pulling his
own weight.

At Purdy's suggestion, their first job would be a late-
afternoon stage. After the holdup, they could then retreat into
the mountains under the cover of darkness. Waylaying a stage
between Central City and Denver merely increased their
chances of hitting a gold shipment. Among the mining camps,
Central City was the major producer of bullion. Since Denver
had the only bank, daily shipments were forwarded for de-
posit and safekeeping. The trick was to guess which stage—
morning or afternoon—carried the strongbox. Quintin agreed
that the afternoon stage was the better bet.

The spot selected was a wooded stretch on an uphill grade.
Quintin studied it with the eye of a man who knew something
of tactics. Then he posted his older hands, Tobert and Johnson, on the south side of the road. He next found a vantage
point for himself and Purdy on the north side, behind a large
boulder. Their horses were tied well back off the road, hidden
in the trees. With everything in order, they settled down to
wait.

Quintin was somewhat foreboding in appearance, almost
brutish. He was a gnarled, lynx-eyed man with a straight
mouth and a jutting chin. He affected a military bearing, and
by the way he rapped out orders, he was accustomed to being
obeyed. His purpose in taking a position with Frank Purdy
was all too clear. Today, quite obviously, was a test of sorts.
Should anything go wrong, he wanted the new man nearby.

The robbery went off without a hitch. On the uphill grade,
the stagecoach driver was forced to hold his horses to a walk.
At Quintin's signal, the gang stepped into the road just as the
lead horses topped the grade. They spread out, two at the front

and two at the sides, with the stage neatly boxed. All of them were masked, their guns drawn, and Quintin's commands were obeyed instantly. The express guard dropped his shotgun and obligingly tossed down the strongbox.

Quintin blew off the lock with his pistol. The contents, lumpy pouches of gold dust, were quickly transferred into saddlebags. The passengers, who had been forced to dismount, were relieved of their pokes and several hundred dollars in coin. Then everyone was ordered back aboard and the stage was allowed to proceed on its way. The holdup, start to finish, had taken less than ten minutes.

After the stage was out of sight, Quintin led the way back into the woods. No one spoke as Tobert and Johnson lashed the saddlebags on their own horses. Watching them, Purdy got a sour feeling in the pit of his stomach. His apprehension was borne out only a moment later. Quintin pulled his gun and placed the muzzle to Purdy's head. He slowly cocked the hammer.

"I was wonderin'," he inquired easily. "You reckon anybody on that stage might've recognized you?"

"Not a chance," Purdy said, licking his lips. "I never saw none of them boys before. Besides, I was masked, the same as you."

Quintin smiled, wolfish ridges at the corners of his mouth. "Why should I believe you?"

Purdy grinned weakly. " 'Cause I wouldn't hang around if I'd been spotted. I'd make tracks for elsewhere."

"Sounds reasonable." Quintin paused, fixed him with a baleful look. "Anything goes wrong, you'll wish I'd killed you now. You get my meanin'?"

"I ain't lyin'," Purdy said, his eyes round. "Honest to Christ!"

"Then I reckon we're in business, Frank."

Quintin laughed, lowering the hammer on his gun. He ordered everyone mounted, and Purdy, with a sense of deliverance, jumped to obey. A moment later they rode out of the woods.

25

THE HOLDUP GOT BANNER headlines. The September 4 edition
of the *Rocky Mountain News* devoted half the front page to
the robbery. On street corners and in saloons, no one talked
of anything else. The railroad, for the moment, was yesterday's news.

According to the newspaper, the haul from the robbery was
seven thousand dollars. Ben Holladay, owner of the Overland
Stage Line, was quoted as saying that the robbers would be
apprehended and brought to justice. Few people doubted his
sincerity, but the comment was regarded with skepticism.
Quotes from the driver and the express guard indicated that
none of the highwaymen had been identified. Hardly anyone
seriously believed they would be caught.

Holdups were by no means rare in the mining camps. On
an average of once a month someone would attempt to waylay
a gold shipment. For the most part, however, the holdups
were the work of a lone bandit, occasionally a pair of desperadoes. And more often than not, the bandits were killed
or driven off by the shotgun guard. Four robbers, working as
a team, was a sensation. Nothing like it had ever happened,

and people's imaginations were fired by the daring act. The word "gang" suddenly became part of their lexicon.

The morning after the holdup, Clint entered the First National Bank. A note, delivered by a messenger, had asked him to drop by the office of Walter Tisdale. His first reaction was that the banker wanted to discuss some matter involving Virgil. On second thought, he'd decided there was small likelihood that Tisdale would ask his advice on family affairs. All of which left him a bit mystified as to the reason for the summons.

Tisdale greeted him with reserved politeness. A tall, heavily built man seated before the desk rose as Clint entered the office.

The banker motioned Clint forward. "Clint Brannock," he said, indicating the other man, "I'd like you to meet Ben Holladay."

"Marshal." Holladay stuck out a hamlike hand. "Pleased to make your acquaintance."

"Mr. Holladay," Clint said, accepting his handshake. "Glad to know you."

Tisdale asked him to be seated. Clint took a chair beside Holladay, and the banker resumed his place behind the desk. After they were settled, Tisdale looked across at Clint.

"As you know, Mr. Holladay owns the Overland Stage Line. Yesterday one of his stages was robbed between here and Central City."

Clint nodded. "I read about it in the paper."

"We've asked you here," Tisdale went on, "to request your assistance. We feel you might be of some help in solving the robbery."

Somewhat astounded, Clint shook his head. "You just lost me, Mr. Tisdale. How would I be of any help?"

"Suppose I let Ben explain. He has all the particulars at his fingertips."

Holladay turned in his chair. "Well, first off, let me say I've heard good things about you, Marshal. You've made quite a name for yourself here in Denver."

"I don't know about that," Clint said. "I'm just doing the job."

"And doing it damn well, too! It's high time we had a marshal who's not afraid to bust some heads."

"Glad to hear you approve."

A pained expression came over Holladay's face. "I wish to hell the U.S. Marshal had some of your grit. Sorry bastard doesn't know his butt from a bunghole!"

Clint appeared surprised. "That's the first I've heard of a U.S. Marshal. Where's he keep himself?"

"Over in Golden," Holladay said in disgust. "He got the appointment as a political handout. So far as I know, he's never set foot outside the capital."

"How's he do his job, then?"

Holladay laughed out loud. "The son of a bitch doesn't even try! He'd wet his pants if he came face to face with a real live desperado."

Walter Tisdale seemed to wince at Holladay's language. "What Ben's saying," he cut in smoothly, "is that we can't depend on federal officers. We have to look to the problem ourselves."

"Hallelujah!" Holladay rumbled. "Unless you help yourself, you'll wind up with hind tit every time. Never seen it to fail."

From stories Clint had heard around town, the statement was characteristic of the man. Shrewd and somewhat coarse in manner, Holladay had begun as an Indian trader. When the Mexican War broke out, he had turned teamster and freighted supplies for the army. Later, he'd become involved with the Pony Express, as well as hauling contract goods for Western military posts. In 1862, he had organized the Overland Stage Line, obtaining a government mail contract for Colorado and Montana. Over the next three years, he had extended his stage routes across the Rockies into Utah, Idaho, and Oregon.

What intrigued Clint most was Holladay's attitude about local politics. According to the grapevine, there was long-standing enmity between David Hughes and the Overland's owner. While Holladay was one of the wealthiest men in Denver, he took little part in civic affairs. The railroad, in particular, was a project that drew neither his support nor his financial backing. He saw it as a threat, direct competition for his stage line. His opposition had done nothing to endear him to Hughes and city hall.

"Well, anyway," Holladay rambled on, "we'll get no help from that pisswillie in Golden. So I thought maybe you'd lend a hand."

"How?" Clint said, meeting his gaze. "I'm just a town marshal."

"Yeah, that's true," Holladay agreed. "But you've got your ear to the ground down in the sporting district. You hear things."

"Like what?"

"Like all the local dirt," Holladay ventured. "The sporting crowd loves a juicy piece of gossip. All the more so if it's about some hard-ass who's thumbed his nose at the law."

"And you think I'll hear something about the stage robbers?"

"Hell, you're bound to! Whoever heads that gang pulled it off smooth as silk. Anything that slick is sure to get talked about."

Clint's eyes narrowed. "Suppose I do hear something? What then?"

Holladay smiled. "I'm offering a thousand dollars' reward—on each of them—dead or alive."

"Four men works out to four thousand."

"Kee-recto," Holladay affirmed. "Or if that game doesn't interest you, I'll pay a handsome price for information—the right names."

"Apart from the money," Tisdale added hastily, "you would be doing the town a service as well. Denver depends on this bank for business loans, and our major depositors are the mining camps. Your help might well make the difference.''

Clint was silent a moment, considering. "All right, I'll keep my ears open. What happens if something does turn up?"

Holladay chuckled. "You come see me."

"And then?"

"What else?" Holladay roared. "We catch 'em or we kill 'em!"

Tisdale looked like he had an acute gas pain. He ended the meeting as quickly as possible and saw them out of his office. Later, it would occur to him that Ben Holladay and Clint Brannock were a matched pair. Neither of them believed in half-measures—or the velvet glove.

Quintin and his men rode into Denver the following day. Frank Purdy thought it was a bad idea, foolhardy and dangerous. His protests had been greeted with amused contempt.

Years of guerrilla warfare had convinced Quintin that the bold move was generally the unexpected move. He argued that no one would look for them in Denver, where the stage had proceeded after the holdup. Instead, the search for the robbers would focus on Central City and the other mining camps. Tobert and Johnson, as usual, went along with his opinion. Purdy was reduced to disgruntled silence.

After stabling their horses, they took rooms in a seedy southside hotel. At Quintin's insistence, most of the loot from the robbery had been buried some miles outside town. The quickest way to arouse suspicion, he'd warned the others, was to go on a wild spending spree. Still, they'd earned a celebration, and good times cost money. He allowed each of them a thousand dollars in gold dust. If anyone asked, they were prospectors on a lark to the big city.

A walk through the sporting district put Quintin in high good humor. He decided that he liked the looks of Colorado Territory. Since fleeing Kansas, he'd seen little that struck his fancy. In New Mexico, where he had recruited Tobert and Johnson, the prospects were limited to rustling cows and stealing horses. Denver, with the mining camps nearby, was an altogether different matter. Gold dust was plentiful, and stagecoaches were easy pickings for a man versed in guerrilla tactics. In mountainous terrain, as he'd quickly noted, a holdup was quite similar to a well-planned ambush. He thought perhaps he'd found a place to light awhile. So far, Colorado looked hard to beat.

The balance of the afternoon went quickly. After a few drinks, the men parboiled themselves in a bathhouse, followed by haircuts and shaves. Drenched in bay rum, they next visited a whorehouse and spent a few hours cavorting with the girls. By midevening, with a steak dinner under their belts, they were ready to cut loose and see the elephant. No wingding was complete without a stopover at the gaming tables, and they wandered over to Blake Street. On a whim, Quintin chose the Bella Union. He figured a plush dive was more their speed.

Frank Purdy decided to keep his mouth shut. It bothered him that the owner of the Bella Union was Clint Brannock's brother. Yet, were he to say anything, he knew the others would peg him a faintheart, or worse. Added to that, there was no reason for him to pussyfoot around town. He'd been posted from Denver for a week, and the week had ended yesterday. He was entitled to do whatever he pleased, go anywhere, and to hell with the marshal. All the same, he told himself to take it easy.

The Bella Union was crowded. Quintin and his men found a spot at the end of the bar and ordered drinks. For a time, they surveyed the elegant barroom in thoughtful silence. Then, after a second round of drinks, their boisterous mood returned. Tobert, who was already feeling his liquor, happened to glance toward the rear of the room. Through the doorway, he saw Monte Verde behind the twenty-one table. His eyes brightened and he let out a whoop of laughter.

"Quintin, would you looky there! They got theirselves a lady dealer."

"Shore do," Quintin said, twisting around for a better look. "And she's easy on the eyes, too."

On his way past the bar, Earl caught the name. "Quintin." He almost halted in midstride, but instead kept walking. At the door to the gaming room, he stopped and lit a cheroot. Casually, as though counting the house, he let his gaze drift back to the bar. He studied the man called Quintin, wondering if he also answered to the name of "Jack." Stranger things had happened, and he recalled Clint saying the guerrilla leader had headed west from Kansas. On the spur of the moment, he decided to play a long shot.

Inside the gaming room, Earl paused briefly at the twenty-one table. He stood behind Monte, pretending to watch the play, and spoke to her in a low tone. Her eyes skittered to the bar, touching on the four men, and she nodded imperceptibly. Earl smiled, as if satisfied with the play, then walked off. He made a tour of the room, inspecting the tables, and stopped to talk with Joe Dundee, one of the floormen. Finally, looking preoccupied with other matters, he left the gaming room and went to his office.

A few minutes later the four men wandered in from the bar. As they moved through the door, Monte finished dealing a hand to the players at her table. She paid off one bet, collecting on two others, and glanced up at Frank Purdy. She gave him a dazzling smile.

"Hello, Frank," she said pleasantly. "Where've you been keeping yourself?"

Purdy appeared dumbstruck. He knew her from the mining camps and more recently as the Bella Union's star attraction. Yet he'd spoken to her only in passing, and never with any familiarity. He finally found his tongue.

" 'Evening, Miss Monte," he said awkwardly. "Good to see you again."

"It's mutual," Monte said, still smiling. "You shouldn't

stay away so long, Frank. You're always welcome at my table.''

Purdy preened at the attention. He hooked his thumbs in his vest, aware that the other men were watching him with new respect. ''Well, now, I might try a few hands. Could be my night to howl.''

''Never know till you try,'' Monte said engagingly. ''Introduce me to your friends, Frank. The more the better, I always say.''

''Well, sure,'' Purdy said, gesturing grandly. ''This here's my new partner, Jack Quintin. The ugly one is Bob Tobert and the other gent's Bill Johnson.''

Monte batted her eyes at Quintin. ''You boys new to Denver?''

''Pretty much,'' Quintin said, moving closer. ''We've been prospecting up in the mountains. Struck ourselves a right nice claim.''

''Good!'' Monte bubbled. ''I like a man with a fat poke. Care to try your luck?''

''Don't mind if I do.''

Purdy led Quintin and the others to the cashier's window. After exchanging gold dust for chips, they returned and took places at the table. Monte quickly discerned that the one named Tobert was too drunk to mind his tongue. She alternated between playing on Quintin's male vanity and Tobert's dulled wits. Dealing seconds, she let them win while she asked innocent-sounding questions. It proved to be no contest.

An hour later Monte excused herself. The men groaned, but she got a laugh when she said, ''Nature calls.'' She left them in the hands of a relief dealer and hurried to the office. Earl looked up from his desk as she came through the door. He seemed unusually tense.

''Well?'' he demanded.

''You were right,'' she said gravely. ''He's Jack Quintin . . . from Kansas.''

Earl stiffened. ''How come you're so sure?''

"Simple," she said with a slow smile. "One of them's drunk and I got him talking. Before Quintin could shut him up, I got their life story."

"I guess there couldn't be *two* Jack Quintins from Kansas."

"No, not likely."

"How about Purdy?" Earl asked. "Where'd he meet up with Quintin?"

"Good question," she replied. "As near as I can tell, they got together in Central City. Quintin says they're partners in a gold claim."

Earl let go a harsh bark of laughter. "I'd lay odds that bunch never prospected anything."

"You wouldn't get any takers."

"Are they still downstairs?"

She nodded. "I'm supposedly taking a break. They're waiting for me to get back."

"Hold them as long as possible. If they leave, tell Joe Dundee to follow them. I want to know where they're staying."

"You sound like you're going somewhere."

"I won't be long."

Earl stood, moving past her. The door opened and closed before she thought to ask. But then, almost as quickly, she decided the question was pointless.

She knew where he was going.

26

LATE-NIGHT CROWDS THRONGED BLAKE Street. Horses lined the hitch racks and a steady stream of men clogged the boardwalks. Every dive on the street was packed to capacity.

Outside the Bella Union, Earl turned uptown. His destination was Virgil's new house west of the business district. Before anything else he wanted to discuss tonight's development with the family elder. His every instinct told him to avoid Clint. He knew where that would lead.

Happenstance dictated otherwise. As Earl approached an intersection, Clint rounded the corner. They were on one another before Earl could take evasive measures. He reminded himself that Clint was a hothead and seldom given to prudence. Any mention of Jack Quintin would provoke immediate trouble, and the odds were all wrong. Still, he thought it would be wise to get Clint off the streets. There was always the risk of a chance encounter.

"What's the rush?" Clint asked. "You look like your pants are on fire."

Earl tried for a casual tone. "I'm headed over to Virgil's place. Why don't you walk along with me?"

"At this time of night? Hell, Virge is probably already sawing logs."

"No, it's not that late."

Clint looked skeptical. "What's so important that it won't wait?"

"Come along and find out. I think you ought to be there."

"Be there for what?"

Earl shrugged. "Let's just say it's family business. I'll explain when we get there. You coming or not?"

Without waiting for a reply, Earl stepped around him. Clint was thoroughly mystified, his curiosity aroused. All the way across town he attempted to pump Earl for some clue. But Earl remained adamant, saying little and revealing nothing. Some minutes later they halted on the porch of the house.

Virgil answered their knock. He was in shirt sleeves, suspenders hooked over his shoulders. When he opened the door, a shaft of lamplight spilled out onto the porch. He peered at them with some surprise. "Where'd you boys spring from?"

"Sorry, Virge," Earl responded. "Something came up and it won't keep. We've got to talk."

"Sounds serious."

"I'll let you judge for yourself."

Virgil motioned them inside. "Beth's already gone to bed. We weren't expecting company."

The parlor was tastefully decorated. A sofa and several padded armchairs were grouped around a low table. The floor was covered by a patterned carpet, and a small desk occupied one wall. Virgil waved them to chairs and took a seat on the sofa. He nodded to Earl.

"All right," he said, "what wouldn't keep?"

"We've got problems," Earl observed solemnly. "Jack Quintin showed up tonight."

Clint started out of his chair. "Why the hell didn't you tell me that before?"

Earl met his stare. "Because you would've gotten yourself killed. Quintin has three men with him, and they're a rough bunch. One of them you already know—Frank Purdy.''

''Purdy?'' Clint repeated, somewhat taken aback. ''How'd he get mixed up with Quintin?''

''Search me.''

''Forget Purdy,'' Virgil cut in. ''Let's stick with Quintin. Are you sure it's him?''

''Dead sure.''

Earl went on to explain. He related how the four men had drifted into the Bella Union. Then, after noting how he'd been tipped to the name, he recounted Monte's role in questioning the men. In passing, he mentioned that they were flush with gold dust and spending it freely. He concluded on a somber note. ''No doubt about it. He's the right Jack Quintin . . . the Jayhawker.''

An instant of tomblike silence slipped past. Virgil appeared grave, somehow subdued. Clint's face was rigid and hard, blazing with fury. He looked from one to the other.

''Well?'' he demanded. ''What are we waiting for?''

''Hold your horses,'' Earl counseled. ''Let's hear what Virgil has to say.''

''The hell with that! We wait any longer and they're liable to get away.''

''No, they won't,'' Earl said. ''They'll probably hang around the Bella Union all night. If not, then I arranged to have them followed.''

Clint grunted sharply. ''I don't want Quintin followed. I want him dead. We're wasting time talking.''

''Wait,'' Virgil said, his face drawn and sober. ''Earl's right. We've got to figure this thing out.''

''What's to figure out?'' Clint said in a flat voice. ''I say we go down there and brace them right now.''

''Whatever we do,'' Virgil said forcefully, ''we're not going to brace them. That sort of thing just won't do.''

Clint gave him a frowning look of disbelief. ''What do you mean it 'won't do'?''

''I mean we have to consider our position here in Denver.

How would it look if we gunned down four men in cold blood?"

"Who gives a damn how it would look? Quintin killed the folks in cold blood. Or have you forgot that?"

"I haven't forgotten," Virgil said in a low voice. "I'm only saying there's a lot at stake. Too much for us to turn vigilante."

Clint stared at him strangely. "You're talking about your reputation with the uptown crowd, aren't you?"

"Yes, there's that," Virgil said, averting his eyes. "But there's something even more important. Something I only just found out about." He paused, managed a strained smile. "Beth's in a family way."

Earl and Clint exchanged a quick glance. Before either of them could reply, Virgil went on. "Funny thing," he said, "when you're a family man, it shades the way you think. I'd like to live to see my first child."

"Anybody would," Earl said quickly. "No need to apologize for it."

Clint bobbed his head. "I'll go along with that. For now, you just steer clear of gunplay. We'll handle it ourselves."

"You and Earl?" Virgil said doubtfully. "You wouldn't stand a chance, not two against four!"

"I reckon we'll have to plan a surprise party. Quintin don't deserve an even break, anyway."

Virgil looked at him for a long moment. "There's more than one way to skin a cat. Why not do it legally?"

"I don't follow you."

"You're the law," Virgil told him. "You're duly sworn and you've got a badge pinned to your shirt. Use it to get Quintin."

"How?" Clint said, baffled. "There's no charge against him."

"Turn over a few rocks and you'll likely find one. His kind are always involved in something crooked."

Clint's face twisted in a grimace. "Waiting's not my game.

I'd sooner see the bastard dead and gone to hell.''

"Virge has a point," Earl interjected. "Stop and think about it a minute. Frank Purdy never earned an honest dollar in his life. Harness him with Quintin and what've you got?''

Clint studied on it a moment. "You said they're flush with gold dust. Any idea where they got it?''

"For what it's worth, Quintin says they're prospectors. Why are you interested in gold dust?''

"Ben Holladay asked me to keep my ears open. He's offering a thousand dollars apiece for those stage robbers, dead or alive.''

"It fits," Earl said slowly. "There were four robbers and there's four of them. And they're damn sure celebrating something.''

Virgil cleared his throat. "Clint, let's suppose you had your choice. Would you rather shoot Quintin or march him onto the gallows?''

"Well . . ." Clint smiled, aware he'd been euchred. "Forced to choose, I reckon I'd rather see him swing. But that's neither here nor there. He's not the type to surrender.''

"You never know," Earl remarked, "until you try.''

"And if he won't surrender," Virgil added, "you can always kill him . . . legally.''

"Sounds good," Clint admitted. "But there's no way to tie him to the holdup. I've got no proof.''

"Get some," Earl said in a jocular tone. "I thought that's what lawmen are for.''

"Easier said than done.''

"Look at it this way," Virgil suggested. "If they robbed once, they'll rob again. You could catch them in the act.''

"Only one trouble with that. I'd have to wait till they pull another holdup.''

"Wouldn't it be worth the wait"—Virgil hesitated, underscoring the thought—"to see Quintin hang?''

Clint lapsed into a brooding silence. His brothers watched

as he toyed with the idea for several moments. At length, he shrugged and spread his hands.

"All right," he agreed. "I'll wait a week . . . see what happens."

Virgil looked relieved. He swapped a glance with Earl and knew they were thinking the same thing. Far from settling anything, tonight was merely a delaying action.

They'd bought a week—nothing more.

Late the next morning Quintin and his men emerged from the hotel. Their eyes were bloodshot and they walked with a peculiar stiff-legged gait. All of them were suffering vicious hangovers.

Downstreet they entered a grungy café. The windows were flyblown and the interior reeked of warm grease. Without being asked, a waiter brought them mugs of steaming coffee. The men swilled it thankfully, as though consuming some magic restorative. Only after a refill were they able to consider breakfast.

Across the street, Clint was posted inside a saloon. Through the window, he'd watched as they trooped out of the hotel and walked to the café. There was bitter anger in his eyes. From Earl's description, he had easily identified Jack Quintin, and he'd been tempted to step outside, end it on the spot. Still, he had given his word last night and he would hold to the agreement. A week of waiting and watching, and then . . .

Clint suddenly started alert. Ed Case's chief enforcer, Hank Newcomb, appeared on the opposite side of the street. Newcomb was short and chunky, with a barrel chest and a head like a cannonball. Fast for his size, he was chain lightning with his fists, and no slouch with a gun. He entered the café as though he owned the place.

Quintin was halfway through a plate of ham and eggs. His fork paused in midair as a large shadow fell over the table. He looked up and found himself staring into the beady eyes of Hank Newcomb. The men around the table abruptly fell silent, their food forgotten.

Quintin gave the stranger a rather indifferent once-over. Then, stuffing a bite of ham in his mouth, he nodded. "Do something for you, friend?"

"Yeh," Newcomb said gruffly. "Mr. Case wants to see you—now."

Quintin looked at him with mild disinterest. "Who's Mr. Case?"

"He's the man that sent for you. That's all you gotta know."

"You tell Mr.—"

"Jack," Frank Purdy cut him short, "don't say nothin' you'll wish you hadn't. Ed Case is the he-wolf of the sporting district. He's nobody to mess with."

"So what?" Quintin said, clearly unimpressed. "If he wants to see me, he knows where I'm at."

Purdy darted a nervous glance at Newcomb. Lowering his voice, he leaned closer to Quintin. "Listen to me, Jack. Case won't take no backtalk off nobody. You cross him and we'll all be swimmin' in deep shit."

"Well?" Newcomb said impatiently. "What's it gonna be?"

Quintin shoved his plate away. He hitched his chair back and stood, glowering at Newcomb. "Awright, let's get to it."

When the café door opened, Clint felt an unaccountable chill. He peered through the saloon window, watching intently as Newcomb and Quintin proceeded along Blake Street. He gave them a slight lead, then moved out onto the boardwalk. A block upstreet they turned into the Progressive Club, one of Ed Case's gambling parlors. Walking on, Clint stepped into the doorway of a saloon on the opposite corner. Staring across the street, he wondered why Denver's vice lord would summon Jack Quintin. All of a sudden, he was glad he'd agreed to wait.

Inside the Progressive Club, Quintin was ushered into

Case's office. He saw a dapper man seated behind a large walnut desk. No one spoke, and he suddenly stiffened as the snout of a gun was jabbed into his backbone.

Newcomb relieved him of his pistol and then nudged him forward. Stepping aside, Newcomb nodded to the man behind the desk. "You want me to stick around, boss?"

"Wait outside," Case said, "I'll call if I need you."

After the door closed, there was a moment of tense silence. Case motioned to a chair. "Have a seat, Mr. Quintin."

"You've got a helluva nerve! Why'd you have me brought here?"

Case waited until he was seated. "Let's get something straight. You're in my town, and I'll do as I damn well please. Understood?"

"Like hell!" Quintin bristled. "Nobody shoves me around."

"I do," Case said softly. "And if that doesn't suit you, then stay out of Denver. It's just that simple."

Quintin's mouth tightened in a narrow line. "You brought me here to say that?"

"No," Case informed him. "What I wanted was a look at the man who robbed the Overland stage."

"What stage?" Quintin shifted uneasily. "I don't know what you're talkin' about."

Case smiled. "You shouldn't throw gold dust around so liberally. It makes people talk."

"How'd you hear about that?"

"I hear everything," Case said matter-of-factly. "Next time bring your gold dust to me. I'll exchange it for paper money, dollar for dollar. That way tongues won't wag."

Quintin eyed him suspiciously. "Why would you do me any favors?"

"Why else?" Case shrugged. "One day I'll expect a favor in return."

"What sort of favor?"

Case spread his hands. "A man of your considerable talents always proves useful, Mr. Quintin."

"How'd you know my name, anyway?"

"No matter." Case dismissed him with an idle gesture. "Just behave yourself when you're in Denver. We'll talk from time to time."

Quintin took a tight grip on himself. No man had ever spoken to him in that tone and lived. Yet, for the moment, he decided to play along in order to get along. On his way out, he told himself that Case had things slightly bass-ackwards. If anybody got used, it wouldn't be him.

It would be Ed Case.

27

IN SUBSEQUENT DAYS, IT became apparent that Jack Quintin was no piker. He and his men flung money about with an easy-come, easy-go attitude. Their spree quickly became the talk of the sporting district.

Clint fell into a daily routine. Around noontime he would stroll past the café where the gang took their meals. Seated around a table, nursing their hangovers, Quintin and his men showed up by twelve at the latest. Satisfied that they were still around, Clint then went on about his normal business. He usually checked on them once or twice during the afternoon.

Daytime presented Clint with a sticky problem. The sporting district on Blake Street was roughly three blocks long. Whenever he went to check on the gang, he had to do it in a way that wasn't too obvious. The job was further complicated by the fact that Frank Purdy knew him on sight. While Purdy had seen him a couple of times, he was always on the opposite side of the street and appeared to be headed somewhere else. He took care to make his presence look like the ordinary conduct of business.

With nightfall, the problem lessened somewhat. The crowds were larger, and even with the streetlamps lit, there was less chance of being spotted. Clint quickly discovered that the gang members were very much creatures of habit. After supper, they stopped off at a saloon for a round of drinks. Before long, with their boilers fired, they headed for Holladay Street and the parlor houses. The girls, along with several rounds of drinks, generally kept them occupied until midevening. Then, already half-drunk and in dazzling good humor, they returned to Blake Street. The balance of the night was spent at the gaming tables.

Apart from shadowing the gang, Clint was still faced with policing the town. Their pattern of activities, which were somewhat predictable, made it easier. Once he had them placed in a whorehouse or one of the gaming dives, he was able to go about his customary duties. Between arrests made at night and afternoon court appearances, he devoted every spare minute to surveillance. His only respite was somewhere around three or four o'clock in the morning, when he trailed them back to their hotel. He was then able to catch a few hours' sleep himself.

Through Earl, he was kept well advised on their gambling activities. As one of the sporting crowd, Earl was privy to every tidbit of gossip. While the Bella Union was their favorite hangout, the gang frequented other dives as well. From all accounts, Earl was able to determine that they'd lost upward of three thousand dollars in only four nights. Clint did a quick calculation, adding food and whores and whiskey. He figured the total was pushing four thousand.

Early the fifth afternoon, Frank Purdy and one of the other men rode out of town. Clint debated following them, but quickly abandoned the idea. His sole interest was Jack Quintin, and after breakfast, the gang leader had retired to a saloon. Several hours later Purdy and his companion returned, and Quintin joined them at the hotel. Within minutes Quintin emerged onto the street and walked directly to the Progressive

Club. No more than ten minutes afterward he was on the street again, walking back to the hotel. At dusk, the gang started out on their usual nightly routine.

Clint was somewhat baffled by the day's events. Later that night, however, the meaning became clear. From Earl, he learned that the gang was now spending greenbacks, not gold dust. In several hours at the Bella Union, they had dropped more than two thousand dollars. According to Earl, they were betting wildly, with a go-for-broke attitude. Upon reflection, Clint put together what seemed a reasonable explanation.

The haul from the stage holdup had been seven thousand dollars. In four nights, the gang's gambling losses, along with other expenses, had approached four thousand. Then, after Purdy's return to town, Quintin had paid an unexpected call on Ed Case. A logical conclusion was that the gang had buried part of their loot somewhere outside Denver. And for whatever reason, Case had obligingly converted the balance of the gold dust into greenbacks. Of that amount, most of it had been lost at the Bella Union tonight. Which meant the gang was down to a thousand dollars, or less.

Ed Case's role in the affair was only of passing interest. Whatever his association with Quintin, it seemed unlikely that the vice lord would be involved in stage robbery. What interested Clint most was that the gang's bankroll had dwindled almost to nothing. From all appearances, they had become accustomed to living high on the hog. So the next step, if they were to replenish their funds, seemed all too clear. They would have to pull another holdup.

Clint awakened earlier than usual the next morning. He'd averaged less than four hours' sleep a night for five nights running. His eyes felt burnt out, almost scratchy, and his nerves were stretched tight as catgut. He was weighed down by a dull and grinding weariness, and there was a leaden feeling in his chest. As he left his hotel room, he was oddly unassured that his logic would hold. In large degree, he'd second-guessed Quintin's next move, with no certainty that he was on the right track. He still hadn't uncovered an iota of proof that Jack Quintin was a stage robber.

Shortly after eight o'clock, he walked into the Overland Stage office. Ben Holladay, who was already hard at work, observed that he looked like "death warmed over." Clint merely nodded and launched into a somewhat sanitized tale of Jack Quintin. He omitted any mention of Jayhawkers or guerrilla raids during the war. Instead, he explained that his suspicions had been aroused by the gang's lavish ways with gold dust. He concluded with what he believed was about to happen.

"Within the next few days," he said, "I think they'll rob another stage."

Holladay appeared thoughtful. "Wouldn't that take a lot of brass? It's only been a week since they robbed the last one."

"Quintin has more than his share of brass."

"You talk like you know him."

"I know the type," Clint said carefully. "He figures he's got the whole world outfoxed."

Holladay nodded. "So how do we outfox him?"

"I'll get word to you when the gang leaves town. However you manage it, you ought to alert your drivers to be on the lookout for a holdup."

"That won't give me much time. I'd have to send messengers to every camp in the mountains."

"Guess that's the best we can do."

"What about you?" Holladay inquired. "Is there any way you could lend a hand?"

"Yeah, there is," Clint said. "I aim to follow them when they leave town."

"By yourself?"

"I prefer to work alone."

Holladay stared at him a moment. "I get the feeling there's something personal involved. Are you planning a little surprise for Quintin and his bunch?"

"Any objections?" Clint asked directly. "I recollect you said dead or alive."

No elaboration was needed. Holladay bobbed his head, chuckling softly. "Good hunting, Clint."

They shook hands and Clint walked from the office. Holladay leaned back in his chair, hands locked behind his head. He thought the man named Jack Quintin was not long for this life. For whatever reason, dead or alive no longer applied. There was just dead.

He wondered why.

Around ten o'clock, Quintin and his men emerged from the hotel. They were carrying their saddlebags and they appeared somehow rushed as they walked to the café. After a quick breakfast, they proceeded to a livery stable one block west of Blake Street. There, they began saddling their horses.

Clint tailed them only as far as the livery stable. Once he saw they were preparing to leave, he hurried back to his office. From the gun rack, he selected a Henry lever-action carbine and stuffed extra cartridges in the pockets of his vest. He told the jailer to cancel the day's court hearings.

A few minutes later he approached Virgil's warehouse. Since arriving in Denver, he'd kept his horse in the livestock pens out back. Upon spotting him, the gelding whinnied and trotted over to the gate. He gathered his gear from the harness shed and propped the carbine against the fence. Bridle and saddle in hand, he eased through the gate of the stock pen.

Virgil appeared on the loading dock. He called out as Clint finished saddling, and got no answer. Somewhat confused, he jumped down from the dock and quickly walked out back. He halted as Clint led the gelding through the gate.

"What's going on?" Virgil demanded.

"Law business," Clint said, grinning. "Quintin and his boys are set to leave town."

"And you mean to follow them?"

"No two ways about it. I figure they're planning to rob another stage."

Clint gathered the carbine and prepared to mount. Virgil took hold of his arm. "Just wait a minute, now! You can't tangle with that bunch all by yourself. Hell's fire, it's four to one. You'll get yourself killed."

"I like long odds," Clint said, shrugging off his brother's hand. "You could do me a favor, though."

"What's that?"

"Get word to Ben Holladay. Tell him I'll stick on their trail till hell freezes over."

Virgil looked worried. "What about your job? You can't just leave the town in a lurch."

"Virge," Clint said quietly, "I'll do whatever it takes to get Jack Quintin. Tell the mayor he'll have to make other arrangements."

"I won't let you do it," Virgil declared. "You'll wind up dead, and for what? It's not worth it."

"We'll argue about it later. I'm pushed for time right now."

Virgil grabbed his shoulder. "Damn you—!"

"Take your hand off me, Virge. I won't tell you again."

Virgil saw something cold and implacable in his eyes. He slowly let his hand fall to his side, aware at last that there was nothing to be done.

Clint stepped into the saddle and reined the gelding sharply about. He rode off at a brisk trot.

Virgil stood there a long time. Finally, his head bowed, he turned and walked back to the warehouse. He looked curiously defeated.

Frank Purdy rode in the lead. He set a ground-eating pace, and the other men were strung out behind him. Their direction was northwest.

The Black Hawk road was lightly traveled. Located some thirty miles outside Denver, the mining camp was off the beaten path. An occasional supply wagon was sighted, but few men traversed the road on horseback. Anyone with the fare much preferred to travel by stagecoach.

Quintin had personally selected Black Hawk. Earlier that morning, he'd told the men it was too soon to hit another Central City gold shipment. Instead, after questioning Purdy, he had decided to rob the Black Hawk stage. Purdy was familiar with the route, and a quick check of the Overland schedule revealed that there were two stages a day. Last time out, they had scored a large haul on an afternoon stage. Today, they saw no reason to change tactics.

A short way behind them, Clint doggedly trailed the gang. Since leaving Denver, he had allowed the terrain to dictate his pace. On an open stretch of road, he would sometimes drop off a mile or more to the rear. Where the terrain turned hilly or on curves, he would close the gap to a quarter-mile or less. They rode at a steady clip, and he became all the more convinced that they were operating against time. Some inner certainty told him that the time involved had to do with the Black Hawk stage. He managed to keep them in sight without being seen himself.

Any lingering doubt was dispelled around midafternoon. Some fifteen miles from Denver, the road took a bend to the right and immediately dropped off on a sharp downgrade. The terrain south of the road was broken and rough, and to the north there was a rocky outcropping strewn with boulders. Quintin called a halt and sat for several minutes studying the landscape. There were no trees to conceal their horses, and it quickly became apparent that he'd decided on a mounted holdup. One man was posted as a lookout, and the others remained hidden just around the bend. They settled down to wait.

Clint left his horse a half-mile to the rear. Hefting the carbine, he began a slow climb up the hillside to the north. Once on the high ground, he took a circuitous route westward, paralleling the road. As the sun heeled over toward the mountains, he stopped at a point directly above the mounted men. Cautiously, he eased into position behind a flat-topped boulder and peered down the rocky outcropping. His eyes fixed on Quintin, who was closest to where the road curved. He judged the range at slightly less than fifty yards, and smiled. It would be an easy shot.

Some while later, the lookout scampered back to his horse. The men pulled bandannas over their faces and drew their guns, waiting expectantly. A minute or so passed, then the thud of hoofbeats sounded in the distance. The stage slowed on the upgrade and rounded the bend with the six-horse hitch straining in the traces. Quintin fired a shot in the air and led the gang from behind the outcrop. The men fanned out across the road as the stage driver hauled back on the reins. A sharp command from Quintin produced immediate results. The express guard tossed his shotgun over the side.

Clint saw no reason to delay. Waiting for the strongbox to be surrendered seemed to him a needless waste of time. He shouldered the carbine and centered the sights on Quintin's shirtfront. No emotion stayed him, and he felt nothing for the man he was about to kill. The thought uppermost in his mind was to do it cleanly, dead center through the breastbone. His finger tightened on the trigger.

As the carbine roared, Quintin's horse skittishly took the bit and pranced sideways. The slug whistled past Quintin and dropped Bob Tobert's horse dead in the road. Clint chambered another shell and hurriedly aligned the sights as Quintin booted his mount around the far side of the stage. The shot missed by inches and whanged off a rock some distance beyond the road. Working the lever, Clint looked for another target and saw that he was too late. Tobert swung up behind Johnson, and with Purdy in the lead, they disappeared around the bend. The sound of drumming hooves faded within moments to a leaden silence.

Standing, Clint saw the driver and the guard staring up at him. He waved the carbine overhead and then began a slow descent down the rocky hillside. Under his breath, he roundly cursed skittish horses and piss-poor luck. An image of Quintin centered dead in his sights flashed through his mind. Then, almost reluctantly, his gaze went to the horse sprawled dead in the road.

His mouth clamped in a tight bloodless line.

28

VIRGIL LEFT THE WAREHOUSE shortly before nine o'clock. The morning was bright and sunny without a cloud in sight. Westward, the mountains loomed against a brilliant azure sky.

Walking uptown, Virgil appeared lost in thought. His expression was abstracted and he seemed vaguely preoccupied. People who greeted him on the street got an absent stare in return. He looked like a man with problems.

The complexities of the situation were like quicksand. Virgil had the sense of being sucked deeper and deeper into a bog from which there was no escape. Late yesterday, he'd sent his office clerk with a message for David Hughes. The wording of the note was stiffly formal, demanding a meeting with Hughes and Luther Evans early this morning. Hughes' reply was little more than a terse acknowledgment of the request.

Oddly enough, Virgil's personal life had never been more tranquil. Elizabeth was expecting sometime in the spring, and she was radiant in the way of a woman with child. She kept herself busy with the house and church activities and greeted him every night with exuberant happiness. She was, as well, his confidante in all he dreamed, his grand vision of the future. Yet, for all their closeness, there were certain things that Virgil shared with no one. She knew nothing of today's meeting.

On another note, Virgil was somewhat less sanguine. All day yesterday, he'd been distracted by worry for Clint. Then, to his great relief, Clint had returned to town early last night. Talking with him, Virgil realized that the aborted trap had done nothing to quell the younger man's determination. If anything, Jack Quintin's escape had merely inflamed Clint's rage. Virgil had argued far into the night, urging caution and a degree of restraint. His contention was bluntly stated: the killing of Quintin was not worth the life of still another Brannock. He wasn't at all sure that Clint had gone away convinced.

There were times when Virgil questioned his own motives. No less than Clint and Earl, he wanted to see Quintin punished. Yet he genuinely believed that the law, rather than men acting on their own, should dispense justice. The war had soured him on brutality and killing, and revenge no longer seemed an excuse for summary execution. He sought quietude and harmony, a life free of hate and bloodshed and violence. On the battleground of war, he had killed until his soul felt leeched of compassion. He knew the feeling of seeing another man die at his hand, and the memory revolted him. He wanted never to kill again.

For all that, there was nothing passive about Virgil. His opinion of himself was grounded in assurance and the knowledge that he possessed certain attributes. He was a man of determination and integrity, and he never backed off from what he considered to be right. His beliefs stemmed from the conviction that there was no substitute for honor and moral courage. While he set himself up as no man's judge, he had small tolerance for subterfuge and corruption. He knew that the meeting today would put those beliefs to the test.

Hughes and Evans were waiting in the lawyer's office.

When Virgil entered, they greeted him with the jocular warmth of old friends. Hughes waved him to a chair beside Evans and then resumed his own seat behind the desk. For a time, Hughes attempted to make small talk, as though to draw Virgil out. Finally, when there was no response, he gave Virgil a pleasantly inquisitive look.

"Well, now," he said, "what can we do for you? Your note sounded just a trifle imperative."

Virgil nodded soberly. "Yesterday afternoon something came to my attention. It involves you and Luther—and the railroad."

"Oh?" Hughes said in an avuncular voice. "What might that be?"

"I have reason to believe a conflict of interest exists. At the very least, some people might view it as chicanery."

"Indeed?" Hughes' reply was overdrawn, a little too guileless. "Surely you're not referring to Luther and myself?"

"I'm afraid so," Virgil said. "I wanted to give you a chance to answer the allegations."

"Commendable," Hughes said with a patronizing smile. "Exactly what are the nature of these allegations?"

Virgil's expression was unreadable. "I've been told that you and Luther have formed a construction supply company. According to my source, you've already ordered the supplies shipped west by the Union Pacific."

"All quite true," Hughes said blandly. "But why should that concern you?"

"I also understand that you propose to act as sole supplier of construction materials for the town's railroad."

"Does that bother you for some reason?"

"All depends." Virgil paused, eyebrows raised. "Do you plan to provide those supplies to the railroad at cost—or at a profit?"

"Come, now," Hughes said with veiled mockery. "Aren't we allowed a profit on our investment?"

"Some folks might figure you're profiting at the town's expense."

"On the contrary, Virgil. It's simply good business."

"It's *sharp* business," Virgil countered. "And however you spell it, it's conflict of interest. How can you sell the railroad supplies—and call it legitimate—when you're both on the board of directors?"

"No, not really," Hughes temporized. "I think you would find it a fairly common business practice."

"I doubt anyone in town would agree with you."

"You've no reason—"

"Let me finish," Virgil cut him off. "I'm reliably informed that Luther has been paying rummies and drifters to homestead land north of the town." He stopped, looking directly at Evans. "Is that true?"

Evans fidgeted uncomfortably. "What if it is? There's nothing illegal about it."

"Why do you want all that land, Luther?"

"Why else?" Evans muttered aloud. "I'm in the land business."

"Like hell!" Virgil pressed him. "Your homesteaders will deed it to you and then you'll sell right-of-way to the railroad—at an inflated price!"

"Careful now," Hughes cautioned. "You're very close to accusing us of conspiracy."

"Your word, not mine," Virgil said. "But if the shoe fits . . ."

The two men stared at each other in silent assessment. After a moment, Hughes steepled his hands, tapped his index fingers together. "As a matter of curiosity, how did you come by your information?"

"When the sporting crowd wouldn't invest in the railroad, I started nosing around. My brother Earl put me on to Luther's homestead operation. He said it had all the earmarks of a bunco game."

"And the supply company?"

"Yesterday afternoon I received a shipment of liquor. The freighter told me your order was the talk of the town in St. Louis. Apparently the UP forgot to keep it under their hat. I just put two and two together."

"How resourceful," Hughes said with perfect civility. "And I presume you're here today to make some sort of proposal?"

Virgil hesitated a moment. When he spoke, there was an undercurrent of authority in his voice. "I think you'd be wise to disband the supply company. As for the right-of-way, Luther should consider donating it to the railroad. Call it a gesture of civic generosity."

"You're crazy," Evans sputtered. "I've already got a ton of money invested in that land."

Hughes silenced him with a look. Then, with a chilly smile, his gaze moved back to Virgil. "What if we refuse? Am I to assume there's an or-else attached?"

"If you refuse," Virgil said bluntly, "I'll take the story to Will Byers. Once it hits the newspaper, I suspect that'd do the trick."

"You realize what would happen?"

"Well, for one thing, it would bring the railroad to a dead stop. For another, I imagine you and Luther would have to hightail it out of town."

"I rather doubt that," Hughes scoffed. "You seem to forget I'm a man of some influence. No one would seriously believe that I intended to bilk the railroad."

Virgil smiled. "One way to find out, isn't there?"

There was an instant of calculation while Hughes studied him. Virgil stared him straight in the eye, challenging him, and at last the lawyer shrugged. "Let me propose a more amicable solution. Suppose I were to offer you a share in the supply company as well as an interest in the right-of-way profits? Would that dampen your civic conscience?"

"No sale," Virgil said, getting to his feet. "I'll wait till tomorrow for your decision. Then I go to Byers."

"Be reasonable," Hughes protested. "You can't expect me to undo all these arrangements overnight. I'll need some time."

"How much time?"

"Well, I should think a couple of weeks would do it."

"You've got a week, and that's it."

Virgil stalked out of the office. The door closed behind him and an oppressive stillness settled over the room. For a protracted interval the lawyer and the land speculator sat staring into space. At last, Hughes seemed to recover himself.

"Well, well," he said slowly. "It appears we underestimated our young friend."

"Confound it!" Evans fumed. "I told you right from the start we couldn't trust him. Goddamn farmers are worse than preachers."

"He's not a farmer any longer. As you've just seen, he plays a very shrewd game."

Evans hawked as if he'd swallowed a bone. His eyes watered and his face turned red. "You'd better stop praising the bastard and figure a way out of this mess. He's got our butts nailed to a tree."

"Perhaps," Hughes mused. "And then again, perhaps not."

"For Chrissake! Don't start talking in riddles."

"I was just thinking of alternative measures. Perhaps we ought to have a talk with the mayor."

"What the hell does Stodt have to do with anything?"

"Our honorable mayor has the ear of Mr. Edward Case. It occurs to me that we might prevail on him in our hour of need."

"You're not talking about—"

"I believe I am," Hughes said with wintry malice. "Suppose you run down and fetch the mayor. Tell him it's important."

The shadow of a question clouded Evans' eyes. But then, as though he thought it wiser not to ask, he rose and walked toward the door. As he went out, Hughes leaned back in his chair, staring at the ceiling. The corners of his mouth razored in a slow smile.

Ed Case seemed to him the perfect man for the job.

Clint walked from the Denver House shortly before ten o'clock. He turned downtown and proceeded toward the Overland Stage company. Outside Hughes' law office, he bumped into Virgil.

Something about Virgil's manner struck him as peculiar. Oddly distracted, Virgil seemed on edge and unusually abrupt. He sidestepped the question when Clint inquired his business with Hughes. Quickly changing the subject, he asked instead where Clint was headed. He listened with only half an ear to the reply.

As they talked, Luther Evans hurried out of the law office. He looked surprised, as though somehow upset to find them together. Casting Virgil a dirty look, he crossed the street and entered city hall. Virgil pretended not to notice the look, even though his own features suddenly grew overcast. He turned away from the law office and Clint fell in beside him.

A block downstreet they parted. Hesitating outside the Overland company, Clint watched as his brother trudged off in the direction of the warehouse. His instinct told him that trouble was brewing, and he wondered why Virgil had acted so closemouthed. Then, glancing back upstreet, he saw Evans and Mayor Stodt emerge from city hall. His unease deepened when they rushed across to Hughes' law office. He decided to have another talk with Virgil.

Inside the stage-line company, he entered the private office of Ben Holladay. Today's meeting had been arranged after his return yesterday from the aborted holdup. Waiting with Holladay was the territory's chief law-enforcement officer, U.S. Marshal Wilbur Smith. He had ridden over earlier from Golden.

Holladay's introduction was rather perfunctory. While he

was civil, his distaste for the marshal was evident. Smith was a bony man, with shrunken skin and knobby joints, almost cadaverous in appearance. A troubled expression settled over his features as he listened to Clint recount the failed robbery. He looked vaguely critical.

"Anyway," Clint concluded, "the dead horse wasn't any help. Nothing in the saddlebags to tie him to Quintin's gang."

"Is that it?" Smith inquired.

"Pretty much," Clint said. "By the time I got back to my horse, they had a half-hour's lead. So there wasn't much sense in trying to trail them."

"No sense a'tall," Holladay added. "Especially when they had you outnumbered. You would've just got yourself ambushed."

Smith furrowed his brow. "What about the livery stable here in town? Could the owner identify the dead horse?"

Clint smiled faintly. "I've already asked him. Way he put it, one horse looks like another. He's not what you'd call a cooperative witness."

Smith nodded. "And the driver—the shotgun guard . . . any luck there?"

"That's a washout, too. The gang was masked and it all happened pretty fast. Neither of them could make positive identification."

"Well . . ." Smith paused, wagged his head. "Sounds like you haven't much of a case."

"Why the hell not?" Holladay growled. "Clint tailed 'em out there and saw the whole thing. He's an eyewitness."

"Maybe so," Smith said tentatively. "But a court would need some sort of collaboration. It's just his word against theirs."

"Jeezus Christ," Holladay said. "He's a duly sworn lawman. Our town marshal."

Smith shrugged off the objection. "It just don't make no never-mind. A judge would dismiss the case faster'n scat."

"You won't know that till you try."

"Lemme make myself clear, Mr. Holladay. I've got no intention of tryin'. It'd be a waste of time."

"In a pig's ass! I want those bastards arrested."

"Then bring me some proof that'll hold up in court."

"Goddamn political hack!" Holladay exploded. "That's your job, not ours. What the hell do you get paid for?"

Under Holladay's ugly stare, Wilbur Smith jackknifed to his feet. He nodded curtly, flicking a painfully embarrassed glance at Clint, and walked out.

When the door closed, Holladay slammed a meaty fist into the desktop. His eyes were hot with rage. "Worthless good-for-nothin' sonovabitch! He hasn't got the balls of a ten-year-old girl. He's scared."

"Looks that way," Clint agreed. "What was he before they pinned a badge on him?"

"A ribbon clerk," Holladay fumed. "Worked in a mercantile store, for God's sake."

"Guess it never hurts to have connections."

"I've heard the sorry bastard's related to the governor. Nobody else could've got him the appointment."

"Well, no matter," Clint said. "We'll just have to tend to it ourselves."

Holladay fixed him with an evaluating look. "You say that like you've got something in mind."

Clint's eyes were curiously opaque. His voice was barely audible, but there was an undercurrent of deadliness in the words. "Some men are just bound to get themselves killed."

"You're talking about Jack Quintin."

"Let's call him the *late* Jack Quintin."

"Appears to me he's still alive and kicking."

Clint smiled. "No, he's not, Ben. He's as good as dead."

29

ELIZABETH OPENED THE OVEN door. She removed a golden loaf of bread and placed it on a cooling rack. The delicate aroma of fresh-baked bread filled the kitchen.

Beads of perspiration dotted her forehead. She moved back to the stove and closed the oven door. A pot of stew bubbled on top of the stove and she quickly stirred it with a wooden spoon. Dipping into the broth, she sampled it for taste, then shifted the pot to the back of the range. She turned down the damper.

Walking from the kitchen, she hurried through the house. The hall clock indicated ten minutes before twelve, and she'd learned that Virgil was always punctual. In the bedroom, she patted her face dry and applied a light dusting of powder. Her hair was pulled tight in a bun, with puffy curls spilling over her forehead. She brushed a stray lock back into place.

After one last check in the mirror, she bustled out of the bedroom. The noon hour was a special part of her day, and she always tried to make it an occasion. While they'd been married slightly more than a month, none of the glow had worn off. Virgil still came home at noontime, putting aside business to spend a quiet hour with her. She counted herself the luckiest of women. Few husbands were so attentive or loving.

In many ways, Elizabeth considered herself blessed. Her man was ambitious, hardworking, and widely respected. His business alliances provided entrée into the right circles and further enhanced his prospects for success. As Denver grew, his prominence in town affairs, as well as their social position, was virtually assured. With a baby on the way, her life seemed complete, wonderously fulfilled. She felt serene and fortunate beyond measure.

Dinner was ready when Virgil arrived home. Normally a hearty eater, he was a meat-and-potatoes man. Beef stew, thick with vegetables and spices, was his favorite dish. The loaf of bread, along with a plate of butter and a steamy pot of coffee, was arranged around the stew bowl. For dessert, there was chocolate cake, baked yesterday but still moist and fresh. A patterned tablecloth gave the table an inviting look.

Almost immediately, Elizabeth sensed that something was wrong. Virgil bussed her on the cheek when she met him at the door. But his expression was dark and he seemed unusually pensive. His customary practice was to relate the morning's activities while they ate. Today, however, he was moody and quiet, strangely unresponsive to her questions. A still-greater reason for concern was his indifferent appetite. He merely picked at his food.

"Sweetheart?" Elizabeth said at last. "Aren't you feeling well?"

"No, no," Virgil mumbled. "I feel fine."

"Well, you certainly don't act it. Is something wrong with the stew?"

"No, it's not that. I guess I'm just off my feed."

She studied his downcast look. "Something's wrong," she said definitely. "I've never seen you so glum."

"Beth . . ." Virgil's voice trailed away.

"Yes?" she coaxed him. "What is it?"

"Nothing. I've just got a lot of things on my mind."

"Fiddlesticks! You can't fool me, Virgil Brannock. Something's very much wrong."

Virgil seemed caught up in a moment of indecision. His eyes drifted off, avoiding her stare, and he appeared wrapped in gloom. Finally, he dropped his fork in his plate.

"You're right," he said. "Things are about to go to hell in a hand basket. I had a meeting with Hughes and Evans this morning."

"Surely there's no problem with the railroad?"

Virgil's features set in a grim scowl. "Hughes and Evans have it rigged to milk the railroad. I accused them of it to their faces."

"Accused them!" Her voice echoed her dismay. "Accused them of what?"

"Conflict of interest," Virgil said morosely. "A scheme to rob the town blind."

Her breath caught in her throat. "I can't believe it."

"Believe it or not, it's true."

Virgil quickly sketched out the details. He related what was at first a suspicion and then the results of his investigation. He went on to recount the meeting with Hughes and Evans.

"Any doubts," he concluded, "were soon put to rest. Hughes admitted the whole thing."

She stared at him with shocked round eyes. "You couldn't have misunderstood? He actually said he intends to plunder the railroad?"

"No," Virgil said, obviously disgruntled. "He called it routine business. Nothing out of the ordinary."

"Is it?"

"Maybe so. I suppose that's why railroad builders got nicknamed the robber barons."

"Then what he plans," she asked, "it's not illegal?"

"Not against the law," Virgil conceded. "But it's crooked all the same. He means to profit at the townspeople's expense."

Her expression was faintly mystified. "Someone always profits. Why do you object to it being David Hughes?"

There was bitter anger in Virgil's eyes. "Hughes gulled the whole damn town! He made everyone believe this would be the 'people's railroad.' And all along, he had most of the money earmarked for his own pockets."

A sudden cold dread ran through her. She knew that men loved the heroic and often struck postures. In truth, men were the romanticists in life whereas women were practical realists. All too frequently men adopted the noble stance, even if it destroyed them. No woman ever put duty before family, which was why men always started the wars. She wondered if her husband had cast himself in such a role now.

She looked at him seriously. "Would other people feel the way you do?"

"Hughes thinks so," Virgil said. "Otherwise he wouldn't have tried bribing me."

"In that event, why haven't you spoken with Father? Don't you think he should be advised?"

"Not just yet," Virgil said in a resigned voice. "For the moment, I don't want to involve him or anybody else. You're the only one I've told."

"You haven't mentioned it to Earl or Clint?"

"Earl knows I've been digging into it. I haven't told him what I found or anything about the meeting. It wouldn't serve any useful purpose."

A thought flashed through her mind. Some intuitive sense told her that he hadn't yet adopted a martyr's stance. His words were tinged with realism.

"Virgil," she said slowly, "why didn't you go ahead and expose them? Why give them a second chance?"

A vein pulsed in Virgil's forehead. His eyes dulled and appeared to turn inward. "You have to understand something," he said. "Hughes is the only man alive who can bring the railroad to Denver."

"I don't believe that for an instant. You could do it, and do it just as well. I know you could!"

Virgil shook his head firmly. "Nobody else has the political connections. Hughes knows all the right people in Washington, and that's what builds railroads. Without him, there wouldn't even be a land grant."

"And without a land grant," she added, "Denver loses the railroad. So one weighs in the balance against the other?"

"Yeah, it does." Virgil nodded. "Hughes is crooked as a dog's hind leg. But right now the town needs him."

"What happens," she asked in a hushed voice, "if he doesn't meet your demands? Will you really take the story to the newspaper?"

Virgil made an empty gesture with his hands. "At bottom," he said with some dignity, "I have to live with myself. If it comes to it, I'll deliver on the promise. I couldn't do anything else."

"By exposing him, you may ruin your own prospects in Denver. I've heard it said that David Hughes is a vindictive man."

Virgil was silent a moment. "You tell me," he said, his eyes grave. "What would you have me do?"

Elizabeth smiled an upside-down smile. She rose, holding his gaze, and moved around the table. Halting beside his chair, she kissed the top of his head softly. Her voice was strong.

"Follow your conscience," she said. "Whatever you do, I know it will be the right thing."

"Even if it makes an enemy of Hughes?"

"Yes, even that."

Virgil pulled her down in his lap. She put her head on his shoulder and he tenderly stroked her hair. Neither of them voiced what they were both thinking.

He'd already made an enemy of David Hughes.

* * *

A warm breath eddied through the hairs on his chest. He glanced around and found Belle watching him with impish amusement. She shifted in his arms, snuggling closer, and playfully nibbled his earlobe. He laughed and swatted her on the rump.

"Don't get any big ideas."

"Awww, what's the matter?" she purred. "Too pooped to pop?"

"You ought to know," Clint said, deadpan. "You're the one that wore me out."

"Oh, that's easily fixed, lover."

Belle slipped from his arms. The lamp was turned low, but he had a good view as she crossed the room. It occurred to him that she was a flossy woman, showy but elegant. Long lissome legs, a flat-bellied waist, and high full breasts. He admired the look of her, and her spirit as well. Hard as life was on the Row, she always surveyed her world with good-humored irony.

Halting before the wardrobe, she stretched like a cat. She knew he was watching, and she posed, allowing him a good look. Then she shrugged into a filmy housecoat and moved to a liquor cabinet on the opposite side of the room. She poured from a bottle of rye whiskey and returned to the bed with two glasses. She handed him one and scooted back in beside him. She sipped, watching him over the rim of her glass.

"Drink up," she said in an odd vibrant voice. "You're going to need your strength."

Clint groaned. "Hasn't anybody ever told you about too much of a good thing?"

There was a glint in her eye, laughter hardly contained. "Are *you* trying to tell me something, lover?"

"Let's put it this way. You keep at it and you're liable to turn a stout log into a limber twig."

She gave him a sassy grin. "Well, I suppose we could just talk."

"Talk about what?"

"Whatever's on your mind. You've been half here and half there all night."

"You act like you've got a crystal ball."

"Honey, you can't fool a whore. And that goes even more so for a madam. You're like an open book."

Clint saw no reason to dispute the statement. To him, women were pleasurable creatures, one of life's great comforts. Yet he believed they possessed some mystical power, the ability to divine a man's thoughts. Whores and madams, as Belle had so aptly put it, were even more so.

Earlier, after Blake Street closed for the night, he'd walked over to the parlor house. He hadn't seen Belle in several days and she greeted him warmly. Upstairs, in her room, they had spoken hardly a dozen words before tumbling into bed. Like him, her appetites were earthy and not easily satisfied. She'd savaged him like a wildcat on the prowl.

But now, lying beside her, Clint was nagged by uncertainty. No one outside of Virgil and Earl knew the truth of Jack Quintin. How far Belle could be trusted was a matter of speculation. Still, his judgment, backed by some deeper instinct, told him that she wouldn't betray a secret. Then, too, a madam heard all the gossip and Quintin's gang spent a good deal of time on the Row. He finally decided to tell her only part of it, the part that dealt with the holdups and Ed Case. He omitted any mention of Missouri and Jayhawker guerrillas.

When he finished, Belle was silent for a time. She sipped the last of her rye and set her glass on the nightstand. At last, she turned to him. "Every madam on the street knows about Quintin and his men. They're tough on the girls but loose with their money. Otherwise they wouldn't be welcome anywhere."

Clint nodded thoughtfully. "Have you heard anything about how they get their money?"

She wrinkled her nose. "They tell the girls they're prospectors. Nobody swallowed that for a minute.''

"So none of them have talked out of school? When they were drunk or with a girl?''

"Not that I've heard. And I usually hear everything worth repeating.''

A slight, ironic smile touched Clint's mouth. "Guess it figures. Quintin wouldn't tolerate loose talk.''

"What do you plan to do now?''

"This and that.'' Clint paused, and his pale eyes glinted coldly. "One way or another, I'll settle their hash.''

"Omigawd!'' she yelped. "I just thought of something.''

"What?''

"You're not planning to tangle with Ed Case, are you?''

"Nope,'' Clint said with a ghost of a grin. "All I want is a crack at Quintin.''

"Good!''

Belle took his glass and set it on the nightstand. Then she slipped out of her housecoat and gave him a wicked smile. Her allure proved irresistible, and he discovered she'd been right all along. Rye whiskey was indeed a great restorative.

Later, when she'd fallen asleep, he dressed and left the house. He made it a practice never to spend the night, preferring his own hotel room. Yet he'd been sorely tempted tonight, for he felt worn to a frazzle. The walk back uptown seemed a long way to go before he slept.

On the street, he turned toward the far corner. The streetlamps were still lit even though the Row was now deserted. As he approached the intersection, he caught a shadowy movement out of the corner of his eye. In the next instant, the night erupted in gunfire. Slugs snicked past him like furious bees, exploding mortar and brick on the building at his side. He dove headlong to the boardwalk.

Fiery gunflashes blossomed from a vacant lot across the street. Clint pulled his Colt as a bullet splintered the boardwalk beside his head. Arm extended, he thumbed the hammer and sighted over the barrel. As slugs fried the air all around him, he got off three quick shots. A strangled scream echoed from the vacant lot, and the gunfire abruptly ceased. Someone muttered a harsh command and indistinct forms began retreating toward an alley at the back of the darkened lot. He fired another shot to hurry them on their way.

A deafening stillness descended on the street. Clint scrambled to his feet and swiftly crossed to the vacant lot. He moved into the shadows, allowing his eyes to adjust to the darkness, and cautiously searched the ground. He found nothing, neither the man he'd hit nor any trace of blood. Yet, for all that, he still felt satisfied with the outcome. One of the bastards was wounded!

Walking away, he realized that tonight had settled nothing. Quintin was on to him now, aware that he was after the gang. So things were out in the open at last, although it had little to do with enforcing the law. He told himself that it was instead another kind of law. The oldest law known to man.

Who killed who first.

30

ED CASE WAS IN a reflective mood. He sat staring at a spot of sunlight on the wall, hands laced across his stomach. His mind was focused on a puzzle of sorts.

Events of the past few days seemed to him somehow intermeshed. Long ago he'd decided that anything happening in Denver affected his position. Whether uptown politics or downtown vice, his rule of the sporting district was dependent on never being caught off guard. He believed strongly in the adage that action was preferable to reaction. He therefore made it his business to know precisely who was doing what to whom. His squad of hooligans served as his eyes and ears around town.

Ever prudent, Case was the sort who never underestimated anyone, particularly an enemy. Instead, he was at some pains to overestimate any man who posed a threat. His concern regarding Earl Brannock had led quite naturally to an interest in the activities of all the Brannock brothers. He was still of the opinion that there was more to the Brannocks than met the eye. None of them had yet challenged him openly, but that was neither here nor there. He saw the potential for trouble.

By noon yesterday, he'd already received several reports. Word first arrived about Virgil Brannock's meeting with Hughes and Evans. Seen leaving Hughes' office, Virgil had paused on the street with his youngest brother. A minute later Evans had emerged, brushing past the Brannocks with a hostile look. Shortly after that, Evans and the mayor were seen rushing back to Hughes' office. The purpose of their hurried confab wasn't difficult to surmise. Virgil Brannock had somehow antagonized Hughes.

While pondering that, Case got word of still another meeting. Clint Brannock, after leaving his brother, had proceeded on to a conference with Ben Holladay and the U.S. Marshal. Upon hearing this, Case quickly put two and two together. Holladay, with or without the federal lawman's approval, had apparently sicced Clint Brannock on the stage robbers. Which would explain Brannock's actions of the day before, when he'd ambushed the gang during a holdup. Yet, all things considered, there was insufficient proof to warrant an arrest. No effort had been made to take Quintin and the gang members into custody.

Late last night, however, Quintin had taken matters into his own hands. Obviously a man who believed in tit for tat, he'd staged an ambush for Clint Brannock. One of his men had been wounded in the process and was reported holed up in their hotel. The town marshal, to Case's vast disappointment, had emerged unscathed. Still, there was a positive note to an otherwise sloppy attempt at murder. Quintin and his men had proved themselves to be willing assassins.

Thinking about it now, Case considered how he might put the information to use. He was concerned that Clint Brannock might somehow tie him to the stage robbers. By law, having exchanged money for stolen gold, he was an accessory after the fact. There was, moreover, the matter of Virgil Brannock.

From all appearances, the elder brother had broken with David Hughes. Whether that signaled a challenge to Denver's political hierarchy was a question that vitally interested Case.

Were it to happen, then it seemed likely that Earl Brannock would make his move on the sporting district. All the machinery was in place for the three brothers to pull a daring power play. A grab for all the marbles, uptown and downtown.

Case trusted no man to look after his interests. David Hughes, in particular, would sacrifice him on the instant if it proved to advantage. Nor was he all that confident of Hughes' strength, should a power struggle develop. Hughes, as well as Evans and the mayor, was especially vulnerable where the railroad was concerned. Their scheme to siphon off the construction funds had become apparent to him almost from the outset. And if he knew, then it was reasonable to assume that Virgil Brannock had also uncovered the truth. All of which could be used to topple Hughes and his cronies.

Therein lay the crux of the problem. The Brannocks might very well overthrow the uptown crowd. Their next move, logically, would be to link him with Hughes and demand his ouster as well. In that event, his squad of hooligans were hardly adequate to prevent his downfall. No man, especially a vice lord, could long stand in the face of public outrage. So it appeared that he'd been right all along. The Brannock brothers were opportunists and spoilers. And not to be underestimated.

The puzzle seemed to him complete. All the pieces fitted neatly together, and only one question remained: how to defuse the situation and rid himself of the Brannocks wasn't yet clear. He was thinking hard on it when a knock sounded at the door.

Hank Newcomb ushered Mayor Stodt into the office. Case knew instinctively that the visit had nothing to do with their ordinary business. Some visceral hunch told him that the solution to his problem had just walked through the door. He managed to look pleasantly surprised.

"Well, Mr. Mayor," he said, nodding. "What brings you all the way down here?"

Stodt took a wooden armchair before the desk. "I've come at the request of David Hughes. It seems you were right all along."

"Oh?" Case replied. "Right about what?"

"We've decided that three Brannocks are three too many."

Case eyed him with sardonic amusement. "What brought about your change of heart?"

"No one thing," Stodt said blandly. "We just feel they're more liability than asset. A potential problem."

"Someone told me"—Case hesitated, let the silence build—"that Hughes and Virgil Brannock are on the outs. Anything to it?"

"You shouldn't listen to rumors. Our concern has to do with the good of the town. And yours, I might add."

"Hmmm." Case considered that a moment. "How am I involved in your affairs?"

Stodt laughed shortly. "Our concerns are your concerns. We all row the same boat."

"And you think Virgil Brannock might capsize us, is that it?"

"Exactly," Stodt said in a careful, precise voice. "So we want him attended to, along with his brothers. Three birds at once, so to speak."

"Attended to?" Case repeated with a certain amount of sarcasm. "Are you talking about roughing them up—or what?"

Stodt stared at him like a stuffed owl. "What we want is to have them removed."

"Cut the double-talk," Case said cynically. "You're asking me to have them killed, aren't you?"

"Use whatever word you choose. However, it must be done with a degree of finesse. No links to myself or Mr. Hughes—or you."

"I think that can be arranged."

"It must also be done quickly. Any delay would jeopardize certain plans already under way."

"Let me worry about the timing. To do it right, I'll have to organize things just so."

"No," Stodt said sharply. "You have five days to get it done. That time limit is absolute."

"Five days?" Case grinned as if at some private joke. "Brannock must really be crimping Hughes' style. Will the railroad fold if I miss the deadline?"

Stodt fixed him with a baleful look. "Keep your wit to yourself. All we want is a job done well, and done quickly."

Case's eyes went hard as slate. After a moment of deliberation, he leaned forward, elbows on the desk. His face was a mask and his tone was offhand, almost matter-of-fact.

"I'll do your dirty work," he said. "But I want you to deliver a message back to Hughes. Tell him the price for murder is steep. So I'll expect something in return."

"What might that be?"

"Ten percent of everything he steals from the railroad."

"Impossible," Stodt said crossly. "Hughes won't sit still for extortion."

"Then I guess he'll have to do his own killing."

"Don't be a fool! We've come to you in good faith."

"Those are my terms." Case's mouth went tight, scornful. "Take it or leave it."

Stodt glowered at him. "It seems we have no choice. I'll speak with Hughes and suggest that he go along. For now, let's say your terms are acceptable."

"Nice doing business with you, Mr. Mayor."

Stodt ignored the gibe. He rose with a brusque nod and walked from the office.

When the door closed, Case leaned back in his chair. He'd struck a hard bargain, but he felt certain the arrangement would be honored. David Hughes was in no position to negotiate.

After a time, his eyes went once more to the spot of sunlight on the wall. His gaze became abstracted and a slight smile played over his mouth. He began planning murder.

*   *   *

Quintin rolled out of bed. He padded barefoot to the wash-stand and poured water from a pitcher into a cracked basin. He briskly scrubbed his face.

Fully awake, he began dressing. As he stepped into his pants, he wondered about Bob Tobert. Last night, in the midst of the shootout, Tobert had taken a slug through the arm. From his guerrilla days, Quintin was familiar with gunshot wounds. After returning to the hotel, he'd swabbed Tobert's arm with whiskey and wrapped it tightly. He thought there was little chance of infection.

From Tobert, his mind went automatically to Clint Brannock. He still had no idea how the town marshal had tumbled to them. Or why the sneaky bastard had ambushed them on the Black Hawk road. Stage robbery was hardly in the bailiwick of a town lawdog. But Frank Purdy swore that his eyes hadn't lied to him. He'd recognized Brannock as the man on that rocky hillside.

Upon returning to Denver, Quintin had felt reasonably safe. There were no witnesses, apart from the marshal, and it was his word against theirs. The chances of being arrested or brought to trial seemed remote. Still, Quintin took it personally when someone tried to bushwhack him. So he'd arranged a surprise party of his own last night. The upshot was scarcely what he'd expected, and he still couldn't believe all those slugs had missed the mark. He told himself that Brannock must lead a charmed life. Nothing else accounted for the way it had worked out.

Finished dressing, he buckled on his gunbelt. He was hungry and he figured it was time to roust the other men out. Except for Tobert, who would have to rest for a couple of days, there was no reason for them to loaf around in bed. Several things needed discussion, and a damnsight better planning! For openers, since they were almost broke, another holdup would have to be considered. But before that, they would have to figure a way to haul Clint Brannock's ashes. Some things took priority over others.

A knock sounded as he took hold of the doorknob. He pulled his gun and stepped aside, against the wall. With his left hand, he opened the door a crack. Hank Newcomb stood in the hallway.

Holstering his gun, Quintin swung the door open. "What can I do for you?"

"Mr. Case wants to see you."

"What about?"

"Ask him," Newcomb said roughly. "C'mon, let's get a move on."

Quintin's eyes flashed. "You oughtn't to push so hard, friend. Tell him I'll be over after I've had breakfast. Think you can keep that straight?"

Newcomb held his stare a moment. Then, with a dour look, he turned and walked off down the hall. Quintin hesitated, debating whether or not to tell his men. He decided to have breakfast alone.

Some while later Quintin was shown into Case's office. The vice lord waved him to a chair and waited until he was seated. They sat for a moment looking at each other.

Case wagged his head. "Heard you had some hard luck trying to rob the Black Hawk stage."

"Nothin' I can't handle."

"I'd say that's open to debate. You and your boys sure muffed it last night."

Quintin grunted coarsely. "Every dog has his day. We'll get him next time."

"Clint Brannock strikes me as a man who takes considerable getting. Maybe you ought to try the indirect approach."

"I don't exactly follow you."

"You're aware that Earl Brannock is the marshal's brother?"

"So Purdy tells me."

Case gave him a crafty look. "How would you like to own the Bella Union?"

Quintin blinked, sat erect. "You'll have to spell that out."

"It's simple enough," Case said lazily. "You and your boys throw a scare into Brannock. Offer him continued good health for a quit claim to the Bella Union."

Quintin screwed up his face in a whiskery scowl. "What's that got to do with the marshal?"

"I understand Clint Brannock's a hothead. When you threaten his brother, he'll just naturally come looking for you. See what I mean?"

"I'm still listenin'."

"Well, that makes it personal, doesn't it? He'd be acting on his own, not as a lawman. You'll have a legitimate excuse to kill him."

"Sounds a little too pat," Quintin stalled. "What's your interest in the Brannocks?"

"Strictly business," Case said with a sourly amused look. "Earl has some notion he ought to be running the sporting district. I figure he's overstayed his welcome."

"Why not use your own men?"

"Too obvious," Case noted. "Besides, that wouldn't solve your problem, would it? You'd still have the marshal dogging your trail."

Quintin regarded him with squinted eyes. "Purdy says there's a third brother, a liquor dealer. What if he decided to take a hand?"

Case's laugh was scratchy, abrasive. "What's another Brannock more or less? Unless, of course, you're not interested in the Bella Union."

"No," Quintin said with vinegary satisfaction. "I like that idea just fine. Owning a gambling dive would sure beat robbin' stages."

"Good," Case said amiably. "You're my kind of man, Jack. I think we'll do well together."

"Only one thing."

"Yeah, what's that?"

"Suppose Earl Brannock don't scare? Wouldn't that sort of put the quietus on the whole works?"

"I have confidence in you, Jack. You'll think of something."

Quintin gave him a lopsided grin. "I reckon I will at that. Got anything more you want to tell me?"

"One last point," Case said smoothly. "You'll have to wrap it up by the end of the week. Otherwise all bets are off."

"Why's that?"

"Because I want it that way. When you take a chair in my game, you play by my rules. Any objections?"

Quintin laughed a loud booming laugh. "Hell, what's to object about? Consider it done."

Case walked him to the door. They parted with a genial handshake and mutual assurances for the future. After seeing him out, Case looked somewhat like a cat spitting feathers. He congratulated himself on a nifty bit of sleight of hand. All in one day, he had Quintin in one pocket and David Hughes in the other.

And the Brannock brothers a step away from the grave.

31

LATE THAT AFTERNOON, QUINTIN walked through the door of the Bella Union. He was trailed by Frank Purdy and Bill Johnson. They halted midway down the bar.

A single bartender was on duty. With the noon rush come and gone, the place was virtually empty. Three men occupied a table, conversing in low tones. To the rear, the gaming room was dimly lighted and appeared deserted. Quintin signaled the barkeep.

"Where's your boss?"

"You mean Mr. Brannock?"

"He owns the joint, don't he?"

"Sure," the bartender said quickly. "He's back in the office. Want me to get him?"

"Don't bother." Quintin glanced around at Purdy and Johnson. "You boys have a drink. I'll be back directly."

At the end of the bar, Quintin turned down a short hallway. Halting before a door marked PRIVATE, he heard muted voices from inside. He opened it without knocking.

Earl looked up from his desk. Monte turned from a file cabinet on the far side of the office, her expression startled.

Neither of them spoke as Quintin closed the door. He crossed to the desk and stopped.

"How's tricks, Brannock?"

Earl's eyes narrowed. "You have some business with me?"

"The name's Jack Quintin. You might've seen me around."

Leaning back, Earl folded his arms. His right hand slipped underneath his suit jacket, touching the derringer pocketed in his vest. He had no doubt that it was Quintin who had ambushed his brother last night. The odds that today's visit was somehow related seemed to him a virtual certainty. He watched the other man carefully.

"I know who you are," he said. "You and your friends play our tables pretty regular."

"That's a fact," Quintin said agreeably. "Miz Monte can vouch for it better'n most. I don't recollect we've ever beat her."

Monte forced herself to smile. "Your luck is bound to change sometime, Mr. Quintin."

"Yes, ma'am, you're surely right. Way I see it, today's the day."

"How so?" Earl inquired.

Quintin laughed too loudly. " 'Cause today's the day I move around to the other side of the table. I'm here to buy you out."

Earl shook his head in mock wonder. "You want to buy the Bella Union?"

"That's the general idea."

"What makes you think it's for sale?"

"Anything's for sale"—Quintin paused, staring at him— " 'specially for the right price."

Earl returned his gaze steadily. "What would you call the right price?"

"Five thousand," Quintin said with a straight face.

"Little low," Earl observed. "Nowhere near what it's worth."

"All the same," Quintin said with a tight, mirthless smile, "you'd be wise to take it."

"Why is that, Mr. Quintin?"

"For one thing, you'd save yourself a lot of grief. For another, it's the only offer you're gonna get."

Earl kept his tone light. "What if I told you the Bella Union's not for sale—at any price?"

"Wouldn't matter," Quintin said indifferently. "You'll sell."

"Let's suppose I won't," Earl said with a half-smile. "What sort of 'grief' are we talking about?"

Quintin laughed. It was an odd laugh, harsh and rough. "Well, for openers, somebody's liable to wreck your joint to hell and gone. Wouldn't be all that hard to get a brawl started."

"Wouldn't be all that hard to stop it, either. I keep men on the payroll for just that purpose."

"There's ways and there's *ways*. Some would cause you more grief than others."

Earl looked him straight in the eye. "And if none of them worked—what then?"

An angry spark flashed in Quintin's eyes. "Then you and your lady friend oughtn't to hang around. Things would get real hairy real quick."

Monte stiffened. "Listen here—"

"Stay put!" Earl silenced her with a sharp command. His gaze was level and cool, fixed on Quintin. "Take your threats and be on your way. We're through talking."

Quintin jabbed a finger in his face. "Damn right we're through talkin'. You got till tomorrow to wise up. After that, it's tough titty!"

"I'll try to remember," Earl said dryly. "Close the door on your way out."

Quintin slammed the door behind him. There was an uneasy silence and neither Monte nor Earl spoke for several moments. Finally, Earl let out his breath in a low whistle. "I'd say we've been put on warning."

Monte looked stunned. "It doesn't make any sense. Why would he barge in here and put the arm on us?"

"Damn good question," Earl said, clearly perplexed.

"Something stinks." Her voice rose quickly. "Quintin wouldn't pull a stunt like that on his own."

"Probably not," Earl said, almost to himself. "But who the hell put him up to it—and why?"

"I could make an educated guess."

"Go ahead."

A loud crash cut short her reply. The sharp, explosive noise was followed instantly by the sound of shattering glass. Earl bounded out of his chair, turning back toward Monte. He pushed her aside and pulled a sawed-off shotgun from behind the file cabinet. On the way out the door, he thumbed both hammers to full cock. She followed a few steps behind.

In the barroom Quintin roared with laughter. A hurled whiskey bottle had reduced the back-bar mirror to shards of broken glass. Frank Purdy and Bill Johnson looked on with admiring approval as Quintin loudly demanded another bottle. The barkeep, who had retreated toward the front of the bar, took a gingerly step through the debris. He stopped as Earl emerged from the hall entryway.

"Hold it!"

Earl stood with the buttstock tucked into his shoulder. His eyes were steely, and the bore of the shotgun barrels looked big as stovepipes. Halfway up the bar Quintin and his men went immobile. Behind them, the barkeep took a stubby-barreled scattergun from beneath the counter and cocked both hammers. Nobody moved.

"You just bought a mirror," Earl said quietly. "All three of you empty your pockets and be damn quick about it. Careful with your hands."

"Go to hell!" Quintin bristled. "You're not gonna shoot us over a lousy mirror."

Earl wagged the snout of his shotgun. "Open your mouth once more and I'll make your asshole wink. Pay up—now!"

Purdy and Johnson hastily turned their pockets inside out. Coins and greenbacks spilled onto the floor in a bright shower. Quintin hesitated only a moment, then followed suit. He kept his hand clear of the holstered pistol on his hip.

"Turn around," Earl ordered. "Walk out slow and easy. And don't come back."

The three men complied without delay. Earl and the barkeep kept them covered until they passed through the door. Monte stepped from the hallway as Earl lowered the hammers on his shotgun. She touched his arm and he looked around at her. He read in her eyes what he was thinking himself.

Jack Quintin would be back.

"I winged one of the bastards."

"Small consolation," Virgil said soberly. "It's a wonder you weren't killed yourself."

Clint smiled. "Hell, I thought you knew. I carry a lucky rabbit's foot."

"Don't joke about it! We've got to find a way out of this mess. Things have gone too far!"

"You're right there," Clint agreed. "I don't care for a second dose of last night."

Virgil snorted out loud. "Then you'd best stay off the streets at night. Assassins love the dark."

They were seated in Virgil's office. All day Clint had put off dropping by, knowing how it would end. And now, after recounting last night's shooting, he saw that his instincts hadn't played him false. Virgil was in a highly agitated state.

"Way it looks," Clint said at length, "I've played out my string. I've got to get them before they get me."

Virgil frowned, shook his head. "Why not swear out a

warrant, deputize some men? You could have them in jail before nightfall.''

"I've got no proof. It's still my word against theirs."

"Then try the U.S. Marshal again. He'd have no excuse not to act now. They tried to kill a lawman."

Clint smiled bitterly. "Wilbur Smith won't lift a finger. He's already made that plenty clear."

The door opened and Earl hurried into the office. His manner left no doubt that he was in a foul mood. To Virgil's question, he indicated that the problem was Jack Quintin. He briefly outlined the gang leader's visit to the Bella Union.

"Nothing's settled," he finally said. "I got the drop on him and he had to back off. But he'll try again."

"Damn right he will," Clint said coldly. "You should've killed him while you had the chance."

"For breaking a mirror?" Earl countered. "That's not exactly a killing offense."

"For Christ's sake, he threatened you, didn't he? What more do you want?"

Virgil separated them with upraised palms. "What's done is done. Let's not squabble amongst ourselves."

"Suits me," Earl said. "We got all the trouble we can say grace over, anyway."

"And all from one man," Clint said vindictively. "The sonovabitch pops up everywhere you look."

Earl's voice was thoughtful. "I'm not so sure it's one man . . . not anymore."

"How's that again?"

"Stop and think about it a minute. Quintin wouldn't have pulled that on his own hook. Somebody put him up to it."

"By somebody," Clint remarked, "you mean Ed Case, don't you?"

"Nobody else," Earl acknowledged. "Nothing happens in the sporting district without Case's approval. Seems pretty clear he gave Quintin the go-ahead."

"Yeah, you're right. But why would they team up on you? That doesn't make a helluva lot of sense."

"Maybe it does," Virgil interjected. "And it's not altogether coincidence, either. I've got a sneaky hunch who's behind it."

Earl looked at him. "Sounds like you know something we don't?"

A tight fist of apprehension hammered deep in Virgil's stomach. He realized with dark fatalism that their enemies had at last joined forces. Hughes and Case, and now Jack Quintin, had somehow been brought together. And without being told, he knew only too well what it meant. All that he'd worked to build was in danger of collapsing.

Quickly, without elaboration, Virgil revealed what he'd uncovered. Earl and Clint listened attentively as he outlined the scheme to bilk the railroad. Their faces registered first surprise and then admiration as he recounted the meeting with Hughes and Evans. Neither of them interrupted the entire time he spoke.

"That's it," he concluded. "I did what I thought best for the town."

Clint gave him a reproachful look. "You should've told us, Virge. We've never kept secrets before."

"It's not that," Virgil said. "I more or less gave my word to Hughes. I felt obligated to wait until the week was up."

"But *he* didn't," Earl said with sudden insight. "You gave him a week and he put it to good use. The crafty bastard rigged a setup!"

Virgil's face went blank, as if cast in metal. "No question I made a damnfool mistake. I should've known he wouldn't honor the agreement."

"Wait a minute," Clint cut in. "Are you saying he sicced Quintin on Earl?"

Virgil nodded solemnly. "Hughes works in roundabout ways. He probably ordered the mayor to strike a deal with Case. And Case worked his own deal with Quintin."

"So he's using Earl to get at you. Is that the idea?"

"It's more than that," Earl said grimly. "They're out to get all three of us!"

"I'm afraid so," Virgil said with studied calm. "Case wants you out of the way. Quintin has a score to settle with Clint. And Hughes figures I'll get caught in the middle. It's damned ingenious."

Earl cleared his throat. "Let's make sure we're saying the same thing. They're not trying to run us out of town or just put us out of business. They intend to kill us."

After a marked silence, Virgil inclined his head. "It appears Hughes is a bit more sinister than I suspected. With the stakes so high, I guess he couldn't take any chances. He has to shut me up for good."

Clint fixed him with a strange, unsettling look. "Virge, you almost sound like you admire the bastard. Aren't you a little ticked off he's trying to get you killed?"

"Of course I am," Virgil said. "I'm just sorry it's come down to this. Once I expose him, Denver loses its best hope for a railroad."

"Expose him?" Clint's voice dropped. "Wouldn't it be smarter to kill him?"

Virgil shook his head in stern disapproval. "We might be able to work a trade-off of some sort. It's just possible we could still save the railroad. I'll have a talk with Walter Tisdale."

A sudden anger welled up in Clint. His mouth set in a hard line. "The time for talk is long past. I don't like people shooting at me."

"Neither do I," Virgil said. "But Walter Tisdale carries a lot of weight in this town. There's a chance he could work it out."

"You talk all you want," Clint said, getting to his feet. "I think I'll put an end to the shooting."

"How do you propose to do that?"

"I'll brace Quintin. Without him, the whole scheme falls apart."

Virgil forced himself to stay calm. "Clint, listen to me. There's no percentage in going up against Quintin and his bunch. We still have—"

"Save your breath." Clint's eyes went pale and vengeful. "You've stopped me once too often already. Don't try it again."

"Goddammit! You'll get yourself killed."

"The hell I will."

Clint laughed and walked out the door. He didn't look back.

32

A BLOCK FROM THE warehouse Earl caught up with him. They walked in silence for a short distance, neither looking at the other. Abruptly, Clint stopped and turned to face him.

"Virge send you after me?"

"Not exactly."

"What's that supposed to mean?"

Earl lifted his hands in a shrug. "I volunteered."

"To help me," Clint pressed him, "or talk me out of it?"

"Would talk stop you?"

"No."

Earl smiled. "No need to try, then. I guess I'll just tag along."

Clint studied him a moment. "What about Virge?"

Earl had hoped to avoid the question. Since childhood, he had been envious of the relationship between Virgil and Clint. His earliest memory was of the youngest brother being singled out for special treatment. But now, forced to take sides, he found himself standing with Clint. The irony of it gave him pause.

"Virgil's changed," he said in a rueful tone. "Maybe the

war took the starch out of him. Or maybe he's just got too citified. I don't rightly know what happened. I just know he's changed.''

Clint suddenly looked troubled. ''You're not saying he's lost his nerve, are you?''

''Hell, no,'' Earl replied forcefully. ''It took a lot of backbone to tangle with Hughes. Nobody's ever done that before.''

''Then what are you saying?''

''I suppose it's a different way of looking at things. Virge believes there's a peaceable way of settling just about any dispute. He's come to be real law-abiding.''

''Judas Priest!'' Clint swore. ''What's any of that got to do with Jack Quintin?''

''Not much,'' Earl said dismally. ''But he's got it all mixed up inside his head. He figures there's a civilized way to stop Hughes . . . and Quintin.''

''By God, maybe he's off his rocker! Nothing short of a dose of lead will stop Quintin.''

''You know that and I know that. Trouble is, no amount of argument will convince Virge. He'd have to be pushed to the limit before he'll fight.''

Clint knew it was the truth. He saw now that Virgil wouldn't take up the fight until it was the last way out. Yet Earl was of a different mind, perhaps too willing. As he pondered it a moment longer, Clint saw no reason to put either of his brothers in harm's way. He thought it could be settled by one man, and fairly quickly.

''Tell you what,'' he said, nodding to Earl. ''I've got to work things out just so before I make my play. Where will you be later?''

''At the Bella Union,'' Earl said with a skeptical look. ''What is it you have to work out?''

Clint laughed. ''The only thing that counts with a backshooter like Quintin. I want an edge.''

''How do you plan on doing that?''

"I'll let you know after I've scouted around. Look for me sometime after dark."

Clint left him there. Earl had the unsettling feeling that he'd been fobbed off with a half-truth. Yet he couldn't imagine that Clint would try it alone. Not after he'd offered to help.

He headed back to the Bella Union.

Late that evening Clint went searching for the gang. From their past carousing, he knew they would be somewhere on Blake Street. He began a cautious tour of the gambling dives.

One place he avoided was the Bella Union. He had no intention of involving Earl in what he planned. Nor was he willing to risk a chance encounter and be forced into more lies. He figured Earl and Virgil would hear about it soon enough, after the fact.

The Progressive Club was where he found them. Outside, he stopped on the boardwalk and peered through the front window. He saw Quintin and two of the gang standing at the bar. The third man, the one he'd wounded, was nowhere in sight. Still, with the odds at three to one, he would have to move swiftly to gain an edge. He considered it fitting that he'd found them in Ed Case's joint.

Curbing his impatience, Clint waited for the right moment. A few minutes passed before several customers vacated a spot at the bar, moving across to a faro table. The empty spot, which was directly beside the gang, suited Clint perfectly. He stepped through the door and walked straight to the bar. Halting, he casually leaned into the counter, his left boot heel hooked over the brass rail. His right arm dangled loosely at his side.

Frank Purdy spotted him in the back-bar mirror. With a sudden jerk, Purdy elbowed Quintin in the ribs. The gang leader was closest to the door, separated from Clint by less than ten feet. He straightened slightly, leaving his hands on the bar, and slowly looked around.

Clint nodded. "You're Jack Quintin."

A statement rather than a question, the remark took Quintin by surprise. "You got some business with me, Marshal?"

"I'm looking for somebody. Maybe you know him?"

"Who's that?"

"Stage robber," Clint said evenly. "I waylaid him and his men day before yesterday on the Black Hawk road."

Quintin's tone was flat and guarded. "What's that got to do with me?"

"Damnedest thing," Clint said a bit more loudly. "You're a dead ringer for the one who looked to be in charge. Fact is, you must have a twin."

Quintin eyed him with a glassy expression. "I've heard tell everybody's got a look-alike."

"Yeah, but yours sure gets around."

"I don't take your meanin'."

"Last night," Clint said in a rougher tone, "him and his assassins tried to bushwhack me. One of them was your friend there, Frank Purdy."

Purdy snapped erect. "Wait a gawddamn—"

"Shut your trap!" Quintin silenced him without looking around. "You must have powerful good eyes, Marshal. How'd you spot anybody in the dark?"

"Just lucky," Clint said, holding his gaze. "I saw the ring leader there, too. Damned if it wasn't your twin brother again."

Quintin sized him up with a lengthy stare. "Sounds like you're tryin' to accuse me of something."

"Yeah, I am," Clint said deliberately. "You tried to rob the stage and you tried to kill me. By all rights, I ought to arrest you."

Several bystanders abruptly moved away from the bar. Conversation ceased at the gaming tables and a stark silence fell over the room. Quintin stood immobilized, as though frozen in place. His expression was puzzled.

"You sayin' you're not gonna arrest me?"

"Not till I'm finished with my story."

"What story?"

Clint's mouth lifted in a tight grin. "You ever hear of a Kansas guerrilla outfit called the Jayhawkers?"

Quintin's face went chalky. "What about 'em?"

"Back in '61, they raided through Missouri. Hit a farm that belonged to my folks, outside Harrisonville. Killed my pa and my ma."

"So?" Quintin bridled. "What's that got to do with me?"

Clint's eyes took on a peculiar glitter. "You're the sorry sonovabitch that killed them."

All the blood leeched out of Quintin's features. Yet he was not foolhardy enough to mistake the nature of the insult. He knew he was looking death in the face.

Hands still glued to the bar, he met Clint's gaze levelly. "What's your game, Brannock?"

Clint smiled. "Let's keep it between ourselves. Tell your boys to stand aside and we'll settle it man to man. I'll even take the badge off."

Quintin saw that he'd been suckered. The challenge involved a personal matter and obligated him to stand alone. How Brannock had tracked him down and identified him as a former guerrilla changed nothing. With witnesses present, three against one would be viewed as murder. He had no wish to be hanged, and yet he sensed it was a fight he couldn't win. He saw it written in Brannock's smile.

"No soap," he said firmly. "I've got no quarrel with you."

Clint shoved away from the bar. His expression was dark with rage. "C'mon, Quintin, you've killed enough old ladies in your time. Try a man for a change."

"*Marshal Brannock.*"

Ed Case appeared in a doorway at the rear of the room. His voice was sharp with authority and instantly brought the room to a standstill. He hurried forward, positioning himself between the two men. He looked straight at Clint.

"A lawman shouldn't start fights, Marshal Brannock. You ought to know better."

Clint fixed him with a cold stare. "You're awful chummy with the likes of Quintin. What's your stake in this, Case?"

"No stake at all," Case said briskly. "I just don't allow arguments to be settled in my place. Yours or anyone else's!"

Clint took a grip on himself. He'd lost the chance to push Quintin into a fight. Yet now, scored through with anger, he was on the verge of saying too much. One miscue would alert Case that he, too, was under suspicion. It seemed wise to back off and take stock.

"Quintin."

The former Jayhawker looked around. Clint smiled, his expression almost benign. "The next time we meet . . . you're dead."

Nodding to Case, he turned and walked away. As he went through the door, it occurred to him that he'd almost pulled it off. But then, as he had just warned Quintin, there would be a next time. A final reckoning.

The moon went behind a cloud. The town was dark and still, Blake Street closed for the night. Corner streetlamps flickered like erratic fireflies.

Quintin emerged from the rear door of the Progressive Club. Following close behind were Purdy and Johnson. They crossed the alley and halted before a small storage shed. After unlatching the door, Quintin groped around inside until he found the coal-oil cans. Holding two gallons each, there were four cans, normally used to replenish lamps in the gaming dive. He handed out the cans to his men and dropped the latch back in place. Turning, he led them down the darkened alley.

A short time earlier Quintin had met with Ed Case. They were both disgruntled and simmering with anger over Clint Brannock's open challenge. Their original plan, designed to provoke all three Brannock brothers, would have to be scotched. Something more direct was needed, an affront that would goad the Brannocks beyond reason. Quintin had been quick to adopt the new plan laid out by Case. The chance to retaliate for tonight's humiliation was incentive enough. There was, moreover, a pressing need to silence a link to his guerrilla past. Added to all that was a plum thrown in by Case: the promise of a steady job in the vice lord's organization. He'd listened intently as Case told him about the storage shed.

By four o'clock, Quintin and his men were positioned behind the Bella Union. Uncapping the cans, Purdy went one way and Johnson went the other. While they sloshed coal oil on the sides of the building, Quintin methodically doused the rear. A reserve was held back in the last can, and Quintin carefully spilled a trail on the ground as they retreated along the alley. Some distance away, he dug a match from his pocket and popped it on his thumbnail. Stooping down, he touched the flame to the wet earth. The coal oil flared and they took off running.

A thin streamer of fire hurtled toward the Bella Union. When it hit the foundation, the coal oil ignited with a *whoosh* and a second later the entire bottom floor exploded in a holocaust of flame. Fueled by dry timber, the fire spread rapidly to the upper floor. Smoke billowed skyward and tongues of flame leapt toward the roof. Within moments, the sides and rear of the building were engulfed in a solid wall of fire.

Upstairs, one of the housemen was the first to raise the alarm. Hammering on doors, he ran along the hall, awakening others. By the time Earl and Monte rushed from their suite, the upper floor was enveloped in thick, blinding smoke. Still in his nightshirt, Earl hustled Monte down the stairs and through the main barroom. She hesitated, unwilling to be seen on the street in her nightgown, and he physically shoved her through the door. They stumbled outside, gagging and choking, and dropped to their knees in the street. The last of the housemen raced from the door as the building was transformed into a raging inferno.

Denver's volunteer fire department arrived too late. The

walls buckled and the Bella Union settled inward upon itself. Then the roof collapsed, demolishing the upper story in a volcanic roar, and crashed downward. Cinders and sparks leapt skyward, and firebrands were hurled onto adjoining buildings. The fire fighters quickly trained their hoses on a dance hall and a saloon, which immediately flanked the Bella Union. For a time, the flames threatened to spread and turn the sporting district into a smoldering tinderbox. Only with herculean effort were the volunteers able to contain it before the water wagon ran dry. A bucket brigade was quickly formed from the pump at a horse trough.

Earl and Monte watched from across the street. As the bucket brigade went into action, flames lapped at the rubble and fiery timbers flashed a brilliant orange. There was one last flare and then the ruins leveled in a glowing bed of coals. A chill wind fanned the embers and the Bella Union settled into a smoky pyre. An eerie hush fell over Blake Street.

Monte shivered, clutching a fireman's coat around her shoulders. Beside her, Earl's gaze was riveted on the spot where the Bella Union had stood not an hour ago. All about them, onlookers drawn by the fire huddled in shocked silence. Earl's eyes were glazed and his expression was one of blunted disbelief. He seemed rooted in place, unable to look away.

Clint suddenly appeared in the crowd. He bulled a path through the onlookers, glancing at Monte as he halted before them. His gaze shifted then to Earl and what he saw left him momentarily chilled. Across Earl's face was a look of cold black rage. His eyes were dead.

"How'd it start?" Clint asked. "Anybody see anything?"

"No," Monte said softly. "We just barely got out alive."

"But we're alive," Earl said in a strange voice. "And Jack Quintin will live just long enough to regret it."

Clint searched his eyes. "What've you got in mind?"

"Come daylight, we'll hunt him down and kill him."

"Just like that?"

"Yeah," Earl muttered coldly. "Just like that."

33

DAWN WAS STILL A gray smudge on the horizon. Virgil stood looking out the window, hands locked behind his back. In the sallow overcast of light, his features were taut and worried.

Earl and Clint sat slumped in chairs. The parlor lamps were turned low, and the beat of the hall clock was clearly audible. From the kitchen, where Elizabeth and Monte were fixing coffee, there was the sound of muted conversation. A funeral atmosphere hung over the parlor.

Earl and Monte, accompanied by Clint, had arrived only a short while ago. With the firemen's help, Earl had reclaimed his office safe from the rubble. The gold dust he'd salvaged was the only bright point in an otherwise long and dismal night. After borrowing clothes for himself and Monte, he had recounted their escape from the Bella Union. Elizabeth had then whisked Monte off to the kitchen, leaving the men to talk.

Virgil's face was haggard. His eyes were circled with bruised-looking rings and his forehead was etched with lines. Staring out the window, he was overcome with the grudging realization that he'd been wrong. Neither the threat of exposure nor his father-in-law's intervention would force David Hughes to act in good faith. There was no sensible solution to the problem, no compromise. The Bella Union fire eliminated any appeal to reason.

Turning from the window, he crossed to where his brothers sat wrapped in grim silence. He took a chair opposite them and drew a deep breath. His expression was one of absolute resignation.

"I miscalculated," Virgil said. "There's no reasonable way to deal with Hughes. I see that now."

Earl studied him with bloodshot eyes. "You did what you thought best. Let's consider it spilt cream and get on with what has to be done."

"You're talking about Jack Quintin."

"For openers," Earl observed. "After tonight, he damn sure heads the list."

Virgil massaged his jaw, thinking. "Will that force Ed Case to deal himself a hand?"

"I tend to doubt it. Case must've had good reason to stay out of it. Otherwise, why would he have used Quintin?"

"Just the same, we can't assume anything. Case might decide to *loan* Quintin a few of his men."

"So what?" Clint said woodenly. "Whichever way it falls doesn't change a damn thing. We've got no choice now."

"Clint's right," Earl said in a low voice. "Either we stand and fight, or we run. Quintin knows it's personal now, and he won't stop. We're the direct link to his Jayhawker days."

Clint's eyes were fierce. His jaw clenched so tight that his lips barely moved. "You can forget that talk about running. So far as I'm concerned, we take the fight to him. We've put it off too long already."

A worm of doubt still gnawed at Virgil. His temples knotted and he took his time about answering. When he did, his voice had an unusual timbre. "It won't be easy," he said. "Quintin will expect us to come looking for him. How do you propose to do it?"

"Simplest way possible," Clint said impassively. "He'll expect us to try something tricky, like waiting till nightfall. So, instead, we'll catch him out in the open—in broad daylight."

Virgil paused, regarding him with a dour look. "That might be more difficult than it sounds."

"You leave it to me. I know just the place . . . and the time."

Clint stood and pulled out his pocket watch. He consulted it a moment, then looked up. "Be ready to leave a little before ten. I ought to get back long before that."

Virgil watched him intently. "Where are you going?"

"Down to the jail," Clint said with a slow smile. "For what we've got in mind, you boys will need some guns. I'll pick you out a couple of good ones."

The hall clock chimed six as Clint walked out. To the east, the first rays of sunrise appeared over the horizon. As streamers of light filtered through the windows, Virgil rose and doused the table lamps. He nodded solemnly to Earl.

"I want to have a word with Beth."

Some moments later Virgil followed Elizabeth down the hallway. Entering their bedroom, he closed the door and leaned back against it. She turned to face him.

"Poor Earl," she said, her features wretched. "And Monte, too, of course. I feel so sorry for them."

"Monte's a good woman," Virgil said quietly. "I appreciate your taking her in, treating her decent."

"Well, why wouldn't I? Whatever else she is, she's very much in love with Earl. Anyone could see that."

Virgil hesitated, staring at her. "You heard everything Earl said about the fire. How it was probably set by Jack Quintin?"

"Yes . . . ?"

"And you remember what I told you about Quintin. How he killed our folks?"

A pulse throbbed in her neck. "What is it you're trying to tell me?"

Virgil's words were almost inaudible, so quiet she had to strain to hear. "We've talked it out and there's no way around it. We have to go after Quintin."

Her face went slack. A pinpoint of terror surfaced in her eyes and her mouth froze in a silent oval. When she spoke, her voice was strangely tortured.

"You won't try to arrest him, will you?"

"No." Virgil's jaw set in a hard line. "It's gone too far for that."

"Are you—" She choked on the words. "You intend to kill him, don't you?"

Virgil seemed turned to stone. "It's the only way."

She shook her head violently. "You told me you wouldn't have any part of it. You said Clint was wrong and that revenge never solved anything. You promised!"

"Things change," Virgil said, averting his gaze. "I'd hoped to settle it along peaceable lines. But Hughes won't have it that way. He just keeps pushing."

"Go to Father," she pleaded. "Let him try again."

Virgil gave her a bleak smile. "Hughes lied to your father. Told him not to worry, that everything would work itself out. You see where that's led."

"Please," she whispered, desperation in her voice. "Try once more . . . for me."

Virgil's headshake was slow and emphatic. "We've run out of time. Either we get Quintin or he'll get us. Nobody could stop it now."

Tears welled up in her eyes. For a moment she thought she would faint. Then, drawing on some inner strength, she regained her composure. She brushed away a tear with the back of her hand.

"There's no other way—you're certain?"

"I'm certain," Virgil assured her. "Sometimes the only way is the worst way. I reckon it's come down to that."

"Then you must promise me something."

"I will if I can."

She smiled wanly. "Promise me you won't take any chances. No silly heroics."

"Don't worry about that. Only a fool gives a mad dog an even break. And you didn't marry a fool."

"Good! I want you back here safe and sound."

"I'll do my damnedest to arrange it."

Her smile widened, and Virgil thought it the saddest smile he'd ever seen. Yet he knew she was putting on a brave front, and all for his benefit. He moved away from the door and she rushed forward, throwing herself into his arms. She buried her head against his chest and forced back her tears. Her voice trembled.

"Don't you dare forget your promise, Virgil Brannock."

"Wouldn't think of it, Mrs. Brannock. Cross my heart."

It was a sunny morning with a bite of October in the air. Shortly before ten they filed out of the house and turned toward the sporting district. From the parlor window, the women watched until they were out of sight.

Earl carried a sawed-off shotgun. Similar to the one he'd kept at the Bella Union, the scattergun was double-barreled and loaded with buckshot. Virgil was armed with a Henry lever-action carbine, which held fifteen .44-caliber cartridges. The narrow forestock allowed him to take a secure grip with the crippled fingers of his left hand. While selecting weapons for his brothers, Clint had decided on a spare pistol for himself. A Remington .44 Army was stuffed crossdraw-fashion in the waistband of his trousers.

None of them spoke as they moved through the residential area. All that needed saying had been said back at the house. Their thoughts were focused now on what lay ahead and how it might be done in the most expeditious manner. The war had taught them that there was no code of honor attached to killing. It was a matter best approached from a practical standpoint; the veteran took every advantage possible while offering the other man none. Those who placed honor before survival seldom lived to regret their mistake. The idea was to walk away in one piece when the shooting stopped.

Will Byers spotted them as they passed the newspaper. He hurried out the door and fell in beside Virgil. On the boardwalk, several passersby halted to point and gawk as the men crossed the intersection. Byers looked at Virgil's carbine like it was a coiled viper. His face was doughy and stunned.

"What's wrong?" he asked nervously. "Why are you carrying guns?"

Virgil's head swiveled around. "Get off the street, Will. This doesn't concern you."

"For God's sake, Virgil! At least tell me what's happened."

"It's a personal matter. You'll hear about it soon enough."

Byers shook his head as if a fly had buzzed his ear. "You're not serious! You're actually going to kill someone?"

"The someone," Earl interjected, "is a son of a bitch named Jack Quintin. He burned down my place last night."

"Virgil, listen to me," Byers said, trying to match their stride. "You can't take the law into your own hands. People just won't sanction that sort of thing! You'll ruin yourself with everyone that counts."

Clint laughed. "Everyone that counts better find themselves a hole. They're the ones behind Quintin."

"What—?" Byers' jaw fell open as though hinged. "Virgil, what's he talking about?"

Virgil brushed him aside. "Stay out of it, Will. Leave well enough alone."

Byers stumbled and broke stride. They left him standing in the intersection as they mounted the boardwalk on the far side. One block over they rounded the corner onto Blake Street. Clint led the way into a saloon with a plate-glass window up front. From there, they had a clear view of Quintin's hotel, which was on an oblique angle across the street. A block away the burned-out rubble of the Bella Union was visible.

The saloon was deserted. A lone bartender wisely busied himself polishing glasses. Standing back away from the window, the three brothers were all but invisible to anyone on the street. As the sun climbed higher, the morning chill gave way to the crisp warmth of early autumn. It occurred to Virgil that he'd arrived in Denver not quite five months past. He wondered if today was his last day in town.

A few minutes before eleven the hotel door opened. Quintin stepped outside, followed by Purdy and Johnson. Bob Tobert, who appeared to be favoring his left arm, was last out the door. Stretching and yawning, they stood for a moment sunning themselves on the boardwalk. Finally, with Quintin in the lead, they turned upstreet toward the café.

Inside the saloon, Clint moved to the door. He pulled the Colt and held it alongside his leg. Behind him, Virgil cocked the Henry carbine and Earl eared back both hammers on his shotgun. Their eyes met, shifting from one to another, and something unspoken passed between them. Nothing in their look betrayed what they felt; their features were hard and determined. Nodding, Clint pushed through the batwing doors.

Outside, they stepped off the boardwalk. Separating, they moved several feet apart and started across the street. Clint, who was in the middle, set the pace. They angled toward the café, on a line to intersect the gang. All street traffic abruptly stopped and passersby scurried for cover. Some ten yards from the opposite boardwalk, they halted.

Quintin took their measure in one swift glance. The other men, who were fanned out around him, watched the Brannocks with doglike stares. A beat slipped past as the men on the boardwalk and the men in the street eyed one another in tense silence. No one seemed inclined to make the first move. At last, Clint nodded to Quintin.

"Defend yourself," he said roughly. "You won't get a second chance."

"Hold on!" Quintin's voice was tight. "We're not lookin' for trouble."

Clint fixed him with a pale stare. "Want it or not, you've found it, Quintin. Fight or get killed."

"Go to hell," Quintin snarled. "You're not gonna murder us. And we both know it."

Frank Purdy's nerves snapped. He darted behind Quintin, jerking his pistol, and scuttled toward the café door. Clint reacted instinctively, leveling his Colt in a blurred motion. He fired, and Purdy dropped like a puppet cut loose from his strings. In the same instant, Quintin and Johnson, followed closely by Tobert, clawed at their holstered pistols. Virgil and Earl shouldered their weapons in unison.

Gunfire suddenly became general. A load of buckshot sizzled across the street as Earl triggered his scattergun. Tobert and Johnson cleared leather and fired almost simultaneously with the report of Virgil's carbine. Quintin backed away, firing as he moved, and ran toward the far corner. Earl took a slug through the leg, collapsing as he emptied the second barrel. Opposite him, Tobert stumbled backward, clutching at his gut, and fell spraddled out on the boardwalk. A bullet nipped Virgil's left arm and he extended the carbine, firing one-handed. Bill Johnson shuffled sideways, arms flailing, and went down.

Clint fired a snap shot as Quintin neared the corner. The slug drilled through a lamppost and Quintin dodged around the corner, disappearing from sight. All too aware that both Virgil and Earl were wounded, Clint took off in a hard sprint. At the corner, he skidded to a stop and cautiously edged around the building. A short distance away he saw Quintin fumbling with the reins of a horse tied at a hitch rack. He brought the Colt to eye level.

"*Quintin!*"

At the sound of his name, Quintin ducked low and slipped

between the horse and the hitch rack. He bobbed up on the other side and fired a wild shot across the saddle. The horse reared, popping the reins, and backed into the street. Clint feathered the trigger the instant the horse cleared his line of fire. A surprised look came over Quintin's face, then a dark splotch spread outward from his breastbone. His eyeballs rolled back in his head and he vomited a great gout of blood down across his chest. He dropped dead on the ground.

Clint turned away. Upstreet, he saw the fallen gang members sprawled on the boardwalk. Virgil was still holding the carbine, as though covering them, his left arm dangling at his side. A few yards beyond, Earl was calmly cinching his belt around his upper thigh. His pants leg was soaked with blood.

All along the street people began appearing in doorways. Hurrying forward, Clint holstered his Colt on the run. When he was only a few steps away, Virgil wobbled drunkenly, dropping the carbine. Clint caught him as he fell, lowering him to the ground. Looking closer, he saw a ragged hole in Virgil's coat sleeve, wet with blood. He rapped out a sharp command to the bystanders.

"Somebody get a doctor!"

34

WALTER TISDALE HURRIED UP the walkway. He appeared visibly agitated as he crossed the porch. Halting before the door, he knocked loudly.

A moment passed, then the door opened. Gun in hand, Clint looked out and inspected the street. There was no one else in sight, and he finally stepped aside, holstering his pistol. He nodded to the banker. "C'mon in, Mr. Tisdale."

"Aren't you carrying things a bit far?"

Clint locked the door. "I reckon I'll have to be the judge of that."

"Speaking of judgment," Tisdale said in a peevish tone, "you exercised all too little of it this morning. The town won't stand for a lawman who uses the law to his own ends."

"Too bad." Clint gave him a crooked grin. "I'll be hard to replace."

"Indeed!" Tisdale huffed. "I want to see my daughter."

"Try the parlor."

Tisdale turned on his heel and marched across the vestibule. As he entered the parlor, he stopped abruptly, his face arrested in shock. Virgil was slumped on the sofa, the left sleeve of his shirt torn away at the shoulder. Seated beside him, Elizabeth was gingerly wrapping his arm with a fresh bandage. A pan of bloody water was on the floor at her feet.

Through the opposite door, Tisdale's attention was drawn to the dining room. Earl was stretched out on the table, lying on a blood-soaked bedsheet. He was naked, except for undershorts, and appeared to be in considerable pain. Dr. Harry Caldwell was bent over his leg, digging for the bullet with a surgical probe. Assisting him, Monte stood nearby with gauze swabs and a tray of instruments. Her face was a study in anguish.

Clint moved past Tisdale and into the dining room. He stopped beside the table, trading a quick look with Monte. Watching them, Tisdale was reminded of stories he'd heard about field hospitals during the war. He idly wondered if Earl would lose the leg to infection. Then, collecting himself, he turned once more to his daughter and her husband. He took a chair opposite the sofa, nodding to Elizabeth as she tied off the bandage. He looked at Virgil.

"Are you all right?"

"Got lucky," Virgil said. "The bullet went clean through. Earl's the one we have to worry about."

Tisdale glanced toward the dining room. "Why weren't you taken to Caldwell's office? I'd think he would have preferred to operate there."

"Clint figured we were better off here. We might yet have some trouble with Ed Case."

"You're not serious!"

Virgil stared at him. "Quintin was working hand-in-glove with Case. I wouldn't rule anything out."

"Good Lord," Tisdale muttered hollowly. "Four dead men, and you and your brother shot down. Whatever possessed you?"

"Stop it!" Elizabeth snapped. "Virgil only did what he had to do. I won't have him criticized."

Virgil patted her hand. She seemed to calm down and he

glanced back at Tisdale. "We were justified in going after Quintin and his gang. When you hear the whole story, you'll agree."

"Whether I do or don't," Tisdale replied, "has no bearing on the situation. You burned all your bridges this morning."

"What's that supposed to mean?"

Tisdale looked at him with utter directness. "Talk has already started circulating around town. You're being accused of taking the law into your own hands . . . a personal vendetta."

"That's partly true," Virgil admitted. "But any man has the right to protect himself and his family. Quintin meant to kill us."

"Can you prove it?"

"No—I can't."

"Can you prove he was tied in with Ed Case?"

Virgil shook his head. "Nothing that'll hold up in court."

"So there you are," Tisdale said dolefully. "Hughes will play on public opinion. He'll say that a man who shoots other men down in the street cannot be trusted."

"I don't give a damn what he says."

"You should," Tisdale remarked. "He'll use the shooting to have you removed from the railroad's board of directors. I have no doubt he'll also arrange your dismissal as head of the board of trade."

Virgil's features mottled with anger. "Just let him try! I've got a thing or two to say myself."

"No, Virgil," Tisdale said with conviction. "You've lost the fight with David Hughes. By nightfall, you will be an outcast in Denver's business community. And, I might add, a social leper as well."

Virgil stiffened, glanced at Elizabeth out of the corner of his eye. "I've told you the truth, Walter. How Hughes and Evans rigged their railroad scheme. All of it."

"I fail to see your point."

"A public statement from you would set the record

straight. Nobody would believe Hughes' lies then.''

Elizabeth seemed to hold her breath. She stared at her father with a look of fearful expectation. Tisdale studied his hands, unable to meet her gaze. At last, his eyes shifted to Virgil.

''I'm not proud of what I'm about to say. I have my life and a rather sizable fortune invested in Denver. Sound business sense dictates that I not antagonize David Hughes. It's a fight I couldn't win either.''

Virgil regarded him with a thoughtful frown. ''In other words, I'm out on a limb—by myself.''

Tisdale spread his hands in an apologetic shrug. ''I'm afraid you've already sawn the limb off.''

''Yeah, so I have.'' Virgil paused, his mouth fixed in a humorless smile. ''Gets lonely being a crusader, doesn't it?''

A strained moment elapsed, then Tisdale cleared his throat. ''There is a solution.''

''What's that?''

''Suppose I were to buy you out? Your liquor business, the icehouses, everything.''

''Why would you do that?''

''Well, after all,'' Tisdale said lamely, ''you are my son-in-law. I'd be willing to offer you a fair profit on your investment. That way, you and Elizabeth could go somewhere else—start over.''

Virgil hesitated, considering. ''Somewhere else besides Denver, is that it?''

Tisdale nodded. ''Under the circumstances, I believe discretion is the better part of valor. You no longer have a future here, Virgil. It ended on Blake Street this morning.''

There was a long beat of silence. Virgil's features were wreathed in disgust and he seemed to look through the older man. Finally, with a heavy sigh, he turned to Elizabeth. ''What do you think?'' he asked. ''Want to pull up stakes and try it somewhere else?''

She smiled, reached for his hand. ''I think the future is

what we make it. There are lots of places besides Denver.''

Virgil held her eyes a moment. His features softened and he gently squeezed her hand. At length, he glanced back at Tisdale. ''You heard her, Walter. You've got yourself a deal.''

''A wise decision, my boy. You won't regret it.''

Clint appeared in the dining-room entryway. ''Virge, the doc's finished. He got the bullet.''

''How's Earl?''

''Come see for yourself.''

Virgil rose, leaving Elizabeth with her father. Inside the dining room, he found Earl resting easy though somewhat groggy. Across the table, the physician was stuffing instruments into his bag. He looked up at Virgil.

''Your brother should come through nicely, Mr. Brannock. There was no bone damage and the bullet didn't fragment. We'll just have to keep our fingers crossed where infection's concerned.''

''I appreciate everything you've done.''

''Not at all.'' Caldwell snapped his bag closed. ''I've given your brother some laudanum to ease the pain. He's in capable hands with Miss Verde.''

Monte smiled. ''You did a swell job, Doc.''

''I had a good assistant.'' Caldwell moved around the table, nodding to Virgil. ''Your arm shouldn't give us any problems. How's it feel?''

''Sore as hell.''

''I shouldn't wonder,'' Caldwell said, walking toward the door. ''Stay off your feet and try to get some rest. I'll stop by again this evening.''

Virgil approached the table. As Clint moved up beside him, Earl's eyes rolled open. He looked at them with a dopey smile. ''Goddamn sawbones. They all like to hand out orders.''

''Listen to him,'' Virgil said, cocking one eyebrow. ''Sounds awful perky for a man who stopped a bullet.''

"You've got lots of room to talk."

"Well, we're alive, and that's what counts. It could've been worse."

Clint gave him a sidewise look. "What's with your big-time in-law? You two sounded mighty serious in there."

Virgil briefly explained the situation. He ended with an offhand gesture. "Guess it's lucky I'm related to a banker. Nobody else would've bought me out."

"Fall of the dice," Earl mumbled. "Wish I had something left to sell. Not much market for soot and ashes."

Clint seemed to square himself up. "Think I'll take a walk downtown. I've got some personal business to tend to."

Virgil shot him a look. "What sort of personal business?"

"Odds and ends," Clint said, glancing across at Monte. "Want me to help you get the gamblin' man into a bed?"

"We'll manage," Monte said with a knowing smile. "Give my best to Belle."

"I'll do it."

"Watch yourself," Virgil warned. "We still don't know where Ed Case stands."

Clint pulled the Remington pistol out of his waistband. He checked the loads and laid it on the table. "Keep that handy till I get back."

As he turned away, Virgil reached down and picked up the pistol. The solid heft of it felt somehow comforting, and welcome. He stuffed it in the top of his trousers.

With Elizabeth's help, Monte got Earl off the table. He was weak but game, and managed to balance himself on his right leg. Supporting him between them, Monte and Elizabeth walked him slowly toward a back bedroom. He hobbled along on one leg, arms draped across their shoulders.

Virgil followed behind, his left arm now cradled in a sling. In the bedroom, the women jockeyed Earl into position and sat him on the edge of the bed. The covers were already turned down, and Elizabeth took his shoulder, lowering him onto his back. Whatever embarrassment she felt at handling a half-naked man was deftly concealed. Monte gently lifted his legs onto the bed, covering him with a sheet.

Earl's face was beaded with sweat. He tried to smile even though his teeth were gritted against the pain. Elizabeth patted his arm with genuine concern and then joined Virgil at the door. Monte fussed over him a moment, dabbing his forehead with a soft cloth. When his eyelids began to droop, she turned and crossed the room. She looked directly at Elizabeth.

"Thank you," she said gratefully. "Taking us into your home like this—well, it's awfully good of you."

"Nonsense!" Elizabeth protested. "I would have been insulted if you hadn't come here. After all, we're family."

Monte smiled, genuinely touched. "We both know what I am, and it's not family. Just saying it, though, proves you're every bit the lady I've heard."

Elizabeth shook her head. "We're not all that different, Monte. And no matter what anyone says, you're family!"

"Awright, ladies," Virgil said lightly. "Suppose we let Earl get some rest. I could use a little shut-eye myself."

Elizabeth and Monte spontaneously hugged one another. When they parted, their eyes were glistening with emotion. Virgil cleared his throat, suddenly unable to speak, and led Elizabeth into the hallway.

After closing the door, Monte dried her eyes and turned back into the room. As she stopped beside the bed, Earl grinned up at her.

"Sounds like you found a friend."

"Listen, you," she scolded. "Why aren't you asleep?"

"I'll get around to it."

"Maybe you need another dose of laudanum."

"Not just yet," Earl said. "I want to talk to you about something."

"Oh?" she said slowly. "What's so important that it won't wait?"

Earl's smile seemed forced, his voice strained. "I was wondering what we ought to do next. What do you think?"

"I think you ought to close your eyes. You're starting to sound delirious."

"Humor me," Earl said, no longer smiling. "We're right back where we started. We've got our wits and a stake—and that's it."

She gave him a wise, appraising look. "You obviously have something in mind. So why not just tell me?"

Earl searched her eyes. "How would you feel about San Francisco?"

"I'll be damned!" she blurted. "Are you really serious?"

"Hell, why not? We're all washed up in Denver."

"What about Central City or Black Hawk? We could always open another Bella Union."

"Thanks all the same," Earl muttered. "I've had my fill of being an owner. I'll stick to poker from now on."

"Well—?" she hesitated, still slightly bemused. "You always said you wanted to try the big time. And Frisco's as big as they come."

"I figure we've got close to a hundred thousand in the kick. You have a say-so in what we do with it."

"Honey, I can deal twenty-one anywhere. So why not go for broke on the Barbary Coast? We'll take 'em by storm!"

"You're sure?"

Her laughter was musical. "Never more sure of anything in my life. Together, we can't miss!"

"One other thing."

"What now?"

"You'd better give me that whole bottle of laudanum."

"Why?"

"Otherwise I'm liable to ask you to marry me."

She sat down on the edge of the bed. Leaning forward, she cupped his face in her hands. She looked deeply into his eyes.

"If you ask, I'm liable to take you up on it, gamblin' man."

"I think I just asked."

"Yes, I think you did."

She kissed him full on the mouth.

35

DOWN THE HALL, ELIZABETH followed Virgil into their bedroom. His features were gaunt and pale, and he suddenly seemed sapped of strength. He sat down on the edge of the bed.

Elizabeth put her hand over his forehead. He stared at her dully as she satisfied herself that he had no fever. She took a pair of scissors from her sewing basket and deftly snipped away the remnants of his shirt. Then she stooped down, tugging his boots off and dropping them on the floor.

Pulling the covers back, she helped him stretch out in bed. She took the pistol from his waistband and placed it on top of the dresser. Then she unbuttoned his trousers, working them down over his hips, and finally removed his socks. For a moment she debated on his undershorts and then decided he should be allowed some dignity. She covered him with a sheet, draping it lightly across his wounded arm.

"How do you feel?" she whispered.

Virgil frowned. "You want the truth?"

"Of course," she insisted. "You mustn't play the hero."

"That's a laugh," Virgil said, not laughing. "I feel like I lost an argument with a meatgrinder."

"Well . . ." She studied him seriously a moment. "Let's look on the bright side, shall we? You're alive and the doctor says you'll mend quickly. I think we have much to be thankful for."

Virgil nodded. "Remind me to count my lucky stars."

"I will, after you've had some sleep. Now, no more talking, Mr. Brannock. Close your eyes."

Virgil gave her a game smile and his eyelids drooped shut. Within moments, he fell into a deep exhausted sleep. She waited until his breathing became even, watching him with a look of pride and heart-wrenching concern. At length, she turned and walked from the bedroom.

A moment later, she entered the parlor. Walter Tisdale was still seated in the easy chair. He straightened, tugging at his vest as she crossed the room and lowered herself onto the sofa. Neither of them spoke, and they sat for a time wrapped in silence. Finally, he looked at her with a disquieted expression.

"Are you all right?"

Her voice was cool. "I'm fine, thank you."

Tisdale shook his head. "Your mother must be having conniption fits. I can just hear her—"

"Damn mother!" she stormed. "And damn you, too! Have you any idea how incredibly self-centered you are? Do you?"

"How dare you talk to me in that tone!"

"Oh, for God's sake, Father. Don't be such a pompous windbag."

Tisdale flushed bright red. "I won't sit here and be insulted by my own daughter. You listen to me, young lady—!"

"*No!*"

Elizabeth suddenly sat erect on the edge of the sofa. She fixed him with a terrible look. "You listen to me! I'm not your little girl anymore. I'm a married woman and carrying my first child. And I have something to say to you about my husband."

Tisdale appeared stunned by the ferocity of her attack. He

blinked, watching her with wary unease. "I thought we'd settled Virgil's affairs."

"You treated him shabbily, Father. You marched in here while he was hurt and sick with worry about his brother—"

"Confound it! What did you expect me to do? He's the one who hunted those men down and killed them. I'm just trying to salvage the mess he made."

"Yes, you salvaged it." Her voice dripped with scorn. "And don't tell me how generous you were. I imagine you'll profit very handsomely by the arrangement."

"I—" Tisdale snapped halfway to his feet. "I refuse to tolerate this any longer. You're obviously on the verge of hysteria."

"Sit down, Father."

There was steel in her voice. Astonished, Tisdale obediently dropped back into his chair. He looked at her as though confronted by a stranger. He saw icy resolve in her eyes.

"Yesterday," she began calmly, "I was a dithering girl of twenty-three. Today, my husband lies wounded and still very much in danger of being killed. So I'm no longer the girl I was yesterday. Do you understand that, Father?"

"Yes," Tisdale said quietly, "I think I do."

"Good." She nodded and went on with unsettling assurance. "I don't begrudge you profiting on Virgil's misfortune. All things considered, it was probably the most sensible arrangement. We have no choice but to leave Denver."

A frown creased Tisdale's brow. "In that event, I'm somewhat baffled. Exactly what is it we're talking about?"

Her gaze was direct. "You deserted Virgil. He trusted you and relied on your support. Instead, you showed the white feather."

"My God!" Tisdale appeared aghast. "Are you calling your own father a coward?"

"Answer the question yourself. Are you afraid of David Hughes?"

Tisdale seemed to shrink back in his chair. His features

paled, and a long moment passed before he was able to speak. "Yes," he said, lowering his eyes. "And I'm not ashamed to admit it. Any rational man would fear Hughes."

"On the contrary," she said, pressing him, "I think you're very much ashamed of it. And for good reason, too."

"What do you mean?"

"Virgil and his brothers drew the line this morning. You may think them irresponsible and foolhardy, but they proved their point."

"Point?" Tisdale's eyebrows bunched together in a question mark. "What point?"

Her eyes were dispassionate. "A man who has been wronged must ultimately take a stand. Otherwise he's no man at all."

"And if taking a stand gets him killed . . . what then?"

She laughed derisively. "I know the argument only too well. Better a live coward than a dead hero. Isn't that what you're thinking?"

Tisdale winced, clearly stung. "I might have chosen kinder words."

"Why be kind?" she said. "The truth often hurts."

"Is that what you've learned from Virgil?"

"For a long time," she noted, "I thought I preferred a live coward to a dead husband. Virgil taught me that a man without self-respect might just as well be dead. What happened this morning merely reaffirms that belief."

"My dear," Tisdale said in a raspy voice, "you are still very naive about the affairs of men. For all your platitudes, what happened this morning was a waste. It's cost Virgil everything he worked toward and what he might have been."

"You find the price too high, don't you?"

"Compromise is the cornerstone of any endeavor. Virgil's pride blinded him to the realities of a harsh world. In short, a wise man knows when to bend."

She gave him a pitiful look. "Is that the secret of your success, Father? Knowing when to bend?"

Tisdale colored with anger. "Your husband could have profited by the example. Instead, he's burned his last bridge in Denver."

"I know," she said with a sudden fierceness. "And I'll never be more proud of him than I am today."

"Quite frankly," Tisdale told her, "you have me at a loss. You admit he's through in Denver and yet you continue to badger me. What is it you want?"

"I want you to intervene on Virgil's behalf."

"Intervene?" Tisdale said uncertainly. "Are you referring to David Hughes?"

She slowly nodded. "Clint Brannock has an instinct for such things. He believes Virgil's life is still in danger. I want that danger removed."

"How do you propose I accomplish that?"

"Talk to Hughes," she said. "Tell him Virgil has agreed to leave Denver. Let it end peacefully—no more killing!"

Tisdale stared at her blankly. "You overestimate my position in the community. I have no influence with Hughes."

"I don't believe that for an instant."

"Well, like it or not, it's true!"

She forced him to look her in the eye. "Please don't bandy words with me. We both know that you're the most prominent businessman in Denver. Use the power of your bank to persuade Hughes."

"By persuade," Tisdale remarked, "I assume you mean I should threaten him?"

"Yes, dammit," she said angrily. "Take a stand for once in your life. Threaten to withdraw financial support from him and his railroad. Force *him* to compromise."

"Even if it worked," Tisdale said with no conviction, "it would put me in an untenable position. Hughes would somehow twist it so as to put me in his debt. And he always collects a stiff price on favors."

"Have you so little backbone, Father?"

Tisdale visibly recoiled. "It has nothing to do with backbone. I've managed to keep myself above local politics. I refuse to stoop that low."

"Perhaps it's time you dirtied your hands. If nothing else, you have an obligation to Denver. But you have an even greater obligation to me—and your grandchild."

"My grandchild?" Tisdale said weakly. "Are you threatening me now, Elizabeth?"

Her voice was determined, somehow chilling. "I'll leave it to you, Father. Should any child know its grandfather to be a coward?"

Tisdale's features sagged, and he appeared to age under her cool stare. He hunched forward, shoulders slumped, and sat staring at the floor. She waited him out, holding to an iron silence, and he finally looked up. There was defeat in his eyes.

"You've become a hard woman, Elizabeth. I liked you better when you weren't so insensitive."

She gave him nothing. "Would you like me better as a widow?"

"No—"

"Then you'll do as I ask, won't you?"

"Very well," Tisdale said wearily, rising to his feet. "I'll have a talk with Hughes."

She sat perfectly still.

Tisdale waited, as though expecting some final word of absolution. When she remained silent, he collected his hat and trudged slowly toward the parlor door. There he stopped and looked back at her.

"Whatever else you may think, I'm not a coward. I won't have that between us."

Her eyes softened. "I never meant to hurt you, Father. I do love you."

Tisdale wanted to ask if she loved Virgil more. But he knew the answer and dreaded to hear it spoken aloud. He nodded and turned into the hallway.

Elizabeth felt an instant of remorse. She had humbled him, invoking a steely side of her nature that seemed somehow unrefined. But then, as she heard the front door close, she reconciled herself to what she'd done. The alternative was to remain a mewing, witless female, and perhaps become a widow. She quickly suppressed any lingering sense of guilt. She told herself again the very thing she'd told her father. Yesterday was a lifetime ago.

A faint noise startled her. Looking around, she saw Monte move through the parlor entranceway. Something in the other woman's face alerted her, and she knew she wasn't mistaken. Her conversation with her father had been overheard.

"Forgive me," Monte said, crossing to the sofa. "I didn't intend to eavesdrop, honestly! I started up the hall and—"

Elizabeth smiled warmly. "Please don't be harsh on yourself. You've really no need to apologize."

"Well, thanks," Monte said with apparent relief. "I wouldn't want you to think I was a snoop."

"I'll tell you a secret." Elizabeth patted the sofa and waited until she'd seated herself. "If you hadn't overheard, I'd probably have told you anyway. I need to talk to *someone*."

Monte appraised her at a glance. "I guess it's not the sort of thing a woman tells her husband."

"No, never!" Elizabeth laughed softly. "Virgil would be furious. He'd say I was meddling . . . a busybody!"

"You know . . ." Monte paused, her eyes twinkling. "I've always operated on the principle that what men don't know won't hurt them. I suspect it applies to husbands, too."

"I'm so glad you're here," Elizabeth said with sudden feeling. "Somehow it makes it easier, having another woman in the house. I don't feel so alone or drawn into myself. Does that make any sense?"

"God, does it! Sometimes I think I'll bust with all the things I'd never say to Earl. I suppose men just don't make good confidants."

"You've never had close lady friends, a real confidante?"

"Not in a long time," Monte said with a wistful smile.

"You'll pardon my French, but whores and saloon girls are the worst gossips in the world. I wouldn't trust one with the correct time of day."

"You may not believe me"—Elizabeth hesitated, then went on in a rush—"but I just can't tell you how much I admire you."

"You're kidding!"

"No, it's true," Elizabeth said earnestly. "You've made a life for yourself in a world I couldn't even imagine. And it's obvious you've earned the respect of everyone, especially the men. I see it in their eyes when they look at you. Clint and Earl, even Virgil."

"Nothing to it," Monte said, trying to cover her embarrassment. "All you've got to do is make the big lugs toe the line."

"Oh, I'm sure there's more to it than that."

"Say, listen, you're doing all right yourself. From what I overheard, nobody needs to give you lessons. You scared the bejesus out of me!"

"Was I really that bad? Honestly?"

"Honey, you were just great," Monte assured her. "You saw what needed doing, and you did it. Virgil ought to kiss your feet once a day and twice on Sundays."

The image flashed through Elizabeth's mind and she laughed. "Somehow I don't think Virgil would appreciate the sentiment."

"Earl neither," Monte said wickedly. "Some men just don't know a good thing when they see it."

"I suppose we could have done worse, though. Not that I would ever admit as much to Virgil."

"Since we're sharing secrets, I'll tell you one of mine. Earl popped the question just before he dropped off to sleep."

"He *asked* you to marry him?"

"And stone-cold sober, too. Unless, of course, you count a dose of laudanum."

Elizabeth spontaneously hugged her. "Oh, Monte, that's wonderful! I'm so happy for you."

Monte smiled brightly. "To tell you the truth, I deserve a pat on the back. It took me four years to get that knothead into a marrying mood."

"So you see," Elizabeth exclaimed. "I was right after all. You truly are family."

"Holy moly," Monte said with a look of bemusement. "I hadn't thought of it, but you're right. That makes me a Brannock!"

The women embraced in a shared moment of wonder. Tears of happiness streamed down their cheeks and their laughter was choked with emotion. Nothing of what they had endured since dawn intruded on the joy they felt now.

However briefly, they forgot tomorrow.

36

SALOONS THROUGHOUT THE SPORTING district were still crowded. Several establishments offered free lunch with beer or spirits, and the noontime rush generally lasted into early afternoon. Today's crowds were even larger than normal.

News of the gunfight had spread to every corner of Denver. Clerks and workingmen, as well as the sporting crowd, were drawn by some ghoulish preoccupation with violent death. Yet talk in the saloons centered more on the victors than the dead men. Losers were seldom accorded celebrity.

Shortly after one o'clock saloons began emptying of workingmen. As Clint crossed the line into the sporting district, word rushed ahead of him along Blake Street. While his brothers shared the limelight, his notoriety now bordered on legend. No one doubted that Denver's roughhewn marshal had carried the fight to the Quintin gang. That he had emerged from the shootout unscathed merely added to his already formidable reputation.

Few of the men on Blake Street took exception to Clint's motives. It was widely known that he'd braced Quintin last night in the Progressive Club. Hardly anyone was unaware that the former guerrilla had been accused of murdering the Brannocks' parents. Nor were they unmindful of the rumor that the Bella Union had been torched by the gang. A rough code governed such matters, and most men considered the Brannocks entirely within their rights. By frontier standards, Jack Quintin had gotten no less than he deserved.

The barroom in the Progressive Club was packed. When Clint stepped through the door, a sudden hush swept over the crowd. As he moved toward the staircase, a path opened before him. Several men spoke to him, and one old-timer, somewhat ossified with liquor, pounded him heartily on the back. He accepted their congratulations without comment, never breaking stride. A buzz of conversation erupted as he mounted the stairs.

On the upper landing, Clint turned down a short hallway. Ahead he saw Hank Newcomb posted outside a closed door. Unlike many of Case's hooligans, Newcomb's reputation deserved respect. Clint reminded himself that the man was quick with his fists and even quicker with a gun. As he approached, Newcomb seemed to bristle like an evil-eyed watchdog. Clint decided to play by his own rules.

"I don't want any trouble, Newcomb."

"Suits me," Newcomb rumbled. "Just turn around and head back the way you come."

"Now, look," Clint said amiably, "no need for us to butt heads. Why not tell your boss I'd like a word with him?"

"Gawddammit, hold'er right where you are!"

Another step brought Clint to within striking distance. Still smiling pleasantly, his hand seemed to move not at all. The Colt appeared out of nowhere and he laid the barrel upside Newcomb's head. The squat gunman went down like he'd been poleaxed. He was out cold.

Clint threw open the door. Ed Case looked up from his desk and his face went ashen. He sat perfectly still as Clint reached back and grabbed Newcomb by the collar. One eye on Case, with the Colt held loosely at his side, Clint dragged the gunman into the office. He dumped Newcomb on the floor and relieved him of his pistol. Holstering the Colt, he kicked the door shut and walked forward. He idly waved Newcomb's pistol at Case.

"You carry a gun?"

"No."

"Maybe you've got one in your desk drawer?"

Case blinked. He spread his hands on the desktop. "I wouldn't be dumb enough to try."

"Go ahead," Clint said easily. "I'd just as soon kill you as not."

A startled expression crossed Case's features. "You're not going to kill me?"

"All depends."

"On what?"

"How you cooperate," Clint told him. "Just for example, Quintin burned down the Bella Union, didn't he?"

"Yes."

"Acting on your orders, right?"

"You'll never prove that."

Clint slowly cocked the pistol. He leaned across the desk and hooked the front sight into Case's left nostril. "Here's your judge and jury. Got anything to say before I pronounce sentence?"

"All right," Case said hoarsely. "It's like you said. I ordered it."

"And you were acting on Hughes' orders, weren't you?"

Case nodded, a slightly dazed look in his eyes. "What do you want, Brannock?"

"How about a full confession . . . in writing?"

"Go to hell," Case croaked. "I'd sooner you shoot me than get myself hung."

"Don't blame you," Clint said without surprise. "I'd feel pretty much the same way myself."

"So where does that leave us?"

"How about a cash settlement?"

"What are you talking about?"

"You burned Earl out," Clint observed. "I figure fifty thousand ought to square things."

"Fifty thousand!" Case bleated. "For a pile of burnt lumber?"

A wintry smile lighted Clint's eyes. "Call it a good-will payment."

"It's robbery! I won't pay it, by God!"

"Yeah, you will." Clint rumpled his nose with the gun muzzle. "Especially when you consider the alternative."

A few minutes later Clint walked out of the Progressive Club. His coat pockets as well as his hip pockets were stuffed with wads of greenbacks. Still, all things considered, he thought Ed Case had gotten the better of the bargain. Fifty thousand was a cheap price to go on living.

Uptown, he turned into city hall. He marched through the door of the mayor's office with a broad grin. Amos Stodt sat bolt upright in his chair. His Adam's apple bobbed like a fish cork, but he seemed unable to speak. Clint unpinned his marshal's badge and tossed it on the desk.

"No need to fire me, Mr. Mayor. I quit."

"Y—you!" Stodt stammered. "You and your brothers broke the law. I've a good mind to press charges."

"Be my guest." Clint's grin widened. "Before you do, though, I'd suggest you have a talk with Ed Case."

Stodt's voice was guarded. "What's Case got to do with it?"

"Few minutes ago, he gave me a full confession. Told me how you and Hughes were behind the whole thing. Guess he wanted to purge himself of guilt."

"I don't believe you," Stodt said. "Besides, that wouldn't hold water in court anyway. You're bluffing."

"Never bluff," Clint said in dead earnest. "Case spilled his guts like it was Judgment Day. You and Hughes ought to be more picky about your friends."

Stodt went white around the mouth. "Why are you telling me all this?"

"Want you to carry a message to Hughes."

"A message?"

"Virgil's leaving Denver. Tell Hughes to let him go in peace. No more trouble."

"That sounds vaguely like a threat."

"Nothing vague about it." Clint's voice suddenly turned abrasive. "Unless Hughes behaves himself, I'll kill him."

"Kill him?" Stodt repeated weakly.

"Deader'n a doornail."

Stodt appeared on the verge of saying something more. He sputtered, swallowing the words, and abruptly changed his mind. Clint waited a moment, watching him with a look of amused contempt. Then he turned and walked out of the office.

On the street, he could scarcely constrain himself from laughing. His revelation about Ed Case would reach Hughes within the hour. By nightfall, the whole bunch of them would be at one another's throats. He thought it was poetic justice. Fitting as hell!

Outside the Overland station he ran into Ben Holladay. The stage-line owner greeted him with a warm handshake and a sly, furtive look. His eyes contained a devilish glint.

"By the Christ!" he said expansively. "When you come unwound, you go whole hog. I heard the bastards was shot to pieces."

Clint shrugged. "Let's just say Quintin's luck ran out."

"Luck, hell!" Holladay roared. "Way I got the story, you forced 'em to fight. No goddamn choice."

"Well, nobody ever accused me of halfway measures."

"Clint, you're a man after my own heart. And there's not a helluva lot more like us around these parts. How'd you like to come to work for the Overland?"

"Funny you'd ask," Clint said, somewhat taken aback. "I just now turned in my badge. What did you have in mind?"

"Stage robbers," Holladay said with a wolfish grin. "I got the sonsabitches runnin' out of my ears! You could be my ace troubleshooter."

"Sounds like a polite way of saying 'hired killer.' "

"Not by a damnsight," Holladay objected. "You'd be in charge of security for the whole line. Hell, I'd even give you a title. How's Special Agent strike you?"

"Not so fast," Clint said. "Are you talking about Colorado Territory or what?"

"I'm talkin' five thousand miles of stage line. Colorado, Montana, Oregon, the whole shebang! You wouldn't hardly have time to take a leak."

Clint liked the sound of it. "What would a job like that pay?"

"Dollar a mile," Holladay said magnanimously. "Five thousand a year and a bonus every time you bury one of the bastards. What d'you think of that?"

Clint laughed. "I think you just hired yourself a Special Agent."

"God's blood! Let's have a drink on it."

An hour later they parted outside Murphy's Saloon. Holladay shook his hand with an ore-crusher grip and left him on the street corner. Somewhat bedazzled by his own good fortune, Clint saw no reason to end the celebration. He rounded the corner and walked toward the Row.

Belle's parlor house wasn't yet open for business. The maid admitted him only after he'd pounded on the door several times. He was shown into the parlor and asked to wait. A couple of girls wandered in from the kitchen, still attired in negligees and housecoats. They looked at him with open curiosity, which left no doubt that the gunfight had been a topic of conversation around the breakfast table. He took a seat on one of the sofas as they disappeared up the stairs.

Summoned by the maid, Belle bustled into the parlor a moment later. She threw him a quick, enigmatic glance as she crossed the room and seated herself beside him on the sofa. She touched his arm. "Are you all right?"

"Fit as a fiddle," Clint said, mocking her concerned look. "Why, were you worried?"

"Who, me?" she said innocently. "What's to worry about?"

"Well, a feller could always hope."

"Oh, I suppose I had a twinge or two. But then I heard you'd come through it alive."

Clint smiled. "Good news travels fast."

She mimicked his cocksure expression. "You look awfully pleased with yourself."

"Hell, yes," Clint said with a chuckle. "I killed Jack Quintin and lived to tell about it. I've got reason to be pleased."

"What about Ed Case? Will you have trouble with him?"

Clint burst out laughing. He briefly recounted his conversation with the vice lord. Then, as a capper to the story, he pulled a wad of bills from his coat pocket. Her eyes got big and round, and her mouth dropped open. She stared at him as though he were a magician who had just performed some staggering sleight of hand.

"Good God!" she said softly. "You actually took him for fifty thousand?"

"Squared the account," Clint replied genially. "He shouldn't have burned down the Bella Union."

"Will that end it, though? Case has been known to hold a grudge."

"I suspect I made a believer of him. One more go-round and it's his ticket that'll get punched. I guaranteed him of that."

She was silent a moment. "How are your brothers? I heard the doc had his hands full."

Clint waved the thought aside. "They'll pull through just fine. Wild horses couldn't keep 'em down for long."

"Will Earl rebuild the Bella Union?"

"I tend to doubt it."

Clint went on to tell her that Virgil was leaving Denver. He then expressed the belief that Earl wouldn't be far behind. After the dust settled, he noted, Ed Case would still control the sporting district. Earl would likely look for greener pastures.

She searched his face. "How about you?"

"Well, I've quit my job as marshal. Figured I'd beat city hall to the punch."

"So you're leaving, too."

"Not exactly," Clint said, watching her reaction. "I've signed on with Ben Holladay. You're looking at the Overland's new Special Agent."

Her laugh was a delicious sound. "You mean you're staying in Denver?"

Clint nodded. "I'll be headquartered here. Holladay wants me to act as troubleshooter for the whole line."

"One of these days," she said with a warm, beguiling grin, "I'll have to thank Mr. Holladay personally. He's a regular Saint Nick."

Holding her gaze, Clint silently congratulated himself. He preferred women of zest and laughter and earthy physical appetites. She was just such a woman, and he felt himself fortunate that the attraction was mutual. All in all, it was a day to be marked by celebration.

"Matter of fact," he said at length, "that's why I dropped by. Thought we could celebrate my new job."

Something mischievous sparkled in her eyes. She looked him up and down. "You know something, lover?"

"What's that?"

"You look plumb tuckered out."

"I don't recollect ever being *that* tired."

"Oh, no?" she insisted. "How long's it been since you slept?"

Clint's eyes suddenly felt gritty. Thinking back, he realized he hadn't been to bed since night before last. Almost unwittingly his mouth opened in a wide, jaw-cracking yawn. He covered it with a sheepish grin.

"You might have a point. I doubt I'm just exactly up to snuff."

She patted his hand. "Why don't you stretch out in my room for a while? I could wake you . . . later."

"Sounds promising," Clint said slowly. "What've you got in mind?"

Her lips curved in a teasing smile. "I'll think of something."

She led him upstairs. In her room, she helped him undress and then tucked him into bed. He was asleep when his head hit the pillow.

37

Virgil stared listlessly out the window. He watched a roiling bank of clouds with a farmer's eye for the weather. He thought it would be an early winter.

A week had passed since the shootout on Blake Street. While his arm was still in a sling, he was all but recuperated. Yet he felt cooped up in the house and couldn't seem to shake a sense of brooding. He was bothered by loose ends.

Yesterday he'd met with Walter Tisdale. After affixing his signature to the contract, all his business interests, as well as the house, had been transferred to the banker. In exchange, he had received a draft for a sum in excess of a hundred thousand dollars. By all rights, the transaction should have pleased him greatly. He was departing Denver a far richer man than when he'd arrived. Yet his mood was dark and strangely defeated.

Thinking about tomorrow only made it worse. Their tickets were already bought and he would depart with Elizabeth on the morning southbound stage. Earl, who was hobbling around on a cane, was scheduled to leave at about the same time. He and Monte were ticketed on the westbound, their final destination San Francisco. For Virgil, the only note of levity was the added fifty thousand in Earl's bankroll. He still chuckled at the thought of Ed Case being sandbagged by Clint.

Turning from the window, he walked back through the house. He found Elizabeth in their bedroom, packing clothes in a large carpetbag. All their other belongings had been crated and would be held for shipment by freight wagon. Elizabeth looked around as he appeared in the doorway. She blew a stray curl off her forehead.

"Almost done," she said. "One more bag and we're all packed."

"Good," Virgil replied without any great interest. "Think I'll take a walk. You don't need me, do you?"

"Where are you going?"

"Nowhere special. Just thought I'd get a breath of air."

A sudden foreboding swept over Elizabeth. Fear was an emotion with which she was all too intimate. She felt weighted with dread that the violence would somehow flare anew. Her one hope was to put Denver behind them, without more killing. She'd already come too close to being a young widow. She wanted Virgil alive.

Yet now the expression in his eyes touched her with a cold chill. All week she'd watched his mood worsen and his temper grow shorter. Some dark complex of fear and premonition told her that his brooding had nothing to do with tomorrow's departure. Nor was she convinced that being forced to leave his brothers was the sole cause. The thought jumped through her mind that it was something else entirely. The thing she feared most.

In a small voice, she said, "You're not considering anything foolish . . . are you?"

"Like what?"

"I don't know," she said softly. "I just hope it's not your conscience bothering you. Is that it?"

Virgil's tone was severe. "Got me all figured out, huh?"

"You promised Father!" She entreated him with her eyes. "You said you wouldn't do anything to upset the arrangement."

"I promised nothing," Virgil said, his voice strained. "What people assume is their own lookout."

The problem stemmed from Clint's talk with the mayor. Clint had warned the city-hall crowd that Virgil should be allowed to depart in peace. David Hughes, after being contacted by Walter Tisdale, had interpreted all this as an overture for a truce. He'd asked Tisdale to pass along a message. So long as Virgil kept quiet about the railroad, no further trouble would develop.

When Tisdale delivered the message, Virgil had immediately put things straight. No truce had been requested, and he felt himself under no obligation to remain silent. Tisdale had argued long and persuasively; he urged Virgil to think of Elizabeth and their new life together. Why jeopardize all that, he'd asked, when exposing Hughes would accomplish nothing of lasting value? Unwilling to quibble over it, Virgil had agreed to consider the argument. But he'd promised nothing.

"What difference does it make?" Elizabeth said now. "We're leaving here tomorrow. What happens is no longer our concern."

Virgil gave her a hangdog look. "You're probably right. I just have a hard time convincing myself of that."

"Why bother?" she said in a hushed tone. "You can't save the world."

"A man has to live with himself, Beth."

"What about our new life? Don't spoil it at the last minute—for nothing!"

"You worry too much. All I said was, I'm going for a walk."

"Virgil."

"Yes?"

"I love you," she said with unclouded simplicity. "Please be careful . . . for me."

Virgil brushed her lips with a kiss. "Stop your fretting. I'll be back soon."

Outside, he paused for a moment on the porch. His eyes were drawn westward, to the mountains. Towering against the horizon, the snowcapped spires stood like a column of majestic sentinels. Even after all these months, it was a sight that still held him somewhat spellbound. He hated to leave it.

A brisk walk brought him to the warehouse. He resisted the urge to step inside and have a last look around. His father-in-law had already hired a local man to manage the business and everything appeared in order. Still, it rankled that he was now an outsider, no part of an idea he had nurtured into reality. He felt gripped by bitter resentment.

Turning away, he headed uptown. He was surprised by the intensity of his own feelings. Like some storybook dream, Denver had captured his imagination. He'd visualized himself as a community leader, a man of prestige and prominence. In his mind's eye, the vision had included the railroad and a town grown to a flourishing metropolis. All that would happen. Denver would become a financial center and a hub of development, but he wouldn't be around to share in the realization. For him, the dream was dead.

Walking along, he wondered if it wasn't sour grapes rather than conscience. He was embittered at having lost, and that bitterness was directed at David Hughes. Then a greater truth registered, jolted him into a state of acute awareness. His conscience had nothing to do with being drummed out of Denver. He was simply unable to compromise principle with pragmatism. The town and the people who had come to trust him were part of it. But he owed himself even more. His honesty was not for sale.

Uptown, he proceeded directly to the *Rocky Mountain News*. As he stepped through the door, Will Byers turned from talking with his pressman. The mechanical crank of the press jarred the floor and drowned out all street noise. Byers waved and hurried forward.

"Good to see you, Virgil. How's the arm?"

"On the mend," Virgil said. "Ought to be good as new by the time we get to Texas."

"You're actually leaving, then?"

"Bright and early tomorrow."

Byers waved him to a chair. After seating himself, the editor stared across his desk. "I heard you were going to Texas. But no one seems to know the reason."

Virgil smiled. "Guess I got bit by the railroad bug. Figured I might put one together down there."

"Texas?" Byers said doubtfully. "Are any of the major lines building in that direction?"

"Not yet," Virgil admitted. "But I calculate it's only a matter of time. Lots of cows in Texas."

"What do cows have to do with railroads?"

"Well, right now Texans trail-drive their herds. It'd be lots easier to ship by rail, and more profitable, too. I plan to get my foot in the door before it happens."

"Sounds ambitious," Byers remarked. "Where will you start?"

"Austin," Virgil said. "That's the capital, and nobody builds a railroad without a charter. Guess I'll have to learn something about politics."

"How do you plan to finance the venture?"

"I'm no greenhorn on that score. Once I've got the state charter, I'll head for Washington. A land grant ought to attract plenty of investment money."

Byers nodded. "You've certainly done wonders here, Virgil. Except for your fund-raising efforts, Denver might never have had a railroad."

"Now that you mention it," Virgil said, suddenly somber, "that's why I dropped by. I'd like to give you an earful about the Denver Pacific."

"An earful?" Byers said blankly. "I don't understand."

"Suppose we start with David Hughes."

Virgil wasted no words. In short order, he outlined Hughes'

scheme to establish a separate construction company. He then revealed Luther Evans' plan to acquire right-of-way north of town. Conflict of interest, he noted, was far too charitable a term. They intended to bilk the railroad.

When he finished, Byers sat as if nailed to his chair. So complete was the editor's astonishment that his eyes were like those of a blind man. He looked oddly disoriented.

"I can't believe it." His voice was shocked. "David Hughes and Luther Evans! It just isn't possible."

"Yeah, I know," Virgil said gloomily. "That's how I felt, too. I got over it quick enough, though."

"Good Lord, it boggles the mind! How can you be so certain?"

"Easy," Virgil observed. "They admitted it straight to my face. Hughes even tried to buy me off."

"You couldn't be mistaken? He actually attempted to bribe you?"

"No bones about it. He outright offered me a share of the spoils."

"What was your response?"

"In so many words, I told him to go to hell."

"And then?" Byers asked, a hitch in his voice. "Was that the end of it?"

"No," Virgil said shortly. "When he couldn't buy me off, he tried to have me killed. That gunfight last week was rigged especially for my benefit."

Byers gave him a bewildered look. "I understood it was a personal affair. Something to do with the war and your parents . . . a border raid."

Virgil nodded wearily. "I'm not denying the personal side. I'm only saying he used Quintin to get at me. It was a put-up job."

"How do you know?"

"Will, let's not get sidetracked. What Hughes tried to do to me isn't here nor there. It's what he's done to the town that counts."

"What is it you're suggesting?"

"I want it made public," Virgil explained. "A story in your newspaper seems like the best way to do it."

"You—" Byers stopped, suddenly flustered. "You want me to expose David Hughes."

"Yeah, I do," Virgil said resolutely. "Otherwise he won't be stopped."

"I'd need proof! I can't libel a man in print with allegations."

Virgil stared him in the eye. "How about a sworn statement? You can quote me word for word."

Byers pondered it a moment, and then, almost as though he was thinking out loud, he raised the critical point. "What about the town? Do we serve Denver's interests by exposing Hughes? We must have that railroad, Virgil!"

"You'll get it," Virgil assured him. "The story will force him to ditch his scheme. He'll have no choice but to play it square."

"Won't he be forced to resign from the railroad as well?"

"Not likely," Virgil said cynically. "It's his railroad, and Denver's his town. I found that out the hard way."

Byers studied his downcast expression. "I notice you've started wearing a gun. Are you still in danger?"

The butt of the Remington pistol protruded from the waistband of Virgil's trousers. He tugged at his jacket to cover it from view. "Hard times demand hard measures, Will. A man has to look to his own defense."

"In that event, maybe I should buy a gun. I might need one after I run the story."

Virgil grinned. "I knew you wouldn't let me down. You're too good a newspaperman."

"Here!" Byers shoved pen and paper across the desk. "Start writing your statement."

"Glad to, Will."

Byers bounced out of his chair. He rushed toward the rear of the room. "Hold the press! We've got an extra to get out."

Some while later Virgil emerged from the newspaper. His conscience was clear, even though he knew he'd catch hell when he got home. Elizabeth was sure to pitch a fit.

Turning upstreet, he suddenly tensed. Luther Evans was walking toward him, and he had the uncanny impression that it was no chance meeting. He took a tight grip on himself.

"Well, Brannock." Evans halted directly in his path. "I hear you're leaving town."

"You heard right."

Evans watched him with a slight fixed smile. "You were wise to keep your mouth shut. Nobody profits from a fight."

"Stand aside," Virgil said quietly. "You're blocking my way."

"Want to ask you something. You don't mind a question, do you?"

"Ask and be damned."

Evans eyed him suspiciously. "You've been holed up with Will Byers for the last hour. What were you talking about?"

Something snapped inside Virgil. He knew he'd been badgered and threatened for the last time. He also knew there was no way around Evans' question. His eyes suddenly turned cold.

"I just told Byers the whole story. He's going to print it in the paper."

"He's *what*?"

"You heard me," Virgil said deliberately. "I gave him a sworn statement. You and Hughes are finished."

"You dirty bastard," Evans muttered, eyes garnet with rage. "You went back on our deal."

Virgil smiled. "Somebody misinformed you, Luther. I don't deal with crooks."

"Goddamn you—!"

Evans' hand dipped inside his coat. He came up with a bulldog pistol and fired as Virgil pulled the Remington. The slug scorched the edge of Virgil's sleeve and shattered a storefront window behind him. He touched the trigger and the Remington belched a sheet of flame. The bullet struck Evans in the chest and his mouth opened in soundless amazement. He took a shuffling step backward and then the light went out of his eyes. He fell dead.

Will Byers ran out of the newspaper. He slowed and walked to where Virgil stood staring down at the body. He tried to speak, but his voice failed him. A moment elapsed, then Virgil looked around. His mouth lifted in a tired smile.

"One down, one to go, Will. Hughes is yours."

38

THE AFTERMATH OF LUTHER Evans' death proved to be revealing. To their surprise, the Brannock brothers discovered
that they had more friends than enemies in Denver. The mood
of the town shifted decisively in their favor.

Several witnesses to the shooting stepped forward. All of
them testified that Virgil had acted in defense of his life. They
told how Evans had accosted him on the street, provoked an
argument, and fired first. The mayor, as well as the new town
marshal, seemed to heave a sigh of relief. No charges were
preferred.

Ben Holladay also voiced support. He let it be known he'd
taken a personal interest in the Brannock family. Any move
against the Brannocks, he declared, would be regarded as outside the law. He left no doubt that harsh reprisals would befall
anyone who ignored the warning. Uptown or downtown, few
people questioned his willingness to deliver on the threat.

The killing prompted still another development. Will
Byers, with the support of Walter Tisdale, arranged a meeting
with Hughes. Upon hearing them out, Denver's political boss
readily accepted their demands. He agreed to disband his con-

struction company and thereby eliminate any conflict of interest. Further, he agreed that all right-of-way acquired to date would be transferred to the railroad at the original sales price. In return, Byers agreed not to print the story on Hughes' shady practices. It was a trade-off that worked principally to the town's benefit. Denver would get its railroad without being robbed.

For all that, there was no celebration in the Brannock home. While Virgil had been vindicated on every count, his time in Denver was nonetheless at an end. Neither he nor Earl had any illusions; their victory was temporary, for David Hughes still controlled the political apparatus of the town. That night, the family gathered for the last time around the dinner table. Later, after the women had retired, the brothers shared a bottle of aged whiskey. They talked of things past and toasted better days ahead.

Early next morning, Clint returned in a buckboard. He collected their luggage and drove off, leaving them to walk the short distance to town. Earl and Monte started down the street, clearly eager to put Denver behind them. Elizabeth paused on the walkway and turned for a last look at the house. An image took shape in her mind, and she saw herself, dressed in a bridal gown, being carried across the threshold. Her eyes misted and she smiled at Virgil, blinking back the tears.

He gently led her away.

By eight o'clock, they were gathered outside the stage-line office. Virgil and Elizabeth were scheduled for a layover in Santa Fe and then on to Texas. Headed west, Earl and Monte would switch stages in Salt Lake City and proceed from there to California. Standing on the boardwalk, they seemed unaware of the other passengers grouped around them. The brothers were solemn, talking in low voices, each wondering when they would meet again. The women remained silent, unwilling to intrude on their last moment together.

Virgil appeared downright glum. As the eldest, he felt the

tug of emotion more than the younger men. He thought back to the day, some five months past, when they'd been reunited. At the time, he had reasonably assumed that they would never again be separated. Events beyond his control had dictated otherwise, and today they would once more part. Yet, with an almost mystical certainty, he knew that their paths would one day merge again. He wanted to believe it would happen soon.

"Guess it's about time," he said to them now. "So let's get our heads together and agree on something."

"Hold your hat," Earl said, winking at Clint. "I think we're about to get a lecture from the elder brother."

Virgil shook his head. "No lecture, just a reminder. You'll recollect I once said we're all the family we've got."

"How could we forget?" Clint said, grinning. "That's the day you made Earl and me shake hands."

"And a damn good thing I did! None of us would be leaving here alive except for the fact we stuck together. Anybody disagree?"

When neither of them responded, he went on. "We're headed off in different directions. I don't like it especially, but I reckon we're grown men. We've each got our own idea about what's best."

"I told you, Clint," Earl noted with a waggish smile. "He's got his mind set on a lecture."

"All right," Virgil grumbled. "I'll make it short and sweet. Wherever we are, whatever we're doing, I'm laying down the law." He hesitated, staring hard at them. "Whenever one yells for help, the other two come running. I want your blood oath on it."

"Only one trouble," Clint observed. "We're all pretty hardheaded when it comes to asking favors. Seems to run in the family."

"Don't give me any arguments. I said I want your oath."

Earl nodded soberly. "Sounds good to me, Virge. I wouldn't have it any other way."

"I'll second the motion," Clint added. "You two can always write me care of the Overland. I'll forward your addresses on to the other one."

"Yeah, that reminds me," Virgil said quickly. "Anytime we lose track of one another, we can always get in touch through Uncle Ezra and Aunt Angeline. Same way we did during the war."

Clint gestured with upraised palms. "Just don't get yourselves thrown in a Yankee prison. The mail service ain't worth a damn!"

Everyone laughed out of nervous tension. Before they could resume talking, the ticket agent called the southbound stage. The women hugged and the men shook hands with an air of solemnity. Then, just as he was about to step aboard, Virgil pulled his brothers into a rough embrace. When he finally let them go, his eyes were moist and clouded. He crawled into the coach and closed the door without looking back. Elizabeth waved through the window as the stage got under way.

There was a long moment of silence. Clint stared after the stage with a thoughtful frown. Monte slipped her hand through Earl's arm and squeezed it tightly. He glanced at her out of the corner of his eye and forced himself to smile. The westbound stage, drawn by a six-horse hitch, moved into position before the boardwalk.

Earl looked across at Clint. "I've been thinking on something."

"What's that?"

"You remember what Ma used to say when times got rough?"

Clint nodded. "She always said: 'And this too shall pass.' "

Earl stuck out his hand. "I've got a feeling we'll all cross trails somewhere down the road. Call it a gambler's hunch."

"Sooner the better," Clint said, clasping his hand firmly. "Look after yourself in the meantime."

"You too, sport."

Earl flipped him a salute and turned away. Monte kissed him on the cheek, then hurried to where Earl waited beside the open door. With a final nod to Clint, Earl assisted her into the coach and climbed aboard himself. The driver popped his whip and the horses took off down the street. Clint watched until the stage rounded a corner a block away.

"I hate goodbyes worse'n any damn thing!"

Ben Holladay stepped through the office door. He'd observed the Brannocks' parting from inside and knew what the younger man was feeling. He halted beside Clint. "How'd you like to have supper with me and the missus?"

"I'd like that fine, Ben."

"Good," Holladay said amiably. "And we won't keep you too late, neither. I know you've got a lady friend downtown."

"Well—" Clint gave him a wry look. "No need to eat and run. You might've heard she keeps late hours."

"By the Christ, don't let on to my missus. She'd think you're a proper heathen. Probably try to save your soul."

"I'll remember to keep a tight lip."

" 'Course you will," Holladay said, nodding to himself. "All the same, you'd do well to make a night of it. I want you to leave for Virginia City tomorrow mornin'."

Clint glanced at him. "Trouble?"

"Goddamn road agents! Sonsabitches sprout like weeds."

"How many stages have they hit?"

"Only one," Holladay replied. "But that don't mean a damn thing. I want them stopped before it gets out of hand."

Clint considered a moment. "What's the law like in Montana?"

Holladay snorted. "Let's just say a little or none. I've seen more law in a catfight."

"In that case . . ." Clint smiled equably. "I reckon I'll have to make my own."

Holladay roared laughter. He slapped the younger man

across the shoulders, then wheeled about and strode back inside the office.

Clint stood for a moment, wondering what to do with himself until supper. Abruptly, he remembered an idle mind serves as the devil's workshop, and his thoughts turned to Belle. It seemed a fitting way to spend his last day in Denver.

He walked off toward the sporting district.